Pirates

G. A. HAUSER

Chapter One

Justin Alexander Taylor had always dreamed of a life at sea. Even as a toddler, he would stand on the very tip of England's west coast, at Land's End, and gaze out at the Atlantic Ocean in absolute wonderment. His bright blue eyes would widen in awe as rough, tanned, leather-skinned men told of their experiences fighting a broadside against violent rogue bands. *Pirates*. Those scurvy dogs of the open ocean who crossed the line from privateer to robber when greed took its hold.

Peering back over his shoulder only once in the direction he had come, he slipped away. Onward he rode, carrying only the clothing on his back, a pocket with a few coins, and his eighteen-year-old desires.

* * * *

The English corvette sloop of war *His Revenge* was in port in Penzance at Mount's Bay. Captain Richard Cornell Jones kept his eyes sharp and his ears alert to any sign of the authorities as his crew gathered fresh water and food supplies, repaired the sails and rigging, and prepared the ship for their next long voyage in search of Spanish treasure.

* * * *

Justin rode his horse with all speed through the darkness. Coming upon the inlet with its shining beacons of light and movement, he walked his mare slowly, watching all the activity around him. When he caught sight of the corvette, his heart jumped under his ribs. "Oh, blimey, there she is...," he sighed. Her double masts stabbed the starlit sky with two towering black needles of hardwood. The shapes of men working on her appeared like spiders creeping on a great rock. Her flags were flaccid, her sails still, and twenty cannons loomed out of her top deck, making her appear formidable against the backdrop of the small fishing village.

Justin dismounted and walked his horse into a stable. Moments later, he appeared with a handful of coins in exchange for her. Burying them in his pocket, he leaned back against the uneven wall of a medieval inn to study his plan.

A ragged, veiled woman had spied him and smiled, showing her crooked teeth. "Hullo, my young beauty, would you fancy an evening with a lady?" She ran her hand through his long, thick, auburn hair.

Blinking at her in surprise, he stammered, "I...I..."

"A farthing could get you into heaven tonight," she purred and smoothed her long bony fingers under his waistcoat, searching for hot flesh.

He swallowed into his dry throat as she leaned closer, pressing her sagging breasts into his chest. Digging her hands deeper into his hair and clothing, she pressed him back against the stone wall with her entire length.

"Oh, Lord..." He shivered, "No, I cannot."

"Yer as pretty as a picture." She ran her hands from his neck down to his breeches. "Like a lovely young lass with your long, black eyelashes and full, pink lips...maybe I shall not charge you a pence!"

"Ohhh...," he moaned. "Free?"

"Yes, my pretty prince." She kissed his neck.

"I...I don't have much time."

"It will only take but a moment. Come quickly." She held his hand and brought him down a black alley.

When his breeches dropped to the cobbles, he panicked and glanced around in intense fear. Instantly she was on her knees before him, sucking, closing her eyes and moaning. Never having anyone do that to him in his life, and previously having only his right hand for satisfaction, his head spun with the sensations. It didn't take more than a minute for him to give into the urge with a rush of pleasure. Justin gasped, his knees weak as he collapsed against the wall in exhaustion.

She set back from him and smiled up into his face. "You are a very pretty lad. Will you meet me again?"

Try as he might, he could not catch his breath, feeling slightly shocked at the obscene act and the intensity of the climax. "I...I cannot. I am leaving."

She raised his breeches and buttoned them for him, then leaned against him to kiss his lips. Twisting away from her mouth in disgust, he loathed the idea of touching her that way. Remembering suddenly why he was there, he panicked at not being able to watch the loading of the ship. As politely as he could he nudged her back and said, "I need to go." He tried not to look at her face, for she was very plain, missing a tooth, and in need of a bath.

She smiled at him and nodded. "What is your name, my lovely boy?"

"Justin."

"Justin," she repeated. "I will remember you."

Watching as she left, disappearing into the night, he thought to himself, "And I shall forget you!" He hurried back out of the alley and finally found the opportunity he was hoping for.

* * * *

"Aye, Captain, there is word of a Spanish galleon set sail fully loaded from Chile, headed home to Spain," Pilot James Peckham whispered.

7

"Do we know her course?"

"Aye, sir. We do. We can intercept her off the coast of the American main. We need set sail within the next two hours when we have the tide in our favor."

"How close are we to making ready?" the captain asked his first mate who was standing near to listen.

First Mate Jack Cromwell scanned the area of working men to assess their progress. "Close, sir."

The captain nodded and stood back as barrels of food were loaded from the dock. "Good, sooner the better, Jack...sooner the better." He eyed the waterfront carefully.

* * * *

The tide lifted the corvette in its shifting waves as the ladders were hoisted and the sails raised. Captain Jones stared at the sky as they planned their route, mapping his course with his pilot and the stars. The water appeared like black glass as they moved out to the strong currents of the massive Atlantic Ocean. The sky was still tinged with violet as the last of the sun's light dipped and vanished beyond the horizon. A cool, refreshing, welcome sea breeze replaced the strong stench of rotting shellfish as it dried the sweat-soaked crew. Summer seas lay ahead. The captain closed his eyes in a prayer as they made their way once again into the unknown. He lowered his eyes from the wind, for it had caused hot tears to run down his face.

* * * *

Justin listened to the movement around him. Cramped inside a barrel of apples, he was making a mash out of them with his shoes. Wearing their sweet scent like an annoying, over-fragrant perfume, he was itching to get out and breathe fresh air. The voices of men and boots faded to a dull heartbeat as he strained to listen. He could feel the swaying of the waves as they set sail and hear the moaning of the planks in the hull. Edging up the barrel top, he waited before lifting it enough to peek out. It was pitch black. Setting the cap down, he climbed out and replaced it as he took a look around. As his eyes adjusted, he could just make out the shapes of things near him. He was in the bowels of the ship, surrounded by the store of beer and hard tack. The soft clucking of chickens could be heard nearby. He could smell odors he recognized, and some that he did not dare to. Smoothing his fingers along the narrow lanes between crates and walls, he found a door, shook it, but was unable to open it. After some violent tugging, he sighed unhappily, aware he would have to wait until someone came in for food. Wondering how long that would be as he began to tire and was in need of some rest, he felt his pockets for his coins and panicked. He turned them out in absolute horror. The whore had picked them clean. "Damn wench!" His forehead broke out in a cold sweat. Sitting down on a pine box, he rested his head in his hands and sighed. "I'm doomed."

Hearing the scurry of a rat, he jolted in surprise, elevating his feet up off the floor in fear. "Can this get any worse?"

Chapter Two

Justin stirred from his sleep to the sound of someone opening the door of the storeroom. He hid behind the crates and held his breath.

A man with a heavy black beard, peppered with specks of gray, had come in. He filled a large wicker basket and then went to check on the chickens. Justin waited, slipping out of the room and down the long narrow passage. A harsh smell of rot filled his nostrils, and he assumed he was heading deeper into the bowels of the bilge instead of upward. Stifling a gag, he backed away, trying to cover his nose and mouth, holding his breath. Having to backtrack, he heard the cook still rummaging through the storeroom and paused. He tiptoed nearer and tried to listen. Hearing voices approach, he stiffened in fright and backed up, with great reluctance, closer to the dank reek. Two more men were coming down the passageway. Justin leaned back against the wall, hoping the dim light was enough concealment.

They were laughing loudly as they greeted the cook and offered to help him carry some of the goods up to the next deck for him. Justin kept still, waiting. Within moments, they headed out of the storeroom and back to the galley.

Assuming the coast was clear as he listened to their footfalls recede, Justin straightened out his back and combed his hand through his long hair, getting it out of his eyes. He gasped, as a man appeared, intent on one more bottle.

"What the devil do we have here?" The large man stood tall as he inspected Justin.

"Sir, I would like to explain." Justin trembled nervously.

The broad, hairy man brought Justin to the light to inspect him; his clean, white knee breeches and brown, pewter-buttoned waistcoat. "Well, shiver me timbers! How did ye get on board? How old are ye, lad?"

"Eighteen, sir...please...I must be allowed to sail with you." Justin put his hands together to beg the man. It appeared all the men on the ship had facial hair and bandanas on their heads. It was difficult for him to tell one from the next.

"Argh! No young boys are permitted on board. Ye have no idea what these dogs are like when they have had enough grog. They would devour ye." The man's voice was as rough as sandpaper.

"They would eat me?" he gasped in horror.

The man laughed. "Aye, but naught the way ye thinks, naught over the spit. Come, lad, we must get ye to the captain and turn back."

"No!" Justin shoved by him and ran down the passage. The man shouted after him as Justin ducked into a dark, narrow opening.

Feeling his way down several cramped passages trying to find a safe route, he could hear men's voices in every direction. *I can't be let off back at port! I just can't!*

Jumping in fear as he felt someone put their hand over his mouth and around his chest, Justin was dragged back into the crew's cabin. When he could free himself, he spun around to see his assailant.

"What a pretty boy! Ye stowaway for some adventure asea?"

Justin swallowed his terror as he studied this man. He was short and heavy-set with a large, protruding, hairy belly and a coarse, brown-matted beard. Equally matted was his greasy hair, tied back from his face with a grimy rag. He had large, gaping holes in his rotting teeth, and foul-smelling breath. Appearing like a hook at the end of his right arm was a hand missing its last three fingers, and his clothing was filthy and stiff from salt and sweat. His once-white breeches were now gray. His red and white knee socks were faded to brown and yellow, and no shirt did he wear to cover his furry obesity.

"Yes, sir, I did. Please don't turn me in." Justin was stalked hungrily and backed against a wall. He tilted his face away from the man when his misshapen hand caressed his cheek. "Agh!" Justin winced in disgust. "Do not touch me."

"There be sixty on board, lad. No women. A pretty young boy hasn't much chance in getting by unmolested. Ye were daft to come on board." In a grotesque gesture of hunger, the man licked his two fingers after they stroked Justin's face.

"What?" Justin gulped. "I want to be just like the other men. I want to help the captain get his gold."

His mouth was covered quickly, and he was pressed back harder. "Ye've a lot to learn, boy, about keeping yar lips sealed. Ye don't speak those words aloud. Ye'll be lucky to leave this ship alive, and I mean 'fore we ever meet the enemy."

Justin managed to get his mouth away from the stifling, deformed grip. He panted to catch his breath. "Let me be. Let me just sail like one of the men."

The grotesque man leaned back and fondled the clean fabric of Justin's clothing. "Ye'll get used to being handled, ye lovely thing. It'll be the reason to keep ye on board." With his hips pressed forward, he ground against Justin's body.

Justin cringed in revulsion. "Oh, bloody hell..."

* * * *

"Captain! Captain Jones, sir!"

"Come in."

"Sir, there be a young lad spotted on board."

The captain narrowed his eyes at Quartermaster John Tucker. "What boy?"

"Down in her hull, sir. The scallywag must have boarded whilst we were in port. He be a stowaway, sir."

"Bring him to me at once."

"Aye, sir, but he still be at large, sir."

"Well, find him!"

"Yes, sir."

* * * *

Justin shivered in disgust as those two chubby, sticky fingers touched the skin under his waistcoat. "Oh, Christ...no..." Shoving back with every ounce of strength Justin possessed, he made for the door. The man was on him again and dragging him back from its safety. "No! Did you not hear me? I said no, you filthy beggar. Get your hooks off me!"

The door swung open and one of the crew stepped in. The crewman grabbed Justin out of the clutching embrace and shoved him down the corvette's claustrophobic passageways.

"Aye! I was just bringing the young lad to the captain, First Mate Cromwell!"

"Sure ya were, Hornbolt." Cromwell said nothing to Justin and physically directed him to the captain's cabin on the upper deck. Justin waited as Cromwell knocked. "Captain Jones, sir?" he shouted and was bid entry. Cromwell nodded for Justin to go first.

Peering in warily, Justin stepped inside, finding someone seated at a desk studying a map. It was a man in his mid-twenties, well dressed, clean-shaven and extremely handsome. His lusciously long, thick brown hair was tied in a ponytail with a blue satin ribbon. When he raised his head and connected with Justin's eyes, Justin felt his insides jump at the intelligence and sensuality of the gaze. With a surge of lightning rushing through his veins, Justin bowed his head in respect and stammered, "Sir...Captain, sir..."

Captain Jones nodded to his first mate. "Thank you. That will be all." The captain waited until he and Justin were alone before he inspected Justin carefully.

Justin lowered his eyes at first but couldn't resist a peek at this handsome ruler. He studied this large, muscular man with three flintlock pistols in his baldric and a cutlass sword at his waistband. It didn't take long until he was in complete awe. This man had the polish of the Royal Navy and exuded an aura of perfect control, absolute power, and unmatched sexuality.

The captain released a long, slow sigh and asked, "What is your name, lad?"

"Justin Alexander Taylor, sir...at your service, sir." He bowed his head again.

"How did you get on board?"

"I hid in a barrel, sir. A barrel of apples." Peeking down at his boots, Justin tried to hide the apple mash still stuck to them.

"Why did you do this?"

Justin wanted to communicate his desire to sail so badly, he was about to cry from the frustration. Dropping to his knees before the man, Justin lifted his hand to kiss his golden seal ring. "Please let me sail with you. I beg it of you. I have waited all my life to do this. I cannot go back. Kill me, but do not send me back."

"There are no boys allowed on board, Justin."

Justin listened to his calm, low voice, but he didn't want to believe it could be over. How could his quest end so quickly? Shivering visibly, he knew exactly what his father would do to him if he were forced to return home. He'd be in agony for weeks from the beating. Tears welled in his eyes as he lay his head down on this man's solid, muscular lap. "Please, sir, I'll do anything you ask. I am a good worker. I will never complain. I will be your servant. I will be your slave. Only, please, don't take me back."

The captain urged Justin's face up to see it. Rivers of tears ran down his jaw in glistening lines. Using his thumbs, the captain softly brushed them away from Justin's cheeks.

Justin connected to his gaze, silently begging. The strength of this man overwhelmed him, his size and his grace. Justin thought he literally oozed with some kind of masculine essence. The master of the ship was debating something, teetering on a decision. Justin remembered what the chubby-clawed creature had said to him. Something about getting used to being handled and being allowed to stay on board. Sneaking a glimpse at the captain's tight breeches, then up into his brilliant sea-blue eyes once more, a thought crossed his mind. *This man, I could tolerate being handled by.* With juvenile awkwardness, Justin cleared his throat and suggested, "I'm at your service, sir. In…in any capacity you please. All I ask in return is leave to remain. Can I beg you any harder? Make it any clearer? Sir?"

Captain Jones raised his eyebrows expressively. "I'll not ask what you are implying. I may take it as an insult." He nudged Justin aside so he was able to stand. So tall was he, he had to stoop over in the cramped space. Commencing a back and forth pacing, he confronted Justin once more, "Why do you yearn for this life? Do you think it is glamorous? It is filled with danger. And I don't mean only from the battles. This boat, it is wrought with filth and disease. The men, they are like inmates, common thieves. They come for the prize and then squander it all on gambling and women in one single night. And you want to live among them? One look at you, and you will be passed from one hungry hand to another. Why, my boy, did you have to be so flaming pretty?"

Justin's face heated up terribly with his blush. After a gulp and a breath, he answered, "If I was plain, would that make the difference?"

Captain Jones rubbed his face tiredly. Inhaling deeply, he found Justin's gaze again. "Justin Alexander Taylor, whatever am I going to do with you?"

"I will walk the plank then, sir." He lowered his head and pouted.

The captain chuckled in surprise. "Walk the plank?" For some reason, it made him roar with laughter.

Justin took great insult. "Is that so funny?"

"Come here, lad." The captain contained himself, dabbing at a tear in his eye. Sitting back down in his chair once more, he reached out his hand. Justin scrambled to his feet and stood before him, clasping it. "I am afraid I am stuck with you for the time. But I cannot watch over you night and day. How will you cope? Do you have a dagger?"

Justin lowered his head. "No, sir."

The captain moved to his wooden chest and unlocked it. After rummaging in it for only a moment, he removed a cutlass sword and handed it to him. "When I cannot be near you, you can defend yourself, but never use this whilst we sail. Let me remind you the code of conduct whilst on board. Every man shall obey my command. No man keeps a secret from the company. No gaming for money, and do not strike another man whilst on board. All quarrels are to be handled on shore with gun or sword. You will walk a fine line in defending yourself, Justin. Remember these rules, or even I cannot protect you."

"Yes, sir." Justin started to grow excited, fingering the handle of the blade.

"You will sleep in here. If you are let loose at

nightfall with that mangy lot, you will have a sexual disease by morning."

"What?" Justin gasped. "Oh, Lord." He dropped to his knees and hugged the captain around his legs. "Thank you, sir! Thank you! I am forever indebted to you, sir." He started kissing the captain's thighs, immaculate in white breeches.

"All right, lad." The captain nudged him. "Let's see if you thank me when we board broadside."

"Yes, Captain. I will fight with you. You can count on me." With a last tight squeeze, he released the captain and raised his chin up to give him a very loving smile.

* * * *

The captain led Justin to the main deck and called out to his men for attention. When they crowded around him as if he were a prophet about to spout Holy Scripture, he set Justin up onto a cannon so he could be seen. "This lad is Justin Taylor. He has managed to stowaway on board our ship. Until we can reach land and return him, he will be here with us."

Justin swallowed nervously as dozens of wild men ogled him. He'd never seen a more ragged bunch in his life. They appeared very raw and dangerous, and more than a few had pieces missing from them. Fingering the hilt of his cutlass, he tried to feel security from it, but it did little to alleviate his fears.

"Leave him be! We won't be at sea for an unreasonably long journey, so curb your appetites. Save it for the whores," the captain stated.

The men glanced around at each other with smirking grins. Justin shifted uncomfortably watching them, unconsciously squeezing his legs tightly together.

"He's going to pull his weight. He'll work as hard as any of you. Just let him get on with it, and let's make this the one broadside that pays!"

The crew hooted in a cheer. Captain Jones turned to Justin and said, "It's no guarantee, lad. You just do your best." He gestured to a tall, slender, clean-shaven, fair-haired man to come forth. "This is James Peckham. He's our pilot, and you need obey him like a captain." Justin nodded obediently. The captain brought over another man, heavy and squat with a dark beard and black, thick, wavy hair. "This here is our quartermaster, John Tucker. If he tells you to do something, you do it."

"Aye, sir. Err, we met briefly," Justin mumbled, knowing this was the first man he had fled from in the hold. He cleared his throat, trying to remember their names.

Another heavyset bearded man was waved over. "This is Thomas Black. He's our boatswain, and Jack Cromwell is our first mate. These are my trusted men. You report any assault to them if I am not at hand. You obey them with the same respect as you would me."

"Yes, sir, Captain, sir." Justin connected to every critical gaze around him.

"Right, carry on. Peckham, come with me." Captain Jones and the pilot disappeared into the captain's cabin.

Justin stood idly and stared up at the sails. A flag was flying. He expected it to be black. How odd. It seemed like a Spanish flag. A lookout was perched aloft the enormous main mast. Justin shivered at how high the man was from the deck. "Blimey!"

"Come on, lad. Ye've work to do." Quartermaster Tucker tapped him. "First ye help out the cook, then ye come back and get busy learning how to tend the rigging."

Justin sighed and followed after him. As he passed many a man on his way down to the galley, several sticky fingers found his rounded bottom. Stiffening up, he tried to ignore them, keeping close to Tucker and swatting his hand like a tail behind him.

The cook was leaning into a large, brick-lined chimney with huge iron pots in it. With sweat beading on his forehead, he peered up from his kettle.

"Aye, Smithy, we got ye a hand." Tucker nudged Justin in front of him.

"Take off yar fancy frock and waistcoat, boy," Smithy yelled.

Justin shed his clean coat and vest and handed them to Tucker. Tucker's eyebrows rose in irritation.

Justin stared back at his agitated expression nervously. "Sorry, sir. What was I to do with it?"

Tucker growled, "Take it to the captain's cabin later. I'm no cabin boy." He tossed the items onto a bench.

"Sorry, sir." Justin blushed crimson. He waited for Tucker to leave and then stood watching the cook.

Smithy shoved a paring knife at him and sat him down at a wooden bench. "Peel." He pointed to a barrel of potatoes.

Justin rolled up his sleeves and sighed. By the time he had peeled about a dozen potatoes, he started to feel seasick. Though he hadn't noticed the rocking of the boat before, having been preoccupied with his fear, suddenly, sitting still, trying to focus, the shifting from side to side became very noticeable. Sweat broke out on his forehead, and a wave of nausea washed over him. His belly was empty, yet he was sure he was about to reject its contents. Grabbing the pail he was tossing peels into, he retched miserably.

Smithy spun around at the sound. As soon as he realized what was happening, he started to laugh. "First time asea, little laddie?"

Justin sat up and wiped his face. "Oh, blimey. I need air."

Smithy smiled sweetly. "Ye go get a breath on deck. Come right back after."

Justin nodded and tried to stand. Grabbing at the

table, he steadied himself as they rode over some rough waves. Immediately he sat back down and leaned over the bucket to gag once more. When he just retched and nothing came up, he tried to stop the spinning sensations long enough to stand. "Oh, sweet Mary, help me. Is it always this rough?"

Smithy roared with laughter. "This ain't rough, me laddie. This is calm seas. Go on, get yarself some salt air."

"I can't." Justin could taste the black water in his mouth.

Smithy made his way over to him and stood him up. He helped him to the passageway and tried to lean him against the wall. "I've got too much to do to be tending ye. Ye make yar way."

"Aye, if I can find me legs."

Smithy shouted for one of the crew to come over. "Samuel! Look after the lad. He's a bit of a landlubber."

The gunner laughed in amusement and wrapped his arm around Justin's narrow waist. "It would be me pleasure. Come on, me pretty boy."

They made it to the open air, and Justin felt immensely better to breathe the sunshine. Leaning against the gunwale, he stared out at the horizon, the only thing that wasn't moving at the moment. "Do you get used to it?" Justin asked over his shoulder.

"Should do. It don't get any better, I fear, me pretty." Without hesitation, Samuel reached out to pet the long fringe back from Justin's eyes. "Sit yarself down."

Justin slid down to the deck as if he were a spineless jellyfish. All the men that were tending the rigging and sails were laughing at him. "I'm the fool," he sighed.

Samuel knelt near to whisper to him and caressed his hair, "Aye, for now. It's a boring road we follow. Nothing for amusement until we spot the galleon's mast. So ye, me pretty, are our entertainment."

Justin rested his head back against the ship's

gunwale. "Lovely. Just lovely." Heated up in his embarrassment, he assumed the color was washing through the paleness of his cheeks like someone had thrown blood on a white sail.

"Aye, that be true. Lovely describes you best." The caressing of Justin's face grew more sensual.

Tucker walked by and paused to peer over the gunner's shoulder at Justin. "Shouldn't ye be in the galley, boy?"

"Yes, sir." Justin tried to get to his feet.

Samuel stood and reached his hand down to help Justin up, smiling at the quartermaster. "Sea sickness, Johnnie."

"Aye, Sam, that it is. Come on, lad, off to work."

Justin nodded and tried to inhale the fresh air a few times before heading back inside. They watched after him with a smile on their lips.

"This will be the voyage from hell for the lad." Samuel shook his head wistfully.

"Aye, as it is for the rest of us," Tucker agreed.

Overhearing their comments, Justin stumbled his way back to the kitchen and found several of the men eating some biscuits whilst their meal was prepared. They instantly stopped talking to stare at him.

Justin sat back down and lifted his knife and a potato. Now that he didn't feel quite as sick, hunger was kicking in. Peeking up shyly as they munched, Justin wondered where he could get himself some of those cakes.

One of the men seemed to read his thoughts. The man brought some biscuits over and sat next to him. "Here, lad."

Justin sighed with relief and thanked him. Biting into it hungrily, he felt the man's leer and was trying to get used to all the lustful ogling. It was very uncomfortable being the object of sixty rough men's desires.

"Justin Taylor, I'm William Davis. One of yar ship's

gunners. Ye can call me Will."

Justin smiled shyly at him. "Will. Thanks again for the biscuit. I felt a bit sick, and now I feel better with this in me stomach."

Will smiled and handed him another one, peeking up at Smithy anxiously.

Justin took it and munched happily. "How'd you lose your ear?" Justin pointed to the left side of Will's head.

Will grinned and boasted, "T'was bit off in a fight. Naught to worry, lad. I won it."

Justin stopped chewing and stared at him curiously. "Why…why do so many men have missing pieces?"

Very gently, Will caressed Justin's long, wavy hair. "Aye, lad, after a broadside there be many a gaping wound that can go bad and rot. The ship's doctor has no choice. He hacks the bad bit, burns what's left, and we go on. Hopefully ye shall keep all yar lovely parts."

Justin tried to swallow down his dry throat. The caressing had gotten more amorous and the gaze more intense. "I have to get back to work now."

"Aye, ye do, before Smithy hollers at us both. If ye are ever hungry, ye come to me. I'll see to it ye are fed properly and without hesitation."

Justin watched in horror as Will's rough, callused hand smoothed down his cream-colored blouse.

"Will! Let the lad finish. I got a shipload of hungry mouths to feed," Smithy roared.

Will laughed at the predicted chastising. When he finally stood up, he gazed down at Justin, smiling sweetly, and reminded him, "Ye have any problems, ye comes to me." He poked his thumb into his own chest proudly.

Justin knew that would never happen, but smiled and nodded politely, not wanting to make an enemy. He got back to his potatoes, keeping his eyes on his work.

* * * *

Everyone was resting after their meal. The deck was loaded with reclining, scratching bodies as the mid-day sun burned too hot for anyone to find motivation to move. Justin felt drowsy as well and wondered where he could close his eyes and feel safe. Several of his shipmates were waving him over, patting the open spots next to them. Desperately, he tried not to catch their drooling sneers. He passed the fair-haired pilot as he made his way down to the captain's cabin.

"You taking a caulk, lad? You look exhausted," Peckham observed.

"Aye, sir. I can't keep me lids open."

Peckham patted his bottom affectionately and went on his way.

Justin scuffed to the captain's cabin and peered in. The captain was there talking with his boatswain, Thomas Black. Justin apologized for the interruption and bowed his head. "I was wondering, Captain, if I could just rest here a bit."

"Come in, lad. Rest your bones." The captain gestured to the bunk.

Justin nodded in gratitude and collapsed on the bed, drifting off to sleep.

* * * *

The boatswain gazed at his captain and whispered, "He's got the men in a right state. Every word exchanged is about the lad. Peckham said several more weeks to the coast of the American main before we even begin to spot her mast."

"He'll be all right. We'll get him back whole." The captain peered over at the sleeping boy.

"What these lads think. Some fairy story adventure asea. He's found out it was a bit more than he asked for."

Black stroked his wiry beard softly as he spoke.

Captain Jones smiled to himself. "We all were lads once, Thomas, looking for a new life. I thought the Royal Navy was my fairy tale. He's not the only one disillusioned, my friend."

Black connected to his captain's eyes, nodding. "I'll leave ye to it then. Get ye some rest, Richard."

After he watched his boatswain exit, the captain turned back to the bunk where Justin was sleeping his worries away. Standing, the captain approached the bed to stare down at him wistfully.

* * * *

Justin stirred after a short hour's nap. With a stretch, he opened his eyes and yawned. Something warm was near him. When he raised his head, he was delighted to find the handsome captain sound asleep next to him. Justin's heart quickened, and a smile played across his lips. Leaning up to gaze down at his gorgeous features, Justin felt very fortunate to have this powerful guardian angel watching over him. He positioned himself comfortably to stare at him as he rested, enjoying his high cheekbones and full lips, his dark eyebrows and long, glittering lashes. That thick brown hair was very full and long, falling out of its ribbon. His cream-colored shirt lay open on his bronze chest, and his breeches stretched tight over his large, muscular legs.

Deep inside, Justin had a tremendous urge to touch him. Finding his courage, he moved one hand so he could trace the line of that huge, rounded chest muscle. Before contact was made, the captain opened his eyes. That hand withdrew quickly, and a bright blue stare attached to his own.

"How long have you been awake?" he asked Justin.

Justin smiled dreamily at him. "Not long, sir. Just

watching over you, sir."

Captain Jones smiled wryly. "Off to work. First check with Smithy, then Boatswain Black."

"Aye, sir." Justin smiled at him, climbing over him, sliding across his body, to get out of the bunk.

When Justin turned back to look, the captain watched him for a moment before he lay back, staring at the wooden beams of the ceiling.

Justin poked his head into the galley. "Oy! You be needin' me?"

"Aye! I could always use the help," Smithy replied.

Justin rolled up his sleeves. "What should I do?"

"Go fetch two chickens, the ones what no cackle fruit are under. Take 'em up to the deck and kill 'em, then down here to pluck."

Justin nodded and made his way to the hold. Balancing with both hands on the walls down the passage, he passed several of the crew who were coming back up after getting some of the bottled beer. He desperately tried not to meet their eyes until one slammed into him with his shoulder. A great growl of rage emerged from Justin in anger, until he realized in disgust that it was the man with the disfigured hand.

"Watch yarself, lad, watch yarself." Ben Hornbolt laughed.

Passing him with a look of complete disdain, Justin sneered in revulsion and avoided him. He found the storeroom and wondered where the chickens were. Quietly listening, he followed the sound of their clucking to a cage. Lifting each one of them off their boxes carefully, he couldn't believe how many had laid eggs. He finally found two that were barren and held one in each hand by the neck. At least he knew how to kill a chicken. His father had shown him that trick years ago.

Carrying them up to the deck proudly, he searched for a likely spot to do the dirty deed. The place was overloaded with male bodies. There was twice the number of crewmen the ship could hold comfortably. That's what they needed to win the battles. Two-to-one ratios. It just felt so crowded all the time. And they stank.

Once again, all eyes were on him—that dreaded sensation. The entertainment, was he? What nonsense. When he released one of the birds to get a hold of the other, it clucked and flapped all over the deck. "Blimey!" he exclaimed as he decided what to do next. The men were roaring with laughter and offering no assistance. Justin figured one bird flapping around was enough. Quickly he drew his cutlass and hacked off the other chicken's head. When he released it and it too ran around the deck, headless, he gaped at it in horror.

Justin noticed the pilot, who must have heard the hilarity as he climbed up the main mast to have a look around.

Peckham shook his head in disbelief. "At least you're keeping the crew amused, Justin."

"Sorry, Mr. Pilot, sir." Justin peeked up sheepishly at him. Like it was a limp rag, Justin picked up the dead bird by its feet and rose on tiptoes to look for the second one.

"How did that one get away from you? He's not got his bleedin' head!" The pilot laughed heartily.

Justin's cheeks were on fire with his blush as the men kept shouting rude things. "I don't know, sir." On feathered feet, he hurried away and searched for the other one.

* * * *

The captain came up behind his pilot and caught the tail end of his laughter. "What passed?"

Peckham twisted around to face him, trying to control himself. "That Justin. He's really quite an amusing lad. I have to say, I'm almost glad he's on board. He makes for high comedy."

The captain's eyes crinkled into a smile. "Yes, he has endeared himself on the crew. So much so, I'd say he'd be a hard one to see leave."

They raised their chins to find him racing by, the white feathers just out of reach. The crew was rolling with laughter. Captain Jones and Pilot Peckham covered their smiles and tried to contain it.

* * * *

Justin finally dove on top of the escaped bird. He gathered it up in his arms and caught his breath. With his lips tight over his teeth containing his fury, he cursed at it angrily and struggled to keep its wings close. As one who has the power of life or death, he carried the second chicken to the same spot he cut the last one and knelt on its body whilst stretching out its neck. Fumbling for his cutlass, he lifted it to hack away at the damned fowl's neck. When he was done, he wouldn't release it lest it run off on him. Cheering burst forth around him. Justin raised his eyes to see the men shouting at him, praising him for finally finishing his job. Not knowing if he should be flattered or more embarrassed, he let up on the dead thing slowly and made sure it didn't move. Sighing with relief at finally completing the task, he carried the limp carcasses back to the galley.

Hands and fingertips touched him, patting his back and handling his bottom, as they appeared to want to congratulate him. It made him grind his teeth, knowing it was a pretext to grope him. When he finally made it past the last fondling, soot-covered finger, he rushed into the galley. His lip curled in disgust, knowing the nasty job of plucking was still ahead.

* * * *

When he was finally released from his chores for the night, he was filthy and exhausted. Smithy held him back and asked him to clean up after the horde. And they were messy eaters. Most used their soiled hands and slopped the tables. First, there was the washing of the bowls, then mopping the floors. The captain insisted on keeping the ship as clean as possible to avoid disease, especially in the galley. When all was done and dusted, he made his way to the captain's cabin and poured a small amount of fresh water into a basin. Stripping off his sweat- and salt-soaked clothing, he began to bathe himself, luxuriating in the refreshing, cool liquid.

When the door swung open, Justin spun around and covered himself quickly.

The first mate gasped, "Shiver me timbers, lad! I thought we had netted a mermaid. What in blazes are ye up to?"

"A bath. I'm a mess." Justin found his blouse and lifted it to cover himself modestly.

Cromwell grinned. "A bath. Ye'll find less and less effort in that soon. There just ain't much fresh water. And she'll turn on us, lad."

"I know. I'm sorry, sir. I'm not used to being so filthy."

"I was looking for our captain. I'll leave ye to it." Cromwell left, closing the door behind him.

Dropping the blouse, Justin stood tall and poured the water basin over his head, letting it wash through his hair. The relief he felt was immeasurable. Finally satisfied and refreshed, he reached for his clothing.

* * * *

The captain had just come from the upper deck, speaking with his pilot to make sure they were still on course. Exhaustion had set in as he stepped through his cabin door, intent on a night's rest. It was at the moment Justin was leaning over to reach for his clothes. When that lovely white rump came into focus, soon to be covered by the light fabric of his pants that were clinging to his damp skin, the captain gasped in amazement, thinking it was a woman. It only took a moment to realize it was Justin. Rubbing his weary face, the captain sighed to himself, "And I've not been at sea more than a day. Lord, help me."

* * * *

Justin twisted around and smiled adoringly at him. "Captain, sir. Just a quick rinse. Sorry, sir."

The captain tossed off his hat and coat. "Don't apologize, lad. Use the water before she turns on us. It's no good full of mold and slime."

"Right then. I will." He climbed onto the bunk with a bounce and felt cool and refreshed with his head wet.

The captain sat down and unbuckled his boot.

"Let me help you, sir!" Justin scrambled to assist, kneeling before his captain to remove his boots as if Captain Jones were a king. When Justin felt a light touch on his back he froze, head down, heart in throat.

"Who did this to you?"

"Me father."

"Your father beat you this way?"

Justin bit his lip and nodded.

"Turn 'round."

Justin obeyed, feeling emotional suddenly.

Captain Jones ran his fingers over the deep scars marring his back. Whipping marks from obviously several extremely severe thrashings. "Why would a father do this to his son?"

Justin didn't know the answer. As he blinked, it caused tears to spill down his cheeks.

When he received no reply, the captain tried to urge Justin to face him. Justin did with great reluctance, wanting to hide his tears. The captain's index finger raised Justin's chin up to face him. "You're a good lad," he told him softly.

Justin burst out crying. He had never cried about it before, choosing to bottle it in, toughing out the abuse and trying to let it harden him into a man.

The captain drew him closer onto his lap and held him in an embrace. With a deep exhale, the captain squeezed and rocked him, rubbing his back gently, shushing him. "All right, lad. All right."

"I'm sorry, Captain. I'm not man enough for this crew. I've made a fool of myself."

"Shhh, you have not. You have done very well today. Better than I expected."

Justin moved back from his embrace to be able to see him and stare into his blue eyes. This man was everything he wanted to be: big, strong, respected, intelligent, handsome, and very well liked.

"Right. Off to bed, now." He gave Justin a little nudge.

"Yes, Captain, sir." Releasing his hold, Justin climbed onto the mattress. Getting himself cozy, he lay on his side and stared at the captain, waiting excitedly to be joined in the bunk.

Clearing his throat, avoiding Justin's eyes, the captain took off his blouse, dousing the lamp, moving next to Justin, facing away from him.

Justin swallowed his emotions and raised his hand. With the lightness of a butterfly, he touched the captain's warm, rounded shoulder. "Thank you, sir."

"Don't thank me, lad. Just go to sleep."

"Captain, sir?"

"Yes, Justin?"

"What is a mermaid, sir?"

"Why do you ask that? Have you been compared to one?"

Justin was glad for the darkness, for he blushed crimson. "Errr, aye, sir."

"She is a lovely maiden, half woman, half fish."

"Oy? Which half?"

"Top half is the lady, lad. Go to sleep, Justin."

Half fish? He wondered if they would see such a creature. With a sigh and a grin, he nuzzled into the bedding happily, stroking that broad, muscular, bronze back lightly with his fingertips. "Aye, my Captain. And a good night to you, sir." Justin dozed off soon after.

Chapter Three

When Justin awoke, he was alone. The sound of men working above filtered into the dimly lit space as he stretched his back and yawned. After relieving himself in a chamber pot, he gathered all his things to ready himself for the day ahead. A stomach grumble urged him on to seek food. With a light airy gait, he headed down to the storeroom for some tack and water.

Rummaging around curiously, he stuck a biscuit in his mouth to crunch on happily, an apple in his pocket, and a flask of water under his arm. Just about to turn and leave, a strong-smelling, sweaty creature blocked him in. When he was able to gather his wits, he yelled, "Get out of me way!"

"Ye'll be wise to stop avoiding me, me pretty," Ben Hornbolt sneered, showing his rotted teeth.

Justin stared into the lecherous leer of the chubby, claw-handed man in complete horror. "You heard the captain! I am to be left alone."

The wretched sod spied behind him, closing the storeroom door. It was in total blackness, but for one covered lamp.

Justin dropped the things in his hand in panic, touching the hilt of his sword. "Let me be! You'll get nothing from me."

Hornbolt slithered closer. "Ye cut me whilst on board, and ye'll see a very painful death."

Justin instantly remembered the captain's warning of the rules on board. Very reluctantly, he released the hilt and backed away into the crates. "No! Whatever you think you shall get from me, the answer is no!"

Hornbolt's condescending laughter revolted and terrified Justin. He moved as far as he could from Hornbolt, deeper into the over-filled room, until he hit some oak casks. "Why, in the name of the King, are you doing this to me?" he cried.

"I've not done a thing to ye yet, lad. Come to me, ye lovely creature, let us both enjoy ourselves." Hornbolt reached out his grubby claws and made some grotesque grunts. The noise reminded Justin of what an oversized snail would sound like as it was plucked off a wooden board, a slimy, sucking sound.

Justin gritted his teeth as the beast took his equally snail-like member out of his soiled trousers. He was fully erect. "No! I will tell you once again! *No!*" he screamed.

Before Justin could react, Ben Hornbolt dove on him and pinned him onto the oak casks, tearing at his breeches and blouse to get at his skin. Justin was pressed painfully against the splintery wood. Growling and battling as fiercely as a young soldier, he was making little headway against a very strongly built fiend who tore open his clothing as if it were paper.

That repulsive, hard thing moved closer. The sensation of it against his legs sickened him. That wheezing, foul-smelling breath in his ear, that protruding hairy belly, and those sucking fat lips, all sought to make him gag and writhe in revulsion. With every twist and turn to wrench away, sharp fingernails and protruding iron nail heads sliced Justin's skin.

With all his might, Justin roared in defiance, denying any defeat though his strength was waning fast as this man was much more mentally fit for battle than was he. As that hard slug-like thing pressed its way between his thighs, Justin clenched his teeth and snarled in rage. Trapped. Trapped like a helpless animal against iron jaws.

* * * *

Smithy made his way down to the hold for the daily task of feeding the crew. Behind him followed a score of men all intent on some tack and ale. As they approached the lower bilge, they heard angry shouting coming from the storeroom. Hurrying their pace, they burst in and found Justin growling fiercely as the beast attempted a savage rape.

At the sound, Ben Hornbolt spun around to a room full of furious eyes. With guilt written all over his face, he stopped to gather himself up quickly and try to explain. "The boy asked me for it! He lured me down here! Honest, me lads. He begged me for it."

Justin collapsed to the floor and covered his face.

Will Davis was among them. He and one of the other gunners grabbed Hornbolt violently. "Ye spineless scallywag! Yar about to be our first keel haul!"

Hornbolt wailed in terror and tried to fight to free himself. Justin curled up into a tight knot, his knees to his chest, his eyes sealed shut. When he felt a light tap on his shoulder, he flinched and snarled up at it. Smithy and the remaining men crouched down to him. "All right, lad. Yar all right."

They urged him to stand. The trembling in his limbs was so extreme, he had to lean on them for support. His clothing was in tatters.

"I got 'im." One of the gunners, Henry, held Justin around the waist and led him up to the captain's cabin.

Tucker and Peckham had heard the tale and hurried to see Justin. The accused man was being detained on deck until a vote and decision could be made.

The quartermaster shoved open the door to find Justin with the first mate and the gunner. "What's passed? Tell me the tale in full."

First mate Cromwell sighed and glanced over at the boy. "Ben Hornbolt attempted to molest our young Justin in the hold."

The pilot asked Justin, "How, lad?"

Justin turned his face away and didn't speak.

Cromwell moved closer to Justin and turned Justin's back to the quartermaster and pilot. Very delicately, he lifted up Justin's torn blouse and showed them the fresh bruising and scratches. "There's more." When he felt Justin shiver, Cromwell rubbed his back in comfort. "I'll just show 'em quick, lad."

Justin barely nodded and bowed his head.

The first mate lowered Justin's breeches to show the amount of force he was subjected to. He was covered in marks and raised scratches.

"Did he get in ye, boy?" Tucker inquired.

He shook his head no, not meeting anyone's eyes.

"That's enough," Peckham snarled, clenching his teeth. "I need no more proof!"

"Where's our captain?" Tucker asked.

"On deck, listening to Hornbolt's tale," Cromwell replied.

"Someone stay with the lad. I need to see the captain." Tucker grabbed Peckham, and they left quickly.

* * * *

Captain Jones listened to Ben Hornbolt's shaky story; how Justin had lured him to the storeroom and made obscene gestures to him. That he had tried to resist Justin's invitation, but he was only human. That the lad had his eye on him from the first time they met.

Will Davis and his mates were holding Hornbolt's arms painfully, allowing him no movement. The rest of the crew were standing around in a tight mass, listening. Tucker and Peckham moved to the center of the crowd to meet with their captain who nodded to them and prompted, "Tell the men whatever you learned."

Peckham raised his head and announced, "Our Justin is covered in welts from this dog! He fought off his best, and this bilge rat was unsuccessful in raping the lad!"

A low, angry murmur encircled them.

The captain knew something like this was inevitable. "Where is Justin?" he asked his pilot.

"In your cabin, sir. Should we put this to a vote?"

The captain scanned the angry mob first, then he glanced back at Hornbolt who was about to meet hell face on. Sweat ran profusely down Hornbolt's pale face, and his hands were clenched and bloodless as the ruthless hold on him constricted his veins.

There was a moving ripple in the mob. The entire crew twisted around to see Justin being led through his shipmates. He had his head down, trying to disappear under his long hair. Justin's tears had dried on his face.

The first mate explained, "We thought the lad had a right to know what was going on and to speak in his own defense if he needed to."

At the very sight of Justin's devastated expression, the crew grew enraged. Ben Hornbolt started to beg for his life. "Have mercy on me soul!" he moaned.

The captain had no energy for this. All he wanted was a bounty of treasure and to retire on it. He rubbed his face in frustration.

Will Davis started demanding, "A vote! A vote!"

The men joined in the chant.

The quartermaster moved front and center. "A vote then. All say aye if ye think sailor Ben Hornbolt is guilty of the attempted vulgar assault on our Justin Taylor!" A thunderous roar filled the air. "All those who think our Justin Taylor lured Ben Hornbolt to entertain vulgar deeds, say aye!"

It was silent as a tomb.

Tucker raised his voice to be heard by all. "Then we find Ben Hornbolt guilty and subject him to punishment!"

Another loud rumbling was heard. Ben Hornbolt lost more color, and his knees weakened and gave out.

"What punishment do ye all see fit?" Tucker called out, "Marooning? Hanging from the yardarm? Or keel haul?" Through the great cacophony of sound, Tucker listened, and then he quieted them. "Keel hauling it shall be!"

Ben Hornbolt wailed in terror.

* * * *

Justin was numb. There were no thoughts left in him, and all he actually heard was nothing more than raucous shouting, which was just distorted to his ears. All he wanted to do was go to the cabin and curl up into a ball and hide.

As the captain made his way back to his quarters, he grabbed his pilot and brought him with him.

Will and his gunner mates started tying Ben Hornbolt up to toss him overboard. They pinned him down and wrapped him up in a cocoon of coiled ropes.

Cromwell stood behind Justin, his hands on his shoulders. "This is for ye, lad."

Justin raised his eyes wearily. "What is for me?"

As he resisted, Hornbolt was thrown into the water with a shriek of fear. The men laughed and jeered in excitement.

Justin's eyes widened in panic. "No! What are they doing to him?"

Hornbolt was hoisted up against the sharp barnacle studded hull and dragged in the deep green water.

Justin heard his screams of agony and covered his ears. "Oh, dear Lord! *Stop! No!*"

* * * *

Captain Jones showed Peckham into his cabin. They paused when they heard the shrieking and then closed the door. "I feared this would happen. I need them to focus on the reason we are all here. That loaded Spanish galleon. Justin is an unhealthy distraction. How many men, you reckon, will we be dragging from *His Revenge*?"

Peckham sat down next to his captain. "No more, sir. This will be their warning. You didn't see what Hornbolt did to our Justin, sir, did you?"

The captain raised his tired eyelids. "No, I did not. The boy is too pretty. He tests these men daily. I wish he'd never come on board. We have lost a man that could be lifting a sword for us."

"One man. It isn't the first time a ship has lost a crewmember. Typhoid is rampant among most. They are not dying off, Captain."

Captain Jones scrubbed at his coarse jaw in contemplation.

"What is it, Richard?" Peckham touched his arm lightly. "You miss your Katherine back home?"

The captain sat back and exhaled a long breath. "Aye, James. That I do. I wanted this to be the one I retire on. I need these men to be at their sharpest. Now look at what we have." They heard another blood-curdling scream.

"You worry too much. Hornbolt was old and full of malice. He is no great loss, Richard."

The captain met the gaze of his trusted pilot. "You get us there, James. Get us there to that flamin' galleon. I want my hands on those pieces of eight."

"You'll have them, sir. You'll have them." The fair-haired pilot smiled, touching his arm.

"What do we do about Justin?"

Peckham shrugged. "Naught. He's a good lad. He does his work with no complaint."

The captain nodded. "Aye, that he does, but now with new battle scars. What good will he be in a broadside if I am to be watching and protecting him from harm?"

"You won't be. He fought off Ben Hornbolt, and the rat was twice his weight. Hornbolt never raped him, Richard. The boy fought well."

The captain met his pilot's sharp eyes, thinking about what he said.

* * * *

Justin covered his mouth in disgust as the lifeless body of Ben Hornbolt was raised for the last time out of the sea. With the help of the strong crew, he was tied to the yardarm where he swung with the rocking of the boat. Hornbolt's skin was almost taken clean off by the ragged hull. Justin turned his face away and stifled a heaving gag at the sight. A hand rubbed his back affectionately. "Come, lad. Methinks ye need an ale."

Will Davis held his hand and brought him to the galley. Leaving him seated at a bench in a daze, Will returned with several bottles tucked under his arms. The men filled up the room quickly and enjoyed a drink after the punishment was completed.

Numb, completely drained, Justin's eyes were distant as he drank the warm beer.

Will smiled at him and then winked at his gunner mates. "Ye needs to develop a stomach, lad."

Reluctantly, Justin looked at him. "Maybe I'm not cut out for this."

"Nay! Yar! Ye've gone on account like the rest of us. When yar pockets jingle with silver pieces, ye'll have that clever grin back on yer Cupid's bow lips." He tapped his bottle. "Drink up!"

Justin gulped the beer down, trying to block out the memory of those hideous screams the tortured man made.

"Do ye need me to look at ye, lad?"

Hardly hearing the question, Justin raised his head up to a slender man with spectacles. "Who are you?"

"I'm Jason, the ship's doctor."

As the tales of amputations and cauterizing flesh flashed through his mind, Justin's eyes widened in horror. "Noooo! Get away from me! Don't hack anything off me!"

The men roared with laughter as the doctor straightened his back and rubbed his chin in surprise. "I merely was offering a salve for yar bruises."

In revulsion, Justin leaned away from him and into Henry, one of the other gunners. "Oh. No. Thank you. I don't need anything."

As if he were protecting him, Henry wrapped his arms around Justin. "I'll save ye, laddie!" Henry laughed and hugged him tight.

Will wiped his eyes from the hilarity, checking the expressions on the rest of the crew around them. They were all smiling and chuckling at Justin. "Lad, ye are as priceless as a letter of marque."

Having no idea what that was, Justin tilted his head curiously at him, then attempted to get out of Henry's affectionate embrace.

"Drink up! Here, have another." A second bottle was placed before him.

Needing no provocation, Justin swallowed the strong beer thirstily as the men around him began chatting to one another in a low murmur. Soon Justin was feeling the effects of the alcohol. With very little to eat, he was happy to drink himself forgetful.

As he came in and out of focus, he tuned into the conversations around him, nodding when addressed and answering any questions as best he could. Will kept him sated with too much beer and very little food as Smithy worked on getting a stew together for the hungry men. In no time, Justin had a silly grin on his face as his level of inebriation soared with the seagulls. He started humming to himself, then singing a tune. The few around him stopped their chatter to stare at him.

Like a little boy who has been set on stage, he grinned at their attention and sang boldly. "Sing a song of sixpence, a pocket full of rye."

Will and his gunner mates nudged each other and urged Justin on.

Hands prodded him to stand. While teetering on his wobbly legs, Justin belted out his little ditty with a robust energy. "Four and twenty blackbirds baked in a pie!"

* * * *

Captain Jones and Pilot Peckham made their way to the galley when they heard the singing. They glanced at each other curiously and stepped in. Justin was leading the song as the men joined in. Captain Jones spied back over his shoulder at a smiling pilot.

"You see? He is good for their morale," Peckham praised.

The captain had to agree. With contented laziness, he leaned against the galley's wall and listened to the singing.

* * * *

"When the pie was opened, the birds began to sing." Justin lovely voice belted out into the stale damp air of the enclosed galley. "Wasn't that a dainty dish to set before a king!"

Once he was done, Justin had a giddy grin plastered on his lips. With his right hand, he raised his half-full bottle in a toast and felt the pat of several hands on his back in gratitude. As one wicked male squeezed his bum, goosing him, Justin choked in surprise.

When he spun around to find the culprit, Justin

spotted the handsome captain in the room, smiling adoringly at him. In an instant, he went into a deep crimson flush of warmth. The man was staring directly at him, his eyes never leaving Justin's, whilst listening to his quartermaster, nodding in understanding.

Instantaneously, Justin could feel the seductive aura of him. The man had enormous presence. So unique was he, he stuck out from the rest of the crew like a cut diamond in a coalmine. With his clean-shaven angular jaw and full head of brown hair, which was pulled back in a ribbon away from his brilliant, crisp azure eyes, he seemed to tower over the rest with his incredible beauty and height. It amazed Justin how some men emanated sensuality. You could feel this man when he walked into a room. A brahman bull of power, the captain was the type you would follow anywhere at any cost. Some men had that magic about them. Captain Jones was one of them.

Feeling a tap on his leg, Justin wrested his eyes away reluctantly from that unbelievable man to tilt over to look at the gunner.

"Aye, ye falling for our captain, me pretty boy?"

"Oy? Me? Don't be daft." Justin sat back down and drank his beer.

Speaking in a hoarse whisper, Will leaned over the table to him. "Don't get yar sight set on him, lad. He's a lovely lady waiting on him."

At the news, Justin felt his heart crack in two. Before it could be detected, he straightened out his features and shrugged it off. "You must be mad. I have nothing but respect for him. He is my captain. Now, when do we get to eat?"

Will studied his shaky denial. "If ye be looking for affection, look no further, me pretty."

Taking a quick glimpse at his filthy skin and missing ear, Justin held back a shiver in disgust, and ignored the comment, reaching for a bowl of stew.

* * * *

As Justin expected, he was assigned clean-up with the cook as the men left to attend their own chores. Efficiently rinsing the wooden bowls, he stacked them in a crate neatly until his back ached. Smithy thanked him and sent him on his way. On very tired legs, he managed to make his way to the upper deck and inhale the cooler twilight into his lungs. With a peek down at himself, he made a halfhearted attempt to tuck in his blouse which had been torn in the attack. Managing to straighten himself up somewhat, he combed his hair back from his face with his fingers, wondering if he looked even remotely respectable at the moment.

The loud chatter of gulls began to annoy him. Moving past the men tending the large main sail, Justin went to see if there was a reason for all the noise. It stopped him in his tracks to find the birds feeding on the body that still hung from the yardarm. Covering his mouth in revulsion, he quickly twisted away from that grotesque vision.

"Aye, it's making me sick as well, lad." Tucker took out his cutlass and hacked at the rope. The body splashed into the sea and vanished. "She's all gone now." The quartermaster patted Justin's head. "Ye've had a trying day. Go to bed, Justin Taylor."

He nodded, trying not to feel completely sick. Once again dragging his feet, Justin made his way to the captain's cabin and found him shaving his face in a looking glass. It was fascinating, watching the handsome man as he tried to time his strokes with the movement of the ship. When he spotted Justin, he ordered, "Oy, dump the chamber pot before you bed down."

Justin curled his lip at the thought. Obediently, he lifted the little latch that held it steady and wrapped his arm around it, holding his breath. The captain held open the door for him before going back to his task.

As if his life depended on it, Justin walked as slowly as he could to the poopdeck, praying he'd not splash any on himself. Gingerly, he made it to the rail and dumped it out, breathing a sigh of relief. With a heavy heart, he brought it back down and into the cabin.

Done shaving, Captain Jones wiped his face clean and smiled at Justin. "You get it there without a disaster?"

Justin re-secured it onto the floor plank and put the lid on. "Yes, sir," he said tiredly.

The captain appeared surprised. "Good job, lad."

"Thank you, Captain, sir," Justin answered softly. With his stare riveted to that perfect man, Justin watched as the captain unfurled the ribbon in his hair and shook out its length, taking a comb to it, still in front of the mirror's reflection. Justin melted at that sensuous sight, afraid to blink.

Captain Jones set his comb aside and started unbuttoning his blouse. With a sweet, patient smile on his lips, the captain raised his head to Justin and asked, "How are you, lad? You've had a terrible day."

His cheeks slightly tinged with embarrassment, Justin shrugged as he stared at this gorgeous man.

The captain exhaled deeply and draped his shirt over a chair. Crouched over from the low ceiling, he approached Justin and pushed the hair back from his face. "I didn't see what Hornbolt had done to you, Justin. I know what you must have endured at home from your father. This attack was brutal to you. I want to see to it you are all right."

"I...I am all right." A catch formed in Justin's throat. As he cleared it, he kept staring into those baby blue eyes.

"Come on, let's have a look," the captain gestured.

Justin lowered his head and opened his blouse, removing it. With a ceremonial gesture, Justin folded it lovingly on the chair, on top of the captain's own.

Making a sound as if he was furious at what he found, Captain Jones snarled through clenched teeth, "Lay down, boy."

Justin shuffled to the bunk and rested, facing the captain, his arms relaxed over his head.

The captain picked up a jar as he sat next to Justin. He took out a slather with the consistency of cooking grease.

Like ice on a boiling fire, Justin felt the cream soothing his angry skin with pleasure. A deep moan came slipping out of him as he relaxed and savored the kind nurturing he'd never experienced before. Not even from his mother.

"Lower this."

Reaching for them quickly, Justin leaned up and opened his breeches, tugging them down his hips.

As if he were stifling a snarl of fury, Captain Jones hissed, "I had no idea how badly you had been bruised, Justin. I am very glad now that Hornbolt has gotten what he deserved. This is grossly unfair to you, lad."

That large, masculine hand rubbed an herbal-smelling liniment over him. Justin was so relieved he could have cried. It unwound his tight muscles and soul with its communicated affection. That palm smoothed over his back, down his spine to his bottom. Justin felt both palms moving in a circular pattern, one on each cheek. The groan of relief changed to delight as Justin grew very excited.

Justin froze as those wonderful hands moved down the back and inside of his thighs. The heat from them made his skin light on fire. They massaged him lovingly, making him forget any ache or pain with the flash of sensuality. Though he tried to breathe normally, Justin started to draw air in and out quickly with his rising desire, swallowing down a very tight throat. He was hard as a rock. Very slowly, he raised his head off the pillow to try and peek over his shoulder. When the captain's contented gaze and softly focused smile came into his view, Justin muttered to himself, "Oh, Lord…"

As Justin felt the shift of the captain's weight on the bed, it appeared as if he was awakened from his daydream.

In the awkward silence, Justin had no idea what to do. As slowly as he could he leaned up and rolled to his side. "Captain?"

"Yes, Justin?" The captain smiled sweetly at him as he wiped off his hands.

Put to it, Justin lost his nerve and edged his breeches up to cover his hardness. "Nothing, sir."

Captain Jones stood and doused the lamp. When he climbed onto the bunk, the captain released a long, tired breath.

After the large man had settled down, Justin moved to lean on his captain's warm side. "Thank you, sir. It felt really nice. I mean, *really* nice."

"I'm glad, Justin. Good night, lad."

Justin didn't answer right away. Very gently, he rubbed his cheek on the captain's hot muscular biceps, then touched it with his lips. Sneaking a quick kiss, Justin lay back, facing the low ceiling. Patiently, he waited until the captain's breathing softened to his slumber before he pleasured himself whilst lying next to that gorgeous god. "Good night, my Captain," he whispered, closing his eyes and falling into a deep sleep.

Chapter Four

The quartermaster assigned a crewmember to climb the mast and use a telescope to search the horizon. He reported nothing sighted yet. The pilot checked his calculations. They were on course, and the seas were passive. The summer was kind, but very hot come mid-day.

Justin was learning how to tend the rigging, but he hadn't climbed the ratlines as yet. The thought of being that high on a rocking vessel horrified him. With his neck craned to the heavens, he was in awe as at least six men scuttled up to trim the sails, never blinking at the task of stabilizing the shrouds. Calluses were forming on his palms as the coarseness of the ropes rubbed them raw. There was something to be said about learning this trade, however difficult, and enjoying the knowledge it gave him. With rapt attention, he studied Boatswain Black as he pointed out how to attach the sails.

After his first lesson on rigging, it was time for him to get acquainted with a pistol. Will Davis loaded the shot and powder, then handed it to Justin, pointing him out toward open sea. Justin bit his lip in concentration, squinted in the glare, taking a wide stance, trying not to sway with the moving ship. With the anticipation of that loud bang making him cringe, he pulled the trigger, only to land square on his rump from the unexpected recoil, the powder spattering his face.

The crew broke into laughter, smacking their thighs in hilarity.

Stunned, Justin sat with the gun still pointed out to the great expanse of water and smoking. "Blimey!"

Will tried to contain his laughter and helped Justin to his feet. "She packs a mean wallop, lad. Ye should try the musketoon, me thinks."

Justin was still in shock. "What a noise! Can I do that again?"

With growing affection, Will patted his back and smiled at him.

* * * *

Back in his cabin, Captain Jones wrote in his log to update it for his own personal use. He heard the pop first, then the group's laughter and had no doubt Justin was up to his usual antics. A very loving grin filled his face as he chuckled to himself and shook his head. A light rap rattled his door, so he shouted, "Enter!"

First Mate Cromwell came in and greeted him.

"You all right, Jack?"

"Aye, aye, Captain. Very all right, indeed." The men exchanged good-natured smiles.

"What's our Justin up to?" The captain closed his journal and gave his first mate his full attention.

Cromwell wiped at a tear as his amusement resurged. "He fired Will's flintlock and landed right on his arse!"

The captain's face brightened up with the image. "I'm sorry I missed it."

"Aye, what a lad, what a lad." He chuckled to himself.

"Did you come here solely to inform me of his latest antic?"

"Nay sir, I didn't. But that was too good to not share with ye."

"Right. Come now, what have you got for me?"

* * * *

In the late evening, Justin went to the galley to help Smithy with his clean-up chores. Smithy brightened up as the lad smiled sweetly and offered his hand. He patted his head in gratitude and gave him some sweet apple cakes when his task was complete. Justin stuffed one into his mouth and chewed it in delight.

"Shhh, just ye and our captain. Don't let the men know." He winked.

"You want I should bring him his?" Justin said with his mouth full.

"That'd be fine, lad." Smithy handed them to him.

Justin smiled brightly and clutched them to himself to hide and protect. He began walking quickly down the passage trying not to shift with the listing hull. In no time at all, he started losing his balance.

Quartermaster Tucker was headed the same way when he spotted Justin about to fall. Justin hit the side of the passageway, then went down. Tucker gripped Justin's collar and pulled upward, trying to prevent it.

Justin ended up on his rump again, the shirt yanked over his head like a tent.

It was all Tucker could do to not explode with laughter. As he covered his grin, he heard Justin's frustrated sigh.

Peckham was passing by and stopped short behind Tucker to peer over his shoulder. "What now?"

No matter how he tried to keep biting back his mirth, the roar of laughter was moving in on Tucker, attempting to escape.

Peckham tried to find Justin under his muddled blouse. "You in there, lad?"

"Yessss…" came a soft reply.

"Can you stand up?" Peckham tugged the fabric down around Justin's head. "What have you got in your hands that you couldn't prevent your fall?"

Woefully, Justin glanced down. The cakes were smashed against his chest. "Something for the captain. Never mind now."

When Tucker found the crumbled mess, he attempted to excuse himself as quickly as he could. Justin and Peckham could hear Tucker roar with the laughter he just could not contain any longer.

Peckham helped Justin to his feet, and they inspected the damaged cakes. "Oh, dear…" Peckham shook his head.

Justin pouted up at him. "Why am I such a clod?"

Peckham smiled sweetly. "It takes time, lad, to maneuver on a moving craft. You've been asea less than a week. Give yourself credit where it's due, and don't be so hard on yourself."

"Aye, thanks, Pilot." He was far from consoled.

Peckham opened the cabin door and allowed him to pass before going on his way.

Justin set the smashed cakes down on the captain's desk carefully. As efficiently as he could, he brushed off his shirt and hands, then tried to get them back together. They were smashed beyond repair. Justin gave up.

With a pout firmly planted on his face, he sat down to stare at them and sighed. Something caught his attention as it lay on the desk, a journal and a quill. With a quick peek up at the door, he tipped it open to read. It was a daily log. It stated time, position, and weather conditions in an absolutely beautiful scrolling hand. Each entry had a small commentary on the crew. It described him as the young stowaway, then on up to the trial and sentence of Ben Hornbolt. The moment Justin heard the latch, he clapped it shut, quickly sitting on his hands and staring up expectantly.

"Justin, lad, you all right?" The captain came in and tossed his hat aside.

"Aye, Captain, sir."

Captain Jones caught Justin's eyes darting to the food on the desk, then back to the floor. "What have we got here?"

"Apple cakes, sir...that I crushed, on accident." Like a guilty little boy, he kicked his boot into the planked floor.

The captain kept a straight face. Lifting one of the larger pieces of broken cake carefully, he brought it to his lips. "Mmm, very good. Did you make it?"

"No, Smithy did. I just ruined it," he mumbled and stared at the crumbling remains.

"No, it's lovely. Not ruined at all."

Knowing he was just being polite, Justin moved his gaze until he caught those laugh lines near his captain's eyes and the perfect white teeth of his smile. Without any conscious encouragement, his body reacted once more. "Why are you so kind to me?"

The captain's gentle expression faded to all seriousness. With the grace of a king, he sat down on the bunk and whispered, "Come here, lad."

Justin managed to get himself upright and walked to his captain.

Captain Jones reached for his hands and clasped them firmly in his own. "Look at me, Justin."

He did with great reluctance.

"I am not your father. You will not find that harsh judge in me. We all find our way in this life, best we can. You are too hard on yourself, and your past is why. Look, you have come on account with us. You are a part of this crew, like it as not. Why should I treat you any differently than any other man under my flag?"

At that soft melodic voice, Justin felt a catch in his throat and could not utter a word. His stare was connected to the one before him, and his hands were clasping those large warm ones tightly.

"In less than two weeks' time we come upon our prey, lad. Who knows who will live and who will die? I've no time for worry or fear. I go with a single purpose. We all do. We fight as a team, a solid group. You are with us now, Justin Alexander. You stand and deliver as we do. What would you do, Justin, if you knew you had less than two weeks on this earth? That is what our reality is, lad. It's no pretty deed boarding an enemy ship, dealing with her cannons, her crew. They may fight to the death or give up. We've no way to know. You are very young, but we cannot guarantee we will not perish."

Justin thought about it. What would he do if this were his last weeks on earth? *Oh, Lord, let me have him!*

Captain Jones studied him. "I don't say this to scare you, lad. I just want to reassure you that these little things you take so hard on yourself are meaningless. Do you see now?"

Moving slowly, Justin unclasped his right hand from the captain's, and raised it up to his handsome face. With very tentative fingers, he hovered over that high cheekbone and rough one-day's growth. Justin's lips parted with a soft breath.

The captain examined him closely. When he felt that light caress tickle his jaw, he asked, "What thoughts are you having, Justin?"

As if he had been caught thieving, Justin felt his face go crimson. His bold hand dropped, and his eyelashes lowered as well. He cleared his throat and stated, "I have never been treated so kindly before. Here, I have boarded your ship like a criminal, caused the death of one of your crew, and distracted the men with my floundering. Yet, you tend me when I am ill, console me when I am miserable, and praise me when I am a buffoon."

The captain smiled gently at his appraisal. "And what do you make of it all, Justin?"

"I love you, my Captain. I want to do you proud on

that broadside. I want to show my loyalty to you. I will fight to the death for you, to protect you and your crew."

Captain Jones replied, "I am honored I have earned such high regard from you. Thank you, Justin."

About to lean forward for a taste, Justin wanted to kiss those lips so badly, he was salivating at the sight of that pink sensuous mouth in front of him.

"You must go to bed now, lad. It's very late, and we need to start at first light as we get closer to our target."

"Aye, my Captain." He stepped back grudgingly and lowered his head, the perfect servant.

"How is your back? Are you healing?"

Justin's face lit up impishly at the thought. "I am very sore."

"Are you? Is the liniment not helping then?"

"No! It helped me a great deal." Hoping for a massage, Justin could not catch his excited breath.

"Did it?" The captain stood and took off his blouse and boots to get himself comfortable.

"Yes. After you applied it, I felt much relief." His heart beat faster.

"Come then, take off your things."

Justin wiggled out of his shirt and breeches, lying on his belly with a delighted whimper of anticipation. The captain sat near him and inspected the scratches. "You are healing well. Very good."

Eagerly, Justin raised his hips up and tugged his undergarment down to his knees, smiling mischievously into the bedding. At first touch of those hands, he groaned in pleasure.

"I don't know what the doctor puts in these things, but it has done the trick. I try to tell by the odor. It smells very herbal to me. What do you think, Justin? Can you tell?"

"Comfrey?"

"Aye, you think so?" Very gently and lovingly, the

captain rubbed the liniment over his back. "I know nothing of plants. My Katherine does."

Wanting to understand his captain's relationship, Justin tilted his head so he could see him. "Tell me about her, sir."

Captain Jones smiled with pleasure. "She is a beauty, Justin. A beauty." With his soft words, he smoothed his hands over Justin's tight bottom.

"Is she?" A shiver of delight ripped across Justin's length.

"Oh, yes, lad. One worth waiting for. She is like a princess to me. Skin like satin, smooth and milky, ginger-colored hair, and lovely green eyes."

Justin took a look at his captain as those large masculine hands grew bolder. "Is she, sir?" he whispered, hoping, against all hope, the captain would not stop massaging him.

The captain let his gaze mist over softly and dipped his finger into the salve for another slather. Nudging Justin's legs apart, he smoothed it over the welts on his inner thighs. "Like a dream, she is, and the body on her is pure delight."

Hoping to be discreet, Justin parted his legs further, attempting to lure him closer, while trying to prevent a full-blown groan of agony at the longing.

"I yearn for her, Justin. You have no idea how I miss her."

Justin was on fire. Though he tried to stay still with a throbbing hardness between his legs, he ended up writhing on the bed, staring at the handsome man. "I do, sir. I do. It must be agony for you both."

With the palms of his hands, the captain smoothed up Justin's bottom again to hold his waist. As he did, the captain smiled, running his fingers up his back and into Justin's head of hair affectionately.

Just when he began to think it was heaven, Justin

thought he had found hell. This unbelievable urge to come was about to make him do something he might regret. That soothing stroking, the quiet sensuousness of the moment, was almost too much to bear. When it ended suddenly, it was as if a sob would escape his chest. As Justin sat up on the bed, he found the captain wiping off his hands and dousing the lamp, only to crawl in next to him in the darkness.

To be so near him, Justin ground his teeth at the craving. He rolled to his side and listened to that soft breathing next to him. "I'll bet she is missing you too, Captain." Justin heard his captain's deep inhaled breath.

"Yes. She was in misery to see me leave and of not knowing if I will return. Then, of course, there is always the hangman's knot out there for me, if we are caught."

"I cannot imagine her pain, sir. You would be impossible to replace." He sensed the captain leaning up to face him in the jet darkness.

"You say very kind things to me, Justin, and I thank you for the comfort."

Justin was in complete agony. Why was the one man he wanted to have touch him, the only one who would not? *Grope me!*

"Good night, lad."

Regrettably, the captain shifted over. Justin moved to make contact with him in the blinding pitch dark. Feeling for his upper arm, Justin wrapped his hand around that solid hard biceps, and brought it over to his chest to hug, like a child would do to a stuffed doll. His pelvis pressed into that large quadriceps muscle, and his head lay upon the captain's shoulder. Only then could Justin close his eyes.

Chapter Five

At daybreak, Justin set out to do his chores. First it was off to help Smithy in the galley, then swabbing the deck and tending the rigging. At the mid-day sun, the men stopped for their rest, taking off their shirts and lying in whatever shade the sails provided.

He leaned over the rail and stared down at the hypnotic deep green water. There were small whitecaps that rose and fell gently. Suddenly with a startled gasp, he spotted a school of flying fish riding the bow. "Blimey!"

Henry came over to see what his reaction was all about. Leaning over his shoulder to take a peek, Henry laughed softly at what he saw. "Aye, fish with wings. I'd give anything for a net to catch them. I'm sick of Smithy's potato stew and salt pork."

"I've never seen anything like them." Justin stared in fascination.

"Ye'll see all sorts of creatures out in the deep ocean, lad. Even whales pass by on their way," Henry said.

"Whales?" Justin choked in surprise.

Henry patted his back and smiled. "Aye, they really do exist."

"Even mermaids?"

Henry was about to answer the question when he lifted his hand from Justin's back. "Oy! Yer a sweaty rat. Why don't ye take off yar blouse to cool down?"

Upset at the possibility of exposing his skin, Justin stared down at his shirt and fingered the buttons. Everyone else on the ship was topless from the intense heat. The thought of others seeing his scarred back shamed him horribly.

"Ye take that off and go sit at the fo'c's'le deck. The wind there will cool ye down. Come on, lad." Henry stood and reached for him.

Justin hesitated, biting his lip.

When his hand wasn't clasped, Henry replied, "Suit yarself then." He shrugged and walked away.

His mood grown foul, Justin leaned back over the rail and rested his head on his arms as he thought about his father and the wicked beatings he endured. Though he had never seen his own back or the damage, he had heard his mother's cries when she did. A single tear fell from his eye as the memory of that day sought to overwhelm him.

With his proud strut, Will Davis walked up to join him and leaned on the spot next to him. He placed his arm around Justin's back to give him an affectionate squeeze. "Aye, lad, ye dreaming of sunken treasures?"

Justin smiled sadly. "No, just gazing at the sea."

"Ye feel overheated. Time to cool down in this heat." Will tugged on the cotton of Justin's long sleeved blouse.

As once again it was the issue, Justin stood off the rail and grumbled, "Oh, bother." Then gave in and started to unbutton it.

Will tilted his head at the odd response. "Me thinks we both need an ale."

In complete agreement, Justin nodded as Will left to get them one. As he removed his shirt, he kept his back facing the sea. As if it were a rag, he rolled the blouse up and held it in front of his waist, feeling very disheartened.

In a minute, Will returned. With little grace, Will plopped down on the deck and gestured for Justin to do the same. Justin sank down and leaned against the ship's gunwale, still self-conscious.

Will handed him his ale and whispered, "Did someone upset ye again, lad?"

"Hmm?" Justin met Will's concerned expression. "No, no, nothing like that."

"What then?" Will brushed the hair back from Justin's face.

"I'm just humiliated to be seen without a top."

At the surprising comment, Will gave Justin's chest a once-over. "Why? Yar lovely! Fit as a fiddle! Ye've nothing to be ashamed of." And as if to prove it, Will pinched one of Justin's small, dark nipples playfully.

Justin flinched and batted his hand away. "No! It's me back."

"Argh? What of it?"

In paranoia, Justin peered around first. There were several crew members spying on them, something occurring constantly to him. The place was so jammed with men, it was impossible to hide.

Will scanned around as well. It appeared most of the crew was asleep. "Go on then."

Justin twisted around reluctantly.

With little effort, Will found the scarring. "Hornbolt do that?" he almost shouted in fury.

"Nay! Nay!" Justin quieted him, then pressed back against the wall and grumbled, "Me father."

Will ground his teeth. "The filthy bugger."

"Aye. He is that." Justin took the ale and drank a swallow.

"What be his name, lad, on the off chance I meet up with him in me travels?"

"Why? What will you do? Kill him?" Justin laughed.

"Nay. I'd give him back what he done to ye."

In surprise, Justin stared into his worn face with that missing ear. "Samuel John Taylor," he announced.

Will nodded. "It comes around, lad."

Justin sighed and drank more ale. "Aye, I know it has for me." He attempted a smile.

* * * *

"I don't want to think past the attack." Captain Jones conferred quietly with Boatswain Black. "But if we are successful, we'll need to replenish our store for the voyage back."

"Aye, sir, we'll confiscate everything on board the galleon, but depending on her own store, I agree."

They studied the map together. "Peckham thinks we'll meet her somewhere off the coast of the American main. Here." The captain pointed. "If that'd be so, the closest safe port to us after such a feat is Portobello."

Instantly, Black lit up with a smile.

"Aye, I knew that wouldn't break anyone's heart. Don't let on. Let's get the broadside out of the way. Once we are victorious, we will find safe harbor."

"Ye thinks it be safe after the crusade of Sir Henry Morgan?"

"You suggest another?"

"Nay. Let's set sight on her. The men are in need of such a release. It has been a long stay asea already with more to come. Me thinks they are eager to spy that mast."

"Aye. And I am ready to set my sights on home."

Black smiled sadly and rubbed the captain's arm. "Aye, Richard. You'll set eyes on yar lady again in this life. Have no fear. She'll be no dowager."

Wanting to change the subject, Captain Jones sat up straight and hardened his expression. "Right. We show no quarter to her crew. No one must live that sees this attack. Whether she surrender or not. Clear?"

"Aye. I agree. We need no bounty on our heads. No one knows our names. Keep it that way."

They both looked up as the door opened. Justin's sad pout was seen.

"Oh, sorry, sir." He bowed his head to back away.

"It's all right, lad. Come in."

Exhausted, Justin plopped down on the bunk.

Black stood and touched the captain's back. "Right. Ye get some rest too, Richard."

"I will. Send me Cromwell, should you come upon him."

"Aye, Captain." Black nodded and left.

He spun around to see Justin's blurred eyes. "You all right?"

* * * *

His expression sour, Justin was a little drunk on the ale and feeling very sorry for himself at the moment.

"What passed? Did someone harm you?" The captain became concerned and sat next to him.

"No, just the old wounds." Justin sighed, thinking of his father. His shirt was on his back, but it was not fastened.

"Come then. Last of the ointment."

In response, Justin raised his head to tell the captain he didn't mean *those* wounds, and then reconsidered as a smile edged through his sadness. "Yes, sir, thank you, sir." With a bounce of joy, he stood and tossed his shirt on a chair, unfastening his boots and breeches. The grin plastered to his lips, he lay down with a sigh and shimmied his pants to his knees.

The captain removed his own shirt instead of rolling up his sleeves. Lifting the jar to the light, he dipped in to collect the last bit of the salve. "The marks are almost gone now, Justin. I think as well, this is making those older scars less noticeable."

"Is it?" In excitement, Justin raised up on his elbows and twisted around.

"Aye. They are less pink."

"Oh, that is very good news, sir." Justin gave him his most charming smile.

The captain scraped out the remainder of the liniment and set the ceramic jar aside. "Yes, I am very sure it has lightened their appearance. I shall ask Jason if he has more." With loving care, he started smoothing the herbal ointment over Justin's back. In bliss, Justin settled down and let out a happy hum as those fingers caressed him.

They heard a knock. The captain shouted, "Enter." Justin tensed up and peeked to see who it was.

"Ye called for me, sir?" First Mate Cromwell stepped in.

"Yes, sit down, Jack." The captain nodded to the chair and continued to medicate Justin.

Intimidated at being seen in this position, Justin held his breath, caught Cromwell's eyes once, then turned his face to the wall. The captain's hand rested on his tight, rounded bottom comfortably as he explained his plans to his first mate. "This is my idea, Jack…tell me what you think."

* * * *

Jack Cromwell worked very hard to listen to what he was told whilst his handsome captain massaged the luscious naked bottom of a very pretty lad. Try as he might to connect his gaze to the captain's serious expression, he could not help but take a glimpse at that very sensual sight. This old seadog knew his captain very well. In his mind, Jack had no doubt as to the innocence of this scene. Justin was beaten and attacked. The captain was medicating his bruises. It was all very simple. But it had been too many days asea. Anything would set a man off. The casualness and comfort the captain had in his contact with this strikingly beautiful boy set his teeth on edge. And with Justin's face turned and that long thick brown hair, narrow hips, and tight bottom; it took nothing to imagine a maiden. Absolutely nothing. He admired his captain for his willpower in resisting this treat, and then doubted his sanity in understanding how he could.

* * * *

Justin tried to focus on the information the captain was sharing with his first mate as well, but he couldn't. The captain's hand would rest on his bottom, then resume its massage, but only in a distracted sense. When he stopped moving and gave one of his cheeks a soft squeeze, Justin knew it wasn't done with any intent. It was like kneading dough whilst having a heart-to-heart conversation. It was just not a conscious effort.

* * * *

Cromwell was having a devil of a time hearing a word. He kept rubbing his beard and nodding, losing himself on that soft, satiny flesh and the large, masculine man near it. Struggling to focus again and find the conversation, Cromwell would only go off track once more when that hand rested on that perfectly tight, snow-white bottom.

He finally gave up. "Aye, Captain. I must be too tired, for not a word is registering in me head. Could we, by chance, start once again in the morning?"

The captain appeared very surprised. "You feeling all right, Jack?"

Cromwell watched that large hand rest on Justin's left cheek, the thumb moving over the line between. "Ah, no. A bit of exhaustion. I'll be ship shape after a night's rest."

Captain Jones tilted his head curiously. "Right. Good night, then."

Cromwell rose to his feet with some effort. After bidding them a good night, he took one last look at that extraordinary image before leaving. As he made his way down the passage with lightheadedness, as if he were drunk on wine, Peckham passed him on his way to see the captain.

"Aye, Jack, you look like you've seen a ghost."

Cromwell met his stare. "Ye headed to the captain's cabin?"

"Aye, why? Is he available?"

"Ye'll see a sight in there, mate, that'll make its mark on yar night."

Peckham was about to ask him something more, when Cromwell brushed past him and left.

* * * *

The captain gave his attention back to Justin and finished up his massage. "There you go, lad."

With intent, Justin rolled over and did not cover himself this time. "Are the scars really fading?"

Appearing preoccupied, Captain Jones stood and wiped his hands. "Yes, lad, they seem less noticeable."

Before he doused the lamp, the captain glanced back at Justin to smile and say goodnight.

When he did, Justin leaned up on his side, his head propped on his hand. He deliberately shook his long hair, making it wild so it covered his eyes and ran down his shoulder. Justin took a quick peek at himself. He was naked down to his knees, where his pants were, and fully aroused. Justin heard the captain's breath catch in his throat and watched the handsome man turn away quickly with a blush hot on his cheeks.

"I wonder," Justin mused out loud, "if you continued to medicate them, if they would eventually disappear. I am so ashamed of them, I hesitate to take off my blouse, even in this horrible heat."

The captain faced the wall and did not answer.

Knowing he was admired, Justin glanced down again

at his body, hoping it was enticing. "Captain? Aren't you coming to bed?"

The captain stared up at the low ceiling rafters for a moment.

"Captain," Justin purred seductively, "It is all right."

Captain Jones turned to look at him. "What is all right?" he asked in irritation.

Slowly, seductively, Justin lay his head down on the bunk and positioned himself more sensually, exposing more of his body to him. Trying to lure the man, Justin opened his mouth and licked his lips.

Captain Jones swallowed audibly down a very dry throat. With bared teeth, the captain rubbed his face.

"I love you, my Captain," Justin whispered. "Please, let me serve you."

"Stop. Please stop," the captain moaned and placed his hand over his eyes.

"Then just sleep. I understand. You are very tired." Justin reached out his hand to him.

The captain let out a long, slow breath and doused the lamp. As if his feet were made of lead, he managed with a great effort to get onto the bunk stiffly, face up.

Having done so every other night, Justin moved once more to lean against him, loving the contact. With his head lying on that broad chest and its thundering heart, beating madly, he smoothed his hand across the captain's overheated flesh. The solidness of his pectoral muscles just underneath was like the arc of a sail blown full, round and flawless.

Justin pressed his pelvis with its erect cock into his captain's thigh while his hand danced lightly over the captain's skin.

"Oh, bloody hell," the captain groaned in agony, then impulsively twisted around and scooped Justin into his arms. Positioning Justin to lay over his chest, the captain devoured Justin's mouth as if to taste the sweet freshness of his youth. After waiting an eternity for his captain's affection, Justin's mind went reeling in pleasure as he wrapped his legs around the powerful hips under him.

The strength and power of this large man completely engulfed Justin. The captain's tongue forced its way into his mouth, causing Justin to whimper in longing. In a breath between kisses, Justin exclaimed, "I love you. I love you, my Captain. Take me. Take what you need."

A deep, rumbling moan from the big man echoed through both their naked ribcages as Captain Jones squeezed Justin tighter. With one movement, the captain had Justin on his back and was sitting over his hips. Feeling the captain's hands running up and down his torso, Justin shivered and fumbled to open the captain's breeches. When his hardened length was released, Justin gripped it in both hands and felt it throb.

"Give it to me!" Justin breathed in desperation, feeling the imposing size of a man's cock that was not his own, in his palms for the first time. And not just anyone's. It was his beloved's body he was holding. Justin began to think he might already be asleep and this was just one of his delirious dreams.

With a sensuous snarl, Captain Jones removed the rest of Justin's clothing. Justin was so pent up, so hard, he knew nothing could prevent what was about to happen. Rushes of tingling pleasure washed over Justin's body, as the captain sated his lust.

He had no idea if Captain Jones was pretending he was his Katherine, or perhaps the big man knew exactly who he was about to enter. Justin only wanted to please him. That was all. At any cost.

As his thighs were spread wide and his hips raised off the bed, Justin gasped in surprise as that hot rod maneuvered between his thighs. The moment the captain's cock began to press into his ass, Justin came, shooting his cream all over his own chest and neck. "Yes! Take it!

Take it!" Justin cried as the captain scooped up that spent cum using it to unite their bodies as one.

Arching his back as his virgin ass was consumed by an enormous cock, Justin strangled the bedding and pushed backwards until his bottom met the captain's pelvis. Once he was completely impaled, Justin panted in deep loud huffs, trying to release his tightly wound muscles so it wouldn't cause him pain. As if sensing Justin's discomfort, the captain paused, his cock pulsating deep inside Justin's body. Then, without a word, the captain began moving his hips. As Justin's hole became accustomed to the sensation of being filled to capacity, something happened. Pure pleasure. "Agh!"

"Justin?" the captain asked in concern.

"Harder!" Justin choked in shock.

Seemingly waiting for that affirmation, Captain Jones let loose, rocking his hips with purpose into Justin. Rumbling, masculine grunting began to echo in the small cabin. Just the sound of Captain Jones' rising climax was enough to bring Justin back to his peak. "Yes! Ah! Captain!"

"Bloody hell!" Captain Jones roared and slammed so hard into Justin, he nearly knocked them both into the wall in front of them.

Bracing himself so as not to hit it, Justin felt a wonderful internal friction, causing him so much pleasure, he blew more cum all over himself. In a choking gasp, Justin jerked his body downwards, consuming Captain Jones' dick to the root.

"Ah! Justin!" The captain's cock shuddered inside his body, and Justin felt him convulse over him.

Moaning in pure adoration, Justin felt honored to be the one. The one to give Captain Jones release. It didn't matter that it felt like heaven on earth for him as well. *From virgin to devil!* Justin smiled into the pillows. *I am so in love.*

With tenderness and care, Captain Jones loosened his grip on Justin and disconnected their union. Dropping down on top of him, the captain whimpered in exhaustion.

Even though they were sticky and sweaty, Justin grinned in bliss, sated and fulfilled.

Chapter Six

When the captain woke at first light, he found a naked beauty in bed with him, nestled in his arms. Untangling himself carefully so as not to wake Justin, the captain climbed out and rinsed his face with a damp cloth. As he stood in front of the looking glass to comb his hair and shave, he connected with his own intense eyes and paused. Staring at himself, he thought about what he had done last night. It was wrong. It was taking advantage of a young one. It was being dishonest to his woman, and it was incredibly satisfying.

"God..." He clenched his teeth as he groaned, sensations of pleasure whipping around him like spirits in a graveyard. He never imagined loving Justin could be so satisfying. It brought a level of attachment the captain had not felt before. Not even with Katherine. And that frightened him.

Twisting back over his shoulder to look at that sleeping seraph, he smiled without an effort. The boy was so eager to please, so loving, so pure, and so very, very pretty.

To have that young man at his mercy, pliable as a rose petal and equally as smooth, brought with it such strong emotions and urges, feelings he hated to admit to himself he had never experienced in all his life. Peering down between his own legs, he knew what those urges did to him.

At the sound of the doorknob turning and a voice calling him, he hurried to Justin and threw a cover over his nakedness, then straightened out his own breeches and bid enter.

His pilot peered in. "Sir?" He paused. "You need a moment?"

"Yes, James, if you would. I just came awake now. Let me wash up and meet you in the galley."

"Aye, very good, sir." Peckham nodded, taking a peek at Justin. It appeared Peckham was absorbing the image of Justin, as he lay prone in delightful sensual repose, his naked upper torso shimmering in the morning light. One last glimpse back to him, and Peckham left without a word.

The captain exhaled; he had been holding his breath. It took a long moment to gather his lost thoughts. Shaking his head at the implications, he knew how the scene looked to his pilot. Did it matter to anyone? He shrugged off the sensation of worry and went to work getting himself cleaned up.

* * * *

Justin stretched and yawned, opening his eyes. He sat up and checked around the empty cabin and smiled to himself. Warm, loving memories of last night washed over him like the tepid, lapping tongue of a Caribbean tide. Humming happily as he dressed for his chores, he whistled a silly tune and headed to the galley feeling as if he were a prism filled with sunshine. A biscuit caught his hungry gaze, and he munched it happily as all the men were handed some mash and salt pork to break their fast. Pushing up his sleeves and tucking his hair into his collar, he went to help Smithy serve. The moment he laid eyes on his captain, who was seated with the pilot and boatswain, Justin lost himself completely; his wonderful smile, the way he gave his entire attention to whomever had his ear, his profile, which was worthy of a Greek coin, and his large muscular arms as they relaxed on the table before him. Forever he would relive last night as if it were a dream. That mouth sucking on his, those large hands running down his sides and that hot, rubbing hardness that eagerly found its way inside him.

"Don't go to sleep on me, lad!" Smithy shoved another bowl at him.

Justin woke up from his daydream and continued serving, flushed with fire at the memory of touching that man.

As Justin served the food, he assumed Captain Jones was going over their location with his pilot. He overheard Peckham say he was sure they were sailing just past the Caribbean Islands, but many leagues east of them, that they were still a few days' journey from where they expected to see the galleon.

As if he had heard someone call his name, the captain raised his head and connected with Justin's infatuated, fixed gaze. When he did, Justin's insides exploded in flames. Suddenly a weight pressed on his chest, and he could not gain enough air. The captain turned away casually and gave his focus back to his pilot.

Free of the connection, Justin caught his breath and panted as if he'd run a marathon. Like a greedy miser who had just found loot, he could not wait to get his hands on his lover again.

* * * *

Come nightfall, the captain finished his rounds and made tiredly for his cabin. There, as he expected, he found Justin with some fresh water in a basin trying to clean himself, his back facing the door, that lovely nakedness once more a treat to his senses. At first, Justin covered himself modestly, sighing when he found his captain's grin. "Ah. It is you," he whispered and let his hands fall to his sides, smiling dreamily.

The captain closed the door and sat down at his desk to enjoy this erotic exhibition. "Go on, carry on."

Justin winked seductively and dipped the rag into the basin, running it over his chest and abdomen, the dancing rivulets making their way to his slender thighs. Hypnotized by the vision, the captain leaned back in his chair to stare at that shining skin. A moan escaped his lips.

Justin washed his legs slowly as the captain gave him his undivided attention. With his foot raised to a stool and with careful deliberation, Justin scrubbed clean the salt and dirt from his day's labor.

As if staring at a sumptuous meal, the captain's mouth started to water, and the dull yearning between his legs grew to an ache. He rubbed his face and combed his fingers through his thick hair, feeling the salt coating him like a crystal layer of frost on a glass pane. "A bath looks very refreshing. I yearn for a hot soak," the captain sighed and leaned over his knees towards Justin.

Justin tilted his face up at him sweetly. "Come here. There is enough clean water for two. You said yourself we must use it before it turns."

A low, amused laugh escaped the captain's lips.

Justin set the cloth down and closed the gap between them as if he were a panther stalking prey. The captain's eyes drank him in, from the top of his long, brown mane to the bottom of his feet. A breath hissed through his closed teeth at the sight, and he had to shut his eyes to try to gain some control of his desires. It was a losing battle. But this man of war was not used to losing. He had never done it before.

Approaching like a well-trained slave, Justin knelt down and unbuckled the captain's tall leather boot.

Captain Jones stared dully as Justin assisted him. Urged to stand, he rose up, and his breeches dropped. As if he were a king, he was brought over to the basin, completely naked, and the rag was rinsed and wrung. Beginning at the top, Justin reached out and wiped his tanned face clean. The captain closed his eyes and tried to relax his tightly wound muscles. With a groan of ecstasy, he expected many things on this journey, but kind nurturing, sex with an angel, and a sponge bath weren't any of them.

Squeezing the rag tightly, Justin allowed the water to roll down his broad chest, his rounded deltoids, and his rippled abdomen. Then he rinsed the rag once more and crouched before him, washing his pelvis, his privates, and his inner thighs. The dark tan stopped short at his waist. The captain's lower half was pure white.

The captain grunted softly as he was handled, fully aroused. It was like a dream to him. In all his life, he had never been treated in this way, like he was indeed royalty. It gave him a headiness he just could not describe. And worse yet, he could grow used to this spoiling.

Justin rinsed the rag clean again and smoothed it down the captain's thighs. They were huge, solid, and covered with a soft brown hair. Sitting back on his heels, Justin stared up at him in awe. "You are so incredibly beautiful, my Captain."

The captain had to laugh. With loving affection, he caressed Justin's hair and whispered, "Enough, lad. It's no good, really. I will be covered in salt again by mid-day tomorrow. When we get to port, I will treat myself to a luxurious soak. But I thank you, for the effort."

"Come, there is a bit more water. Sit here." Justin gestured to the spot in front of him.

The captain sat down and waited. The ribbon was removed from his long hair, and the pure, salt-free liquid felt glorious running through it. Tilting his head back, he whimpered as the cooling sensation of the water caressed his broad back.

Justin dug his hands into the captain's mane,

massaging his scalp. When Justin had his hair soaked, he found the captain's comb and ran it through gently. Wet, the captain's hair came to his mid-back.

Captain Jones closed his eyes and surrendered as sweet memories of his childhood and his mother's doting ran through his mind. Sunshine and fresh baked bread, his five sisters all fawning over the only boy child, his father standing tall and proud in a blue uniform, his dear mother twisting his long hair into ringlets. It felt wonderful, he could not deny that.

Justin set the comb aside and wrapped his arms around his shoulders from behind. The captain rose up and carried him that way to the bunk. He set Justin down on it and turned around to face that angel come down to earth. When he beheld that expression of innocence, it filled the captain with deep adoration and longing, a mirror image of what he was observing in that young man's face.

Justin held him around his neck and smiled. "I told you it would make you feel better." He leaned in so they were touching noses.

"You spoil me." The captain grinned impishly.

Justin answered happily, "You took the words out of me own mouth!"

The captain lay him down and moved next to him. "You are one special lad, Justin. I am very glad you stowed on board. What would I do without you to pamper me?" He toyed with Justin's right nipple until it hardened.

"And make love to you." Justin reached for him and ran the captain's swelling hardness through his palms.

The captain closed his eyes at the rush of fire. "Aye, and that as well."

Justin hopped over him to douse the lamp, scrambling back to his spot. He positioned himself on top of the captain with his legs spread wide. The captain embraced him and pushed Justin's hair back from his face, finding his mouth with his tongue, and groaning in pleasure.

As Justin's teasing fingertips traced lightly over his length, Captain Jones began to feel the urge to come strengthen. Opening his lips for a deep intake of air, the captain cupped Justin's jaw and deepened their kiss, jamming his tongue into Justin's mouth the way he wanted to ram his cock into Justin's body.

Justin pulled back from their kiss gently. The captain heard him gasping and felt a hot, pulsating friction against his hip. Thrilled Justin had climaxed, the captain waited as Justin caught his breath.

In the dark, he felt Justin coating his hardness in the spent come. A moment later, Justin was sitting over the captain's pelvis impaling himself on his length.

Captain Jones inhaled sharply as his body was engulfed in tight heat. Allowing Justin to take his time and slowly sink all the way down against his pelvis, the captain shivered and tried to resist the urge to pound hungrily up into Justin.

"Oh, lad," the captain hissed, tightly gripping Justin in anticipation.

"Aye. Ready now, Captain."

Once Justin began rising and falling on his cock, Captain Jones held onto Justin's hips and allowed himself the pleasure of riding this slender god. Slapping his thighs against Justin's bottom, he began ascending to heaven. Hearing Justin's renewed gasps, the captain could sense Justin working himself feverishly. At the thought of Justin pleasuring himself, he grunted and shot his seed into Justin's tight body. Instantly, the captain felt Justin's cream spatter his chest and abdomen.

As they recovered, Justin reached over his torso and connected to his lips. Welling up with emotion, Captain Jones dug his fingers into Justin's thick hair and deepened the kiss, sliding his tongue in and out of his mouth as he had just done to Justin's body with his hardened length.

His cock softening as it relaxed, the captain felt Justin

rest limply over him. Closing his eyes, Captain Jones caressed Justin lovingly, lulling them both to sleep.

Chapter Seven

The days went on and on, but the nights kept him alive and pulsating. Justin felt he could live this way forever. Easy chores, no beatings, and the loving of the handsome captain. He had no complaints. Now he would be happy if things would stay that way. He knew they would not. Change was in the tropical wind of a pirate round.

Whilst he was swabbing the deck right before the noon rest, the lookout shouted, "Avast ye, men! A mizzen mast!"

Peckham sprinted to the main mast and climbed the ratlines like a squirrel hungry for acorns.

Everyone stood and went to the starboard side to squint over the reflecting waves.

Captain Jones hurried to them and climbed the mast himself. "Aye! Pilot! Give me the bring 'em near!" Peckham passed him the telescope, and they clung there like birds on a tree.

Justin shielded his eyes and stared up at his captain.

"Aye! There she is! All right, lads. Let's get her to her full ten knots. Hoist the white jolly!"

The men sprang into action. Justin stood there with his mop, bewildered, as the Spanish flag was lowered and a white flag was raised. The flurry of movement was astounding. Each man knew exactly what was expected of him and ran to get it done immediately, if not sooner.

The captain handed his pilot the telescope and climbed down; Peckham then handed it back to the lookout and did the same.

Tucker stood next to the captain as he gazed out to the horizon. "Argh, Captain, our luck is high. We're almost there now."

"Aye, mate, and she's enormous. We dare not tempt her cannon. Come in from the stern and get every man visible. We need fear and the devil on our side."

"Aye, sir. That we do."

The captain shouted to his first mate. "Cromwell, batten down, we go full speed!"

"Aye, sir!" Cromwell yelled and took off.

"Black!" the captain roared. "Get your gunners to the deck and load the cannons!"

"Aye, Captain!"

Captain Jones twisted around for his next command and almost ran over Justin. "Lad, go load the flintlocks and musketoons. Go!" He shoved him off.

Justin dropped his mop and went scurrying away in a frenzy.

He sat with a load of shot and a powder horn. He was shaking so badly, he was spilling everything onto his lap. His fingers were dipped inkwell black from the gunpowder. All he wanted was to stay out of everyone's way. The weeks of lounging around in boredom had ended in a clamor of activity, and he wasn't so sure he was up to the challenge now that he was finally faced with it.

The pile of guns was amazing. He knew each man carried one or two. The captain, three! And with nearly sixty on board, that was a lot of loading. He knelt up on his knees, determined to do a good job.

Will Davis finished tending his cannon and almost stumbled over Justin. He sat down with him and gave him a hand. "Aye, lad, most are loaded, just check quickly, but don't pull the triggers!" He laughed.

"Oh, thank the Lord!" Justin cried. "I thought I was to load all of them."

"Nay, lad. Come, let's get ye organized."

As they were set out, the men collected them and placed them into their waistbands. Justin had one left over from Hornbolt. Will smiled and whispered, "That's for ye now, lad. Go on, in the waist belt. Ye've one shot, make it count."

Justin tucked it in and smiled in pride. "Aye, I'm one of the men now."

"Aye, yar. Just come out alive and whole, lad." Will roughed up his hair affectionately.

The lookout hollered down to the captain. "She's spied us! She's come about!"

"Come laddies! Tighten up her sails!" the captain shouted. The wind shifted, and the boat launched ahead full speed. "That's it, lads! Hold her steady. We gaining on her, Pilot?"

"Aye, sir! She's slow and laden!" Peckham shaded his eyes and stared at the merchant ship.

Captain Jones felt a light tug. Peering down distractedly, he found Justin handing him another pistol. His third. "Ah! Thank you, lad. I don't know where I'd be without you." He took it and tucked it into his already heavily armed baldric.

"Are we close yet?" Justin squinted and could now see the galleon plainly. "Blimey! There she is!" He could make out her gaudy colors, red painted scrolls and curtained portholes.

"Aye, there she is, lad. My dreams. You just keep out of trouble. It won't be pretty."

"Yes, sir. I will, sir."

"She's slowing, Captain! She knows we're outrunning her!" the pilot shouted.

"She take down her flag?"

The lookout took a moment with the scope before he yelled, "Not yet, sir!"

"What's happening?" Justin asked the captain.

"She's either decided to engage us or given up. We have no way of knowing yet."

Justin waited in anxiety. *Give up, give up.*

"Her colors are still flying!" Peckham announced.

The captain showed his teeth in rage. "Hoist the red jack!"

At the command, Justin craned his neck as the white was replaced with a red flag, emblazoned with golden skull and crossbones. "What the devil does that mean?"

"No quarter, lad."

"What does 'no quarter' mean?"

"Not now, lad, shove off and get busy." Captain Jones nudged him, never taking his eyes off the galleon.

Attempting to decipher the riddle, Justin backed away and waited, staring at his captain as he planned his strategy.

"Get every man on board and with cannon!" the captain commanded.

"Aye, Captain!" Boatswain Black answered.

"Stay out of her range! Lower the sails!" Captain Jones ordered.

The ship almost ground to a halt with the sails down. It rocked side to side in the current.

"What do you see, Pilot? She lower her flag yet?"

"Nay, sir!"

Justin could not believe the size of the galleon. It seemed so odd to come upon another ship. The ocean's eternal plane of green had been uninterrupted for weeks. How strange to have this massive brown and black beast here before him now. A companion in the deep blue sea. But she was no friend. Her cannons were intimidating, to say the least. Twenty pointed their way. It was deathly quiet but for a lone, lost gull's metallic screech and the creaking of the hull. He twisted around to the main deck and found almost sixty men there, each with a pistol in one fist and a cutlass in the other, glaring at that treasure ship

79

with intense, violent hatred. They were downright ugly.

"Captain! She's lowering her flag!" the lookout shouted.

"Stay back from her portside! If she's bluffing, we go straight to hellfire!" the captain roared, fingering one of his pistols. His bare chest glistened under the diagonally crossed, heavily armed baldric and his white breeches appeared transparent as they clung to his sweat-soaked thighs.

Justin was afraid to blink, shaking in his boots. He had no idea if he was ready for this. In all his life, including his beatings, he had never experienced terror. He wondered if he was feeling it now. Or maybe it was what the galleon's crew was enduring, staring at the frightful felons of *His Revenge*.

"She truly surrendering? Are her men on deck or with the cannons?" Captain Jones hollered to the man aloft.

"Both, sir!" came the reply.

There was a challenge of wills, captain to captain. It was deathly silent, and it felt as if time had slowed to a halt. Justin watched as his captain ground his jaw, his rage building. "No quarter!" he roared. "That's it! Overhaul! Aft! Stern side! Get ready to board!"

The corvette's sails filled and she slipped through the water like a deadly tiger shark. As they came to the stern, a loud cannon boomed from the port side of the galleon. Just one single shot from a nervous Spanish gunner. The ball was way off target and splashed harmlessly into the sea. The noise, however, got everyone's adrenaline surging. The galleon was trapped. The corvette was much more maneuverable and had slipped away from a target's perspective. There was no way for that bulky leviathan of a ship to escape, turn and fight, or avoid a confrontation, so they gave up and prayed for mercy.

"Scuttle up! Get the ropes! Board in mass!" the captain commanded his crew. The sloop of war rubbed the galleon's hull as the men used boarding axes to get on her poop deck and swung ropes onto her, connecting the decks. There was a clashing of voices as they scrambled on, and then the sound of flintlocks blasting.

Justin hurried after his captain to join the fray, trying not to look down at the deep water as he climbed over and onto the enemy ship. When he stood on that merchant ship's deck, he could not believe the turmoil. The galleon's crew was running in every direction, flailing their arms and rending their garments in fear. They could not escape *His Revenge*'s swift, well-trained army. The amount of blood astonished him. The surface of the deck ran with it. It was sprayed on the bleached white sails in a spattering of crimson. A few severed limbs lay in an odd ballet across the red glazing. One hand still held a sword. Justin had to force himself not to stare at that compelling, yet completely revolting sight. With cutlass raised in one hand and the pistol in the other, he tried to tiptoe invisibly into battle, his boot heels sliding on the red current.

The captain fired his first bullet and dropped a man that was rushing for him with an axe raised. With tremendous force, he hacked his cutlass through his neck to make sure he died, then searched for the enemy captain as his own shipmates made fast work of the outnumbered, poorly organized galleon.

Justin was moving along the walls of the large ship, trying to keep out of the way of the slaughter. No one took notice of him. He kept his eyes on his captain, quaking in mortal dread that someone would harm that man.

The captain kicked open a door and aimed his second pistol. He was rushed from within and fired point blank into the chest of the enemy.

At the blast, Justin flinched and then sighed with relief when he realized it was the captain's gun that had gone off and he was still standing tall and proud.

The captain moved on. "Show yourself, you bootless

seawolf!"

On trembling limbs, Justin crept to the cabin door as the captain searched the interior. He was shivering in spasms and holding his breath, praying for courage.

Captain Jones found the Spanish captain, hiding like a rat behind an enormous carved desk. With his arms raised over his head and seemingly empty-handed, the enemy of England came out of his cramped, secret space. Captain Jones snarled into the Spaniard's scarred, bearded face and tilted his head for the coward to get out into the sunlight on the deck.

Justin kept hidden in the shadows just outside the cabin door. Some movement caught his attention behind his captain's back, and he focused on a dark, looming figure with a long, shining, curved cutlass blade in its hand.

The captain jumped out of his skin when he heard a shot behind him. He spun around and found a man lying on his face, the sword still in his grip. Immediately he returned his sneer to the galleon's captain and discovered he had a dagger in his hand. Raising his flintlock, like a reflex of his very nature, the captain shot him in the face, blowing off his nose. The dead Spanish captain fell over like a tree that snapped in a gale and made a loud thud as he did.

Justin had both hands clamped around his smoking pistol and was sitting on his rump from the recoil. With his eyes wide and unblinking, Justin tried to conceive the fact that he had just killed a man. He could feel his face was smeared with gunpowder and sweat. "Blimey!" he gasped in amazement.

The captain made sure the cabin was clear before he helped the others. After his search, he came upon Justin sitting on the floor. His knuckles were pure white under the powder stains from their death grip on the gun.

"Was it you then?" the captain asked in astonishment.

Finding his gaze, Justin nodded slowly. "He...he was going to kill you...he was sneaking up behind you...he had a sword..." Justin was trying to justify what he had done. He didn't want to get into any trouble. After all, everything he did back home, he was punished for.

The captain reached out his hand to help him up and said, "Thank you, lad. Now, we've more business at hand before we can relax." With a bold, confident strut, the captain hurried out to the remaining crew.

When he came onto the quarterdeck, his men had a small band of survivors surrounded. They were begging for mercy. Justin hid behind his captain's broad back and observed with anxiety.

The crew knew their captain's command. He didn't need to repeat it. In one movement, they rushed the last few and cut them up without pity, hesitation, or least of all, mercy.

In horror, Justin gagged and turned his face away. It seemed a terribly cruel thing to do to unarmed prisoners. Without success, he tried to cover his ears as their agonizing cries haunted him. He could actually hear the sound of the blades hitting bone. It made the bile rise in his throat as he struggled not to throw it up.

A search was made for anyone hiding out. When the ship was given the all clear, the crew stood catching their breath, trying to account for anyone missing.

They had done well. They outnumbered the enemy two to one, and their fighting skills were obviously far superior to anything the crew of the merchant ship ever dreamed of encountering. The captain leaned over the rail to his pilot and waved to assure him they had completed their task. The few left on *His Revenge* waved back and hooted in joy.

"All right, lads, check for provisions and loot." The captain gestured to them. Instantly, the men scrambled to the lower decks. Straightening his back, the captain scanned around leisurely. His vision rested on Justin who was crouched in a corner, cowering. Without a second thought, he made his way to him. "You all right, lad?"

When his eyes rose to his captain slowly, Justin moaned, "I've never seen so much bloodshed."

"Come here, my pretty." With a gentle smile on his face, the captain reached out his crimson-and-black-stained hand.

As if thrown a lifeline, Justin scrambled to get near and feel the reassuring grip on his numb shoulder.

"I owe you my life, Justin. Will you help me find her treasure?"

Justin felt so pale from fright he knew the black soot from the gunpowder must be standing out on him like newsprint. The captain wrapped his arm around him in a loving, encouraging embrace, and they went into the bowels of the ship together.

They heard shouting and followed the noise. Quartermaster Tucker had located a storeroom with chests in it, deep in the hull. The captain gestured for them to step back as he pointed one of his pistols at the metal lock, then he realized he had spent all three of his bullets. He turned the empty gun in his hand and held the barrel, trying to knock off the lock. It was too solid and he could not damage anything but the butt of his flintlock. Someone handed him a loaded pistol. He raised his head and made out whom it was. "Tucker, never fired a shot?"

"I prefer me cutlass, Captain." That mischievous grin sparkled, and his fingers still held it in his right hand like it was merely an extension of his arm.

Justin's mouth hung open. Quartermaster Tucker's arms were almost as large as his own thighs. He swallowed in a gulp, wondering what a slice from that man could hew through.

"Aye, Johnnie, all right. You got your blade." The captain laughed at him, then nodded to his men to look aside, blasting off the lock.

Scrambling to cover his ears from the noise, Justin cringed and jumped at the explosion. When he looked back, the captain was opening the lid. He thought he would pass out from the sight.

A great roar went up from the men as they found thousands of pieces of silver and gold, crowns and crucifixes, necklaces and pearls, goblets and oil lamps, and fine porcelain and china. There were golden carvings from the wilds of the Americas, strange gods in the image of the sun and the stars. Justin thought he was hallucinating.

Captain Jones clutched a handful of gold escudos and doubloons as tears fell from his eyes. He addressed his crew with a smile that was too large for his face, "Oy! We shall all be kings!"

They roared with joy and patted each other happily.

The captain removed a crown from the heap and sat it atop Justin's head. It was brilliant yellow gilding, with blue and red cabochons encrusted in its face like a cobblestone path made of gems. It slid down, lopsided, on him as Justin's eyes widened in amazement. The men laughed at the sight.

"All right! Anchor. Get all her treasure on the corvette. Last, we plunder her stores!"

They set up a line of men to transfer the booty to the ship's deck. It took most of the afternoon to unload the bounty. The men ended the search by scavenging for medicines, food, alcohol, and then, lastly, clothing. They tossed the bodies into the sea once they had stripped them of anything of value.

Justin was on the corvette, standing at the rail, toying with a belaying pin. As each member of the Spanish galleon was plunged into the ocean, there was a commotion in the water. An unbelievable sight met his eyes as he found a feeding frenzy of sharks. The red churning water nauseated him. Backing away from it instinctively, he sat facing the opposite way from the galleon. Resting his head in his hands, he mumbled to himself, "Why must everything sicken me?" Then he shuddered in complete disgust.

Justin was waiting for the captain. He needed him back on board. He wanted things calm and boring again. He wanted this dirty deed done.

Within the next hour, he finally got his wish. Captain Jones once again stood on the corvette's deck. They pushed back from the anchored ghost ship and came about to leave her behind. The men threw lit torches onto her deck, and she caught fire and blazed like Erebus into the dusk. Justin gaped in awe as the red Jolly Roger lowered, and the red ensign of England rose. The men were exhausted and filthy, tending their wounds and shredded clothing. A horrendous scream erupted as the doctor amputated and cauterized a torn limb. Once more Justin shivered and huddled into a ball; his captain stood within hearing range but had not noticed Justin yet.

Captain Jones found his quartermaster and patted his back. "You've your work cut out for you, John."

"I don't mind this work a lick!" His smile broadened into a devilish grin.

"You count her up, and we'll see to it everyone has a pocketful before we dock."

"Aye, indeed I shall, sir."

The captain instructed his pilot to shift their course for Portobello. Peckham grinned happily and adjusted the tiller. Pausing, thinking things through, Captain Jones felt he had done everything that needed doing for the moment, and it was time he searched for his Justin. With his sharp vision, he scanned the deck for him and found him looking filthy, pale, and ragged in Will Davis' company.

* * * *

In the crowd, Will Davis searched for Justin. He hadn't seen him since before battle and was getting anxious. When he caught sight of the top of his mop of brown hair, he sighed with relief and sat next to him, leaning against his shoulder. "How'd ye like yar first longside?"

Justin raised his head slowly. His face was covered in gunpowder and soot; his hands were black with it. "Not well, Will. Not well."

Will put his arm around him and shook him gently. "Ye did fine, lad. Ye have all yar limbs. Ye did fine."

In the dimming sunlight, Will caught sight of the captain as his shadow fell over them. The man stood enormous and imposing. With his blood-stained breeches and hands, his soot-covered face, the captain seemed otherworldly. A divine warrior-god from mythology. He was just so bloody huge.

An aura-like glow upon him at the sight of the victor, Justin met the captain's eyes and found the big man's irresistible smile. His success was written all over him.

Will gazed from one to the other. At first, he thought nothing, then something in the length of the attention they gave each other made him take heed.

"We've some more fresh water, Justin. I know how much you hate to be dirty," the captain chuckled softly.

"Am I a mess?" Justin asked him, twisting to check with Will.

They both broke into laughter as Justin's innocent blue eyes peered out from a very smudged face.

He got the point and stood up. "Right. Off to make meself look pretty again."

They watched him leave, grins on their faces. The captain turned back to see Will Davis studying him closely. "Aye, good work, Will. Even though we didn't need cannon, you did very well looking after the lad. Black informed me you helped him with the flintlocks. I thank you."

With an effort and stiff limbs, Will Davis stood and gazed up into that handsome face. "T'was not a problem, Captain. He's a pleasure ta tend. I'm sure ye are well aware of that fact." He scratched at his itchy armpit.

The captain's friendly features vanished. "Is that an accusation?"

"Nay! Naught meant to be as one. He beds down in your cabin, so I assumed ye have gotten closer. How close aren't fer me to wonder."

Captain Jones bristled angrily. "If you think I am going to allow him to sleep on deck with those disease-ridden bilge rats, you are a fool. He is safe with me where I can watch over him."

"And ye watch over him closely, don't ye? Me wonders, Captain, sir, how close that really is?" Will knew his evil smile proudly showed off a few broken teeth. His scratching moved to his chest.

The captain shifted his stance. "Do we settle this on land, William? Or have I had enough of this talk for one voyage?"

"Argh! No offense intended, Captain!" Will knew very well he was no match for this powerful soldier on land or sea, with gun or blade. "We've all been asea too long, and ye know as well as me Hornbolt wasn't the only one with designs on that pretty boy. He's just one fool enough to force himself—" He turned to see the tall pilot's fair blond hair and light eyes and stopped talking, and scratching.

Peckham scrutinized one then the other. "You all right, Captain? Is there a dispute here over something?"

"I think, Pilot, you need ask our gunner that." He narrowed his eyes and crossed two very muscular arms over his broad chest.

Peckham stared at Will Davis in expectation.

"Nay, no dispute here, sir. Naught whatsoever." He

bowed his head and left.

* * * *

After Will disappeared, Peckham studied him. "It's been a long day, Richard. I think once everyone has had some food and sleep we shall be in better temper."

"Aye, right as usual, Pilot. I need to freshen up as well."

"That, and a pocket full of doubloons!"

The captain smiled at him and winked as he went back to his cabin.

When he stepped through his cabin door, he found precisely what he expected, Justin, naked, rinsing the battle off himself.

With a flutter of dark long lashes, Justin turned his brilliant blue eyes the captain's way and smiled in pure delight. "I've brought enough water for two."

"Have you?" The captain started to remove his guns and sword.

"Aye, indeed I have, sir. And soap. From the galleon." He produced a small bar, appearing very proud of himself.

"What a resourceful lad you are." The captain removed his boots and beamed excitedly into that enthusiastic expression.

They heard a light rap. He nodded to Justin to find his breeches. First mate Cromwell opened the door and caught the tail end of Justin's rump as the material was pulled over it. While the captain observed, Cromwell managed to tear his eyes away from that delightful sight and close the door behind him, stepping in with an unopened bottle of rum. As Cromwell held it up and waved it, he grinned invitingly at his captain and then nodded to Justin. "Argh! I found this in that bilge rat's cabin. I couldn't help meself."

"I must have overlooked it. I combed that cabin myself." The captain teased and walked over to sit near Justin.

"Will ye join me? A victory toast?" Cromwell pried the bottle open.

The captain nodded in appreciation, turning back to Justin for him to go ahead and start his bath.

Raising the bottle, Cromwell took a deep swallow and wiped his mouth, handing it to the captain, who brought it to his lips and drank it down. Justin set the basin of water behind him and raised a pouring pitcher. As carefully as he could, he wet the captain's hair and caught the overspill.

Cromwell moved his stool closer to them to be able to pass the bottle easier. "Ye have a nice cabin boy now."

"Yes, he's been a godsend, Jack. He keeps the salt and soot off me skin." The captain sighed softly and handed back the bottle.

Justin happily rubbed the oatmeal soap into the captain's hair and washed it.

"I'd ask ye for the favor, lad, if I thought it would do any good." With a flip of his hand, Cromwell took off his bandana and showed his bald head.

Justin broke up with laughter whilst he massaged the captain's scalp through his thick hair.

Another knock was heard. The captain bid them enter. Boatswain Black came in with a bottle of Spanish wine. "I see the party has just begun!" He spotted the rum in Cromwell's hand.

"Pull up a seat, Thomas. Join us." The captain waved.

Justin asked the captain to lean back again. When he did, Justin poured the fresh water through the captain's hair, rinsing out the soap.

Cromwell and Black exchanged glances. "Ye spoiling our Captain, lad? He won't want to go back to his lass if ye treats him too kindly," Black warned playfully and passed the wine.

"This is the corvette's water. She's about to turn. It'd be a shame to waste it," Justin replied as he made sure all the soap was out of the captain's hair before he took a comb to it.

"Most men would shiver in their boots to get wet like that." Cromwell wiped the rum off his beard. "Me thinks washing too much makes a man vulnerable to disease."

"Ah, not I. Nothing like getting the soot and filth off." The captain groaned at the refreshing feeling.

"Ye want some wine, Justin?" Black offered.

"May I?" Justin set the comb aside after running it through the captain's hair.

Captain Jones felt his wet locks framing his face and dripping gently down his back. He told Justin, "Of course, lad. You did well today. You know, he saved my life?"

The two men raised their bushy eyebrows to that. "No! Tell us, lad!"

Justin blushed and drank from the bottle.

They heard another scratching noise at the door.

"Aye, enter!" the captain shouted.

Quartermaster Tucker and Pilot Peckham came in with two more bottles. When they realized the others had beaten them to it, they laughed and had a seat.

"The one thing that galleon had a plenty was grog!" Peckham opened his bottle and passed it.

"The men are well pleased then." The captain smiled as Justin washed one of his long, grime-covered arms.

"They be on the drink. I have no doubt. Don't ask them to behave themselves," Tucker announced. "I just hopes no one gets too out of hand."

Justin passed the bottle and rinsed the rag, sponging the captain's chest after cleaning both his limbs.

Peckham and Tucker stared at them, then glimpsed at each other as if they were exchanging thoughts.

The captain let out a soft chuckle. "Aye, yes, he spoils me. All right, lad. You can just relax now." He blushed and passed him the rum.

As a last gesture, Justin wiped the captain's broad back dry, whispering into his ear, "I'll finish the job later. When we are alone." Justin sat himself down on the floor by his side.

The seductive words sent an eager shiver over the captain's skin.

* * * *

When the men became absorbed into a conversation around him, Justin listened in silence as he was given a bottle as it passed. The captain petted his hair softly, again with that same unintentional sensuousness and attention. It was as if Justin were a Persian cat on his lap, being stroked as a means of relaxation and comfort. In reality, it was comforting to both.

Justin knew the men tried not to take notice. Perhaps they felt what went on between the captain and his new cabin boy wasn't of their concern. One by one, they came in; the carpenter, the doctor, and anyone else who fancied sharing a drink on that moonlit night.

Justin inspected the ring of shadowy men, illuminated solely by the covered oil lamp's halo. Only his captain and the pilot were clean-shaven. He thought Pilot Peckham appeared elfin with his narrow face, blond hair, and large eyes. The man had a reputation for being able to see and hear things that others could not, faraway masts and siren songs. A very valuable trait indeed.

Then Justin's gaze found Quartermaster Tucker. He was the heavy dwarf type; short, squat, with a thick beard and roughness of manner. The rest were all crossed between man and beast. If he could, he would put animal species to each man's appearance. Boatswain Black was the bear, covered in hair from his toes to his ears, but for the top of his head. First mate Cromwell was the ram, a long scraggy beard and large rounded ears. The ship's doctor was the owl. The only spectacled crewmate on the ship. Justin smiled a silly grin to himself as he wound a fairy tale in his drunken head. All the animals were tended and tamed by the only prince in the room. His fair captain. If he had to put an animal form to that one, he would surely have been a lion. The powerful king of all the beasts. The pride of England. He purred and leaned against those large legs of his, legs that generated an alluring heat.

Justin's eyes went heavy. The alcohol was finally putting him to sleep. He was fatigued from the battle and couldn't keep awake, especially with the captain's soft caress on his hair.

Tucker noticed his eyelids drooping. "Go on, lad, get ye ta bed."

The captain twisted in his chair to be able to see Justin's face. "Go lay down, Justin."

Needing no more prodding, he stood a little unsteadily and made it to the bunk, collapsing down on it.

* * * *

The men smiled and continued to speak softly and pass the bottles.

Peckham leaned over to the captain. "What a brave lad. I'm glad he was your guardian angel today on the galleon. Where would we have been if he hadn't been there?"

The captain glanced back to Justin on the bed, lost to the conscious world. "Yes, I owe him my very life. It is ironic. I wonder if he was sent to this ship for that reason."

Tucker leaned closer when he overheard the conversation. The rest of the men stopped talking and moved into the tight circle to listen. Tucker spoke quietly, "Aye, he is a good luck charm, Captain. The boy shouldn't just be discarded when we get back to England. I do fear for his safety, knowing how his father abused him."

The few who hadn't heard that tale urged to be caught up. They kept peering back at Justin, who was sound asleep.

"Maybe we can recruit the lad on our next voyage," Cromwell offered.

"There is no next for me." The captain handed the bottle off and wiped his mouth. "I have officially retired from pirate life, my boys."

"Until the next whisper of a loaded galleon!" Tucker roared, quieting himself when he remembered the sleeping lad.

"Nay, not this time, John. I yearn the settled life. Some children, a farm," Captain Jones sighed.

"And lovely Katherine." Peckham grinned.

"Aye, yes. And Kath," the captain whispered shyly, a slight blush in his cheeks.

Loud singing was heard from out on the upper deck as they grinned at one another happily.

'...there's spanking full-rigger just ready for sea...give me some time to blow the man down....'

"Argh! Bottomless flagon!" Cromwell raised his bottle in a toast.

"Aye!" Tucker agreed. "A never-empty black jack!"

"I should make sure the men are all right." The captain went to rise.

"Allow me. I've had enough and need to get back to my cabin." The doctor stood and left the bottle behind.

"Oh, Jason. Before you leave, do you have more liniment here on board?" the captain asked.

"Aye, that I do. And more yet from the galleon. Why? Ye have a wound that needs tending?" He took a step toward the captain.

"Nay, not I, the lad. Thank you, Jason."

The doctor nodded and left.

The other men stared at their captain as his eyes

misted over.

"Argh. Ye look dog-tired, sir, ye hanging the jib. I'll be off now." Tucker stood and took two of the bottles with him, singing to the songs he could hear on the deck. "So, I give you fair warning before we belay, to me way aye, blow the man down!" He winked as he sang happily on his way out.

The doctor returned and held out a jar. The captain thanked him and set it down.

* * * *

One by one, they left until only the pilot remained. Peckham swallowed the strong rum and listened to the receding footfalls until it went quiet in the cabin. Peckham moved to sit next to his captain and took a quick peek at a sleeping Justin. When he caught the captain's attention, he whispered, "You've fallen in love with the lad."

The captain's eyes flashed in anger, then it faded away to tired resignation.

"Who could blame you? Look at us. This group of scallywags and scoundrels. Weeks asea with no woman, no tender touch. And you, most of all, Richard, who's remained true to his woman to a fault. You would not be able to prevent your feelings from taking charge. A captain with a greater heart, I have not seen. You have never ruled us by fear or intimidation, but pure love and respect. And the lad is completely enamored by you. He lights up when you come in view. Who could blame him?" Peckham smiled adoringly into that handsome, tired face. "What, dear Richard, will you do about him?"

The captain rubbed his exhausted eyes. "I do not know, James. I don't have time to think of these things now. I only have the bay at Portobello, and then the long journey home. After that?" He shrugged. "Do we know we will not be lost at sea? Why burden ourselves with things that may not come?"

Peckham reached out to touch that long, brown, damp hair, pushing it back from the captain's brilliant blue eyes. The captain seemed startled by the contact.

"The boy is the lucky one to have gained your love and attachment. I envy him."

Captain Jones blinked in surprise. "I think we have all been without for too long!" He tried to make a joke of it.

"The whores at Portobello cannot hold a candle to you." Peckham reached for the captain with his other hand, both dug through the captain's long clean hair.

"Ah, Pilot." Captain Jones held his arms gently and tried to move him back. "We are tired and drunk and say foolish things. Off with you now." The captain grunted in surprise as Peckham's lips met his. Without unnecessary force, the captain tried to back away. When he was able to locate both of his hands, the captain took them down from his hair and leaned away to see his face. "To say I am flattered at best, Pilot. But this is not possible. Please, respect my wishes and get some rest so we may see things more plainly in the morning sun."

The taste of those lips lingering, Peckham moaned softly and nodded. He rose to his feet as the captain stared up at him with deep intensity. Peckham knew the Nordic blood in him was very evident, and he looked different from most of the crew with his golden blond hair and fair skin.

"Keep us on course, and you'll be amply rewarded," the captain whispered.

"I don't crave an extra doubloon. This won't be my final voyage. If you want to show me your appreciation, you know how." He moved his hand slowly over his own britches, feeling how hard he had grown under them.

Captain Jones caught his seductive smile, including the tease of his hand. Peckham winked at him and left.

* * * *

As he watched Peckham exit the cabin, the captain exhaled and scratched his chin stubble absently. "This has been a very long and unusual voyage," he sighed.

With an effort, he finished getting ready for bed and doused the light. On deck, one could still hear the noise. The men were very drunk and singing in the moonlight, most likely with bottles raised. The faint chorus was still in the wind.

'*... Don't ever take heed of what pretty girls say, give me some time to blow the man down...*'

Like a snake, Captain Jones crawled into the bunk and cuddled a sleepy Justin into his arms, wrapping himself around him, inhaling the scent of oatmeal soap on him, clean and fresh. At the sensual caress, Justin stirred and came to the surface. His lips parted with a tiny gasp, and the captain started to get very hungry for him.

"My Captain...," he whispered.

Captain Jones smiled lovingly. "My Justin Alexander, wake up, lad, and please me."

With his head raised, Justin squinted into the dimness. A moan and a stretch of his back brought him to the conscious world once more. "What does my Captain wish?"

The captain's deep laughter rumbled in his chest as he opened his breeches. He knew Justin knew that answer. Justin sat up in the dark and ran his hands down his chest to his pelvis, finding where he'd grown extremely hard.

"There is another jar of liniment, there." The captain felt in the dimness for it, handing it to Justin.

Justin dipped his finger into the jar and covered his length with the lotion. Sensing his movement, Captain Jones reached out to get an idea of his position and realized Justin was on his hands and knees next to him. Grinning in pure delight, the captain knelt up behind him.

"Oh, you are a good lad...such a good lad." Holding those narrow hips delicately, the captain slid inside the tight heat and groaned in pleasure. Slowly penetrating that squeezing ring of muscles, he worked his way inside Justin gently. "You are an angel, Justin," he crooned.

"Ah, my captain. It is a delight to serve you." Justin wriggled backwards, grinding his bottom against the captain's body. "Harder, please!"

"Bloody hell, yes!" He clamped onto Justin's waist and ground full force into his lover. The rush to his loins was so intense, he choked on his moans and felt his body tighten up for the surge.

"Captain!" Justin gasped breathlessly.

As if just remembering to tend Justin, the captain reached one of his hands to surround Justin's cock and worked him eagerly. Hearing Justin's whimpers and feeling his rod pulsate as he spewed out his load, the captain grunted and felt it well up in him. He released a deep, masculine sound that echoed in the cabin.

As the captain gave into the spasms of orgasm, he held onto Justin's body a moment longer, letting the sensations linger. After savoring the afterglow, he pulled out and lay back with a breath, face up. Justin curled onto his chest and nuzzled him happily. The captain petted him gently before he closed his eyes, kissing his hair to whisper, "Thank you, lad."

* * * *

The moonlight glimmered over the sweaty faces of men like a fire ship over the waves. The crew were allowed to get intoxicated on board for the first time since setting out from England. The thought of the whores at Portobello was the main thing on their minds -- that and the gaming and rich food. They were starved for it.

Will Davis and his crewmates were passing the

bottles and splayed out on the deck as the pilot checked the rudder and the sky. "Aye! How many days to the port, Pilot?" he shouted.

"Soon, William, soon," Peckham yelled back.

"Ye getting ready for ye pound of flesh? What do ye fancy?" Will passed the bottle along.

Peckham thought about the question and laughed to himself. "Oy! Just a wet hole! I don't care at this point. I think we've all had enough of the wait."

Will chuckled and scratched himself. "Any port in the storm!"

The men roared with laughter and started shouting rude things. Will Davis smiled at the wit of this rough company. He eyed his fair-haired pilot and asked, "Ye haven't had enough to drink, Pilot!"

"Nay! Someone's got to keep us on course, Will. Look at you dogs. You don't know which way the wind's blowing."

"Come, come! Sit and share a toast with yer maties." Will patted a narrow spot on the deck between bodies.

Peckham nodded and sat near him, thanking him for the bottle.

"There's fresh tack and even some limes if ye care to." He handed over some food the men had been eating.

"Thanks, Will, mate." Peckham ate the fresh food hungrily. "I'm starved for a real meal of roast lamb and carrots."

"Ye tired of Smithy's potato stew and salt pork?" He laughed heartily.

Henry exclaimed, "Now that we are in no rush to port, we find some fish!"

"Aye! Or a turtle!" Samuel added.

Peckham swallowed the dry tack with some rum. "Aye, yes, boys, no more scuttling. You find us some nice seafood come the daybreak."

Will Davis grinned into the pilot's face. "Where's me

Captain and pretty Justin Taylor?"

At the query, Peckham removed the bottle from his own lips too quickly and spilled it down his chin. He wiped it away with his sleeve and stared at the gunner.

Will scanned all the shining eyes of their group, then back at his pilot. "Ye know naught?"

"No, I do know. Sound asleep in each other's arms, no doubt." Peckham cleared his throat and bit into the biscuit.

At the comment, Will bristled and sat up. There was a murmur of disapproval from the company.

Peckham caught the glare in their eyes. "I meant asleep! Don't think more."

Knowing it was far more than sleep, Will felt the jealousy and anger in him rising. With an air of complete frustration, he threw the bottle he was holding aside and stood on wobbly drunken legs.

"Oy! Where ya going?" Peckham chided. "Sit back down, Will!" He grabbed at Will's knees.

Boatswain Black and Quartermaster Tucker headed over to investigate the noise.

"All right, maties, come tell us what the quarrel is about," Tucker asked, crossing his massive arms over his broad chest.

"No quarrel here, John." Peckham tried to stand in front of the drunken, angry gunner.

The one-eared man shoved Peckham aside roughly. Will faced the broad, bearded Tucker and snarled, "Our pilot thinks me Captain and Justin are more than bunkmates!"

"I said naught of the kind," Peckham growled. "It is your imagination what's done it."

Black waved his hands in a gesture to calm everyone down. "He protects the lad. Our Captain Jones has only one set of arms on his mind, his own Kath. It's the rum what's got to ye! Sit yerselves down before ye feels the cat o'nine tails on yer back," he warned.

"That goes double for me! Ye start stirring up this lot, Davis, and ye'll be the scallywag," Tucker added, poking his finger into Will's chest.

"Ye don't even go to see. Ye has no notion. Why don't ye get yerself to that bloody cabin?" Will swiped away Tucker's accusing digit.

"I was just there, me matey! I just now come from sharing a drink!" Tucker puffed up his chest and grew more imposing. "And if our Captain does have the arse of our Justin? So? What concern is it of yars?"

As the commotion grew, Jack Cromwell was now a part of the ruckus, defending the captain along with his trusted men against Will and the other gunners. The shouting grew more explosive and vulgar as tempers caught quickly from too much hunger, sexual tension, and rum.

When the captain's height and broad, bronze chest appeared, the ones who spotted him clammed up instantly. The captain made his way to the large crowd, and it opened for him, allowing him to move into the middle. His hair was now dry and loose from its ribbon, blowing back from his face in the same breeze that filled the sails. He made sure he gave eye contact to each and every man. One never knew if a dagger was hidden in the dark. It was silent but for the wind and the creaking of the mast.

Will swallowed nervously at the intimidation he felt. The man was so powerfully built and fit. So filled with an elegance of movement and an aura of authority, it was painful.

Peckham stifled a groan at the sight of him. "Ahoy, Captain," he whispered sheepishly.

"I find this puzzling after fulfilling our dreams. We've a hull full of booty, and yet we quarrel? Is it simply too much rum? Must I cut off your supply of grog? Enough! Get some rest, and soon you will fill your bellies and replace your tattered rags."

No one said a word. They lowered their eyes submissively.

"Black!" the captain shouted to his boatswain. "Confiscate all bottles! Tucker! You as well! That's it! Back to watered-down grog for this crew."

"Aye, Captain," his men answered obediently.

"Back off!" the captain roared into the very close crowd. "Get to sleep! Why do I have to order you?" He tried to disperse the mob. "I know you are sick to death of each other. When we port, you decide to come back or not. I'm not bothered either way. But whilst you are under my flag, you will settle your quarrels on land. You all know the code of conduct. Why is it you are behaving like a bunch of buccaneers?"

"Aye! Do ye, sir? Know the code? Have ye a secret what needs telling?"

The captain spun in fury to face Will Davis. "Again my gunner has a complaint. You are now assigned careening detail in port," he growled. "Tucker!" the captain commanded.

His quartermaster hurried front and center. "Aye, Captain, sir!"

"You make sure our gunner here is assigned careening detail."

"Aye, Captain, sir!"

The men watched Will's face carefully. He was not pleased.

The captain moved to tower over him menacingly. "So far, that work detail is your only punishment. Open your gob and see what comes next."

The pilot appeared afraid to blink. All the men were watching the test of wills. No one crossed the captain and lived. He had killed several unruly men on land before.

Will Davis ground his jaw, tempted to again spit out his accusations. His shipmates stopped him from stepping once again over the line. They held his arms and tugged him back.

* * * *

The captain watched as Will was dragged to a safe distance. He raised his square jaw and stared around the deck. Bottles were being collected, and the crew was silent. As he walked by his pilot, Captain Jones grabbed his shirt to drag him, making his way back to his cabin. Once there, he threw him inside and closed the door.

Peckham regained his balance and trembled visibly.

Captain Jones approached him and through clenched teeth whispered, "Why do I have a feeling this has to do with you and your attempt?"

"Nay! Captain, you must believe me."

"What then!" he growled.

In paranoia, Peckham spun to look at Justin quickly.

Justin appeared to be asleep.

"Our gunner, Will," Peckham stammered. "He asked where you and the lad were. Honest, Captain."

"And your reply?" Growling, the captain moved another step closer, looming over him.

"I...I merely said in bed together." Peckham's Adam's apple bobbed as he swallowed nervously. "He took it his own way."

Captain Jones grabbed his pilot's collar. "We need one another, Peckham, to survive this voyage. Don't betray me now simply because you have been rebuffed."

The pilot clasped his hands onto the captain's fists and gently squeezed them. "I would never betray you, sir. I am in love with you. It is in Will's mind, this madness, not mine. Please believe me, Richard."

The captain studied his face. Slowly he relaxed his grip and lowered his hands.

"Please, my trusted friend," Peckham whispered,

"There are enough enemies on board and off to deal with. Let us not make one more here and now." He grabbed the captain's hand and kissed it.

"If we breed traitors, we will all dance the hempen jig, Pilot. We have come this far in our quest, let us not lose to the hangman's knot now."

"Of me you have no fear. I beg you to have faith in me. I would die for you. Of our gunner, you have another problem. He looks for ways, I'm afraid, of discrediting you. His jealousy of your relationship with the lad has begun to twist him."

"Yes. I know this. But he will not drive Justin and I apart. I will protect Justin, and he will stay here with me. That will not change. I will not toss him out to the sharks to live in the lice-ridden decks with those bilge rats. No. No matter what the men think, I will not subject our Justin to that."

"I know, Captain. He would not survive it. You're a kind, generous man." He brushed his lips again on the back of the captain's hand, lingering.

"Get some sleep, Pilot, and show the men the bay they crave." He cupped Peckham's face softly.

"I will, my Captain. Have faith in your pilot."

"I do. With all my heart." Captain Jones kissed his forehead softly.

The captain walked him to the cabin door and closed it behind him. Exhaling tiredly, he made his way back to the bunk. As he approached, Justin moved over and rested on his elbows to speak. "I am now causing battles on board."

Not knowing Justin was awake or heard their discussion, Captain Jones leaned up on his side to face him. "No, no more than is normal. The men always quarrel after too much grog. They will be calmer now that it is withdrawn."

"What of Will Davis, sir?"

"What of him?" The captain pushed the long hair off Justin's pretty face.

"I am afraid."

"Do not be. I am here."

Justin reached around and squeezed him, burying into his neck and hair. "Thank you, my Captain."

"Shhh, all right, lad, go to sleep."

Chapter Eight

At first light, Justin and the captain dressed and made ready for the chores of the day. The captain loaded his flintlocks, all three, and tucked them into his baldric, which he laid across his chest. His dagger he hid in his boot, then he attached his cutlass to his hip. Placing his tri-cornered hat on his head, he stepped outside of the cabin where he could stand tall.

Justin stared at him in pride, as it seemed the captain was preparing for another battle, and inevitably, he was. With a wink and a smile in Justin's direction, he left to address his men. Lost, Justin stood still a moment trying to gather his thoughts, which at the time were reflecting on more sensual things. When he snapped back to the present, he moved to the looking glass to comb his hair. Catching sight of his own reflection, he paused to inspect it curiously. Was he too pretty? *Well, pretty enough to attract the handsome captain.*

Though he tried to let that reality lift his suddenly sullen mood, it did not. Too many intruding thoughts invaded, primarily, the incident last evening on deck. Pensively, he set the comb back down only to notice the logbook again. With a quick, impish glance at the cabin's closed door, he sat at the desk to casually flip the pages and read the text. The usual details of their location, the weather, etcetera, were present, so he scanned down to the notes. He found his name.

'I have come to be the guardian of our Justin, which I assume gladly. He is a good worker and I've no

complaints. I worry for him and wonder what to do with him when we finally end this quest.'

A noise startled him into slapping the book shut. He stood and backed away like it was a hissing cobra. Someone was yelling his name, so he hurried on deck.

When he arrived, Captain Jones was addressing the men. They were sober now and had slept, so they appeared to be a more civilized group than the night before. The first mate waved to Justin to get closer to listen. Every man was standing shoulder to shoulder, staring at their captain in anticipation, keeping still, but for the occasional scratch of an itch.

"Aye! A more ragged bunch I have never seen." The captain laughed and shook his head. "Yet, you look better for the sleep and fresh air. You know as I do this ship is run like a democracy. I'm no Blackbeard. I don't rule you with a savage fist. You are granted many freedoms here and come of your own free will. Your work, split between sixty, isn't so demanding. You have food, Smithy's salt pork and stew. You have grog, and now even a pocket full of golden coins." The captain paused to gather his thoughts.

"What you have asked for, you have received. We are all present, save one, who started out with us. Our seas have been calm, and our sails swollen full. More, we cannot have asked or dreamed. Here we are about to dock in the town where you can find pleasure in many places, and many ways, as I have promised. We need some work, as you know. Some careening, some carpentry, some replenishing of stores. But nothing you cannot handle as a group. And a group I have had like no other! You are to be commended for your bravery against the galleon. You faced her broadside cannon and never flinched. What men you are!"

At the brilliant speech, Justin's eyes started tearing as he surveyed all the scarred, dirty faces. Every eye and patch was facing their handsome leader.

"So, this I have said. Now, I ask you. If you are not happy with my command of *His Revenge*, you must vote." A murmur surrounded him. "Quartermaster Tucker!" he called.

"Aye, Captain, sir!"

"Come forth and be heard."

The quartermaster fell in beside his captain. With the wirehairs of his elevated, bearded chin pointing forward, he yelled, "All ye who wish to no longer follow Captain Richard Jones' flag, say aye!"

In anticipation, Justin bit the inside of his cheek. It was silent. With his weak sixth sense, he tried to read their faces.

"All ye who want to remain under the command of Captain Richard Jones say aye!"

When the roar came up, Justin bowed his head in an answered prayer.

The captain quieted his men. He thanked his quartermaster and then announced, "So, you have me once again. I will see you safe into your harbor at Penzance if the seas are willing. Pilot!" he thundered.

"Aye, Captain, sir!"

"Full speed to Portobello! These men need land under their feet!"

Another cheer rang out, and the men dispersed slowly, patting one another's backs and smiling their toothless grins.

Justin noticed Captain Jones inspecting Will Davis' actions with great care. He had voted for the captain, most likely being too frightened not to. Was it the captain's way of assuring his complete command once again and, hopefully, convincing his gunner that his popularity had not waned with the accusations?

As one who has been triumphant in battle, the captain reached his hand out to Justin boldly. Justin brightened up and moved past the opposing stream of men to meet him. With a firm grasp, the captain brought Justin to his side and put his arm around his shoulder. Then as if to incite him, the captain connected to Will Davis' gaze.

Witnessing this deadly exchange, Justin noticed the jealous sneer appear on Will's face, most likely exactly as the captain had expected it would.

Trying to ignore the conflict between men for a moment and savor his captain's touch, Justin knew he was completely love-struck. In adoration, he beamed up at his captain and leaned against his side. Around them, the crew got busy with the sails and rigging.

Justin asked, "What will you do, sir, when we first come to land?"

"Ah, my Justin, a bath and a meal. Then I shall burn these clothes and buy some more."

"Aye! Me too. Will you be on your own there, sir? Or do you want some company, perhaps?"

Captain Jones began laughing. "I would be delighted, Justin, if you would accompany me."

Having held his breath in apprehension, Justin brightened up and jumped into the captain's arms with the impulsiveness of the young man he was, giving him a warm, loving hug.

* * * *

The captain raised his stare to catch that venomous glint from the one-eared man. The captain smiled at Will with complete superiority whilst he rocked Justin in his arms. Everyone was well aware of who was in possession of the real prize on *His Revenge*. This pretty, well-groomed young man had sold his soul to his captain. In some warped way, he enjoyed the growing hatred from Will Davis. Whilst Will glared, the captain ran his right hand down to Justin's solid rump and squeezed it tight, massaging it lovingly. Wickedly, he taunted the gunner, giving him fuel to challenge him. He wanted the chance to squash this growing menace and knew just how to antagonize the man.

* * * *

Justin felt the sensuous grasp and friction in pleasure. It hardened him up instantly, and a small sound of wonder escaped him. This show of public affection surprised him, so he tilted his head up to see his captain's expression. He realized his captain's attention targeted something behind him. For a moment, Justin thought of breaking the embrace to have a peek, then reconsidered when those fingers brought a rushing chill over his skin. "Ah! You are driving me mad," Justin whispered.

Never releasing his gaze from beyond Justin's back, Captain Jones squeezed him closer and hissed, "Good."

About to climax where they stood, rubbing hotly against his captain, Justin clenched his teeth and pressed his hardness into that large thigh. "Will you meet me in your cabin?"

"Aye, my pretty. Go and get ready for me." He nudged him gently.

Justin had to force himself to move back from that hot friction. He smiled lovingly first before he skipped away.

* * * *

At dusk, the corvette was moving into the port amongst dozens of tall mast ships. The captain was at the bow shouting orders. One of the crew swung the lead to see how deep the water was.

"Heave to!" the captain instructed. The corvette slid to a stop. "Anchor! We're here, my pretties! Get her sails down and tie her up before you scurry away."

The crew worked like mad to get her ready, then stood at the bow gunwale eagerly.

"All right, men. Off you go. Tucker has made sure you have your purse. But remember, high tide tomorrow we're off. So, come back to her early and let's get her ready."

"Aye, Captain!" they shouted.

With a wave of his hand, he sent them on their way as they crowded the narrow dock and went off seeking pleasure.

The captain put a hand on Will Davis' chest to halt him before he debarked. "Have we settled our differences, William?" he asked innocently.

The gunner glanced down at that large hand first, inspected the well-armed baldric leather next, then those stern eyes. "Aye, Captain."

"Good. You are too good a man to lose, my friend. Come home with us whole." He grinned.

"Aye. I will, sir."

The captain knew he was baiting him. He judged Will's sincerity, doubted it completely, and then allowed him to pass.

* * * *

Justin hurried to his captain's side. "Are we ready for a feast and a bath?"

The captain embraced him roughly. "Aye, my pretty boy! That we are." They made their way to the land with a lightness of spirit and uncapped jubilation.

When Justin finally stood on the cobbled street, he felt like he was losing his balance. The captain held his elbow and steadied him. "Easy, my boy. It's just sea legs, Justin, my lad."

"Just when I get used to the water, I have to get used to the land." Justin reached out to him for balance. "Is the ground moving, sir?" he asked in all seriousness.

The captain erupted with laughter. "Nay, she's solid as a rock. It be your wobbly knees. Come, lad."

Justin had to concentrate and will his legs to obey. They were shaky from the rocking of the ocean and going without proper nutrition for the last few weeks. Daring not to release the man next to him, he clung to his arm and used him to get himself along. In the pit of his hungry stomach, he was craving fresh meat and vegetables very badly. The captain escorted him to an inn and allowed Justin to pass through the well-worn doors first.

The captain greeted the owner and requested two baths. The owner grinned in delight at the generous number of coins handed to him and hurried to get the water heated. They were led to a backroom as plump working women poured water from buckets into the tubs that waited. A screen was set up separating the two, and Captain Jones winked at Justin as he disappeared behind his.

Justin started disrobing quickly, very excited about a hot scrub. He dropped his dirty clothing into a pile and climbed in with a groan.

The captain heard it and replied, "You enjoying yourself, lad?"

"Aye, my Captain! It is just as good as in my dreams." He sunk down under the water and then popped back up, slicking back his hair.

Justin strained to be able to decipher words at the rumble of his captain's deep voice. It sounded as if it took some time to communicate his wishes. Next Justin heard the rustle of the person leaving. "You still there, my Captain?"

"Aye, Justin."

"Good." He sighed and closed his eyes as he shampooed his hair.

Humming in complete contentment as he washed the

salt and soot off himself, he scrubbed in delight knowing this would be the last for a long while. When two men entered carrying something, Justin was surprised. "Oy! What's this?"

He heard the captain's chuckle and then his soothing deep voice, "New garments, lad. I doubted after your soak you wanted to climb back into those lice-ridden rags."

Justin perked up considerably at that piece of information. He rinsed off and climbed out of the bath eagerly. He toweled dry quickly and nodded to the men as they raised different outfits for him to admire. "Blimey! I feel like a prince!" A pair of cream-colored breeches and blouse, a waistcoat and frock of dark blue velvet, and a tall pair of leather boots struck his fancy. With a passionate groan at the feel of the fine fabrics against his clean skin, he was led to a looking glass to admire himself. In frustration, he ran his fingers through his wet hair to untangle it, only to notice a woman step up to comb it and tie it back in a ribbon for him. He couldn't stop his laughter at the thrill. When they completed their task, he wanted to give them payment, but didn't know how.

On soft, leather-soled feet, he went around the screen and stopped short. A lovely young woman was shampooing his captain's long brown tresses. Her white peasant blouse was low on her chest, exposing her cleavage; her skirt was colorful and printed with hues of reds and oranges. Jealous anger rose up in Justin quickly.

The captain opened his eyes, and the shock of their brilliant blue color jarred Justin horribly for some reason. "Aye? You all right, lad? You look like royalty. What's with the hanging jib?"

Justin attempted a smile though he hated that woman touching his captain. Her face was showing her complete pleasure at being able to serve such a man. She was lost on his profile as the captain addressed him. Justin stared down into the bath and made out his lover's body through the soapy depth. The water had seeped into the woman's blouse, and her nipples were showing through the sheer fabric. Justin dreaded that if his captain noticed it, he'd want her.

Captain Jones squinted his eyes at him, then sighed softly. "Don't be jealous, lad. It's but one bath." After he gave Justin a reassuring smile, he turned to see the woman, noticing her expression as well as her wet blouse.

It snapped Justin out of his thoughts suddenly. "Yes...I wasn't...I didn't...ahh, you almost done?"

As if trying to distract himself from the woman's ardent admiration, the captain tore his attention from her to reply. "Aye. Your stomach is calling you, I fear. Yes, my Justin. I am done." He nodded to the woman who rinsed him off efficiently.

When he stood out of the water, Justin almost felt faint. He had never seen him in the bright light, completely naked, until now. His six–foot, four-inch frame seemed enormous with the extra height of the tub. That luscious dark bronze tan tinted his skin from the waist up and the snow white tone glowed from it down. The mass of him was solid and sinewy. His long brown hair was pasted to his cheek and dripped down his shoulders and back. His legs were powerful and long, the hair at his pubis was almost black, his cock was large, and his balls hung low from being heated.

"Oh, blimey." Justin panted as he feasted his eyes on him, afraid to blink.

The captain took the towel he was handed and started to dry himself, stepping out of the tub. Rubbing it through his hair roughly, he caught the look Justin was bestowing upon him. He took a quick check around them, shaking his head at Justin, admonishing him for openly admiring him. "Behave, lad."

Knowing he should stop staring, Justin tried to turn away. The serving girl was cleaning up, and the two men with clothing were coming in. Step by step, Justin backed up, never removing his focus from that vision until he hit the wall. Leaning against it, he tried not to hyperventilate. He was fully excited and wondering what to do about it. His inspection kept shifting from that face, to that chest, to that cock, those legs...

Captain Jones got busy choosing his new clothing, trying not to acknowledge the hungry ogling he was receiving from this very pretty eighteen-year-old lad.

Justin's mouth was watering. *This is what loves me every night?* He groaned silently and felt his excitement stirring between his legs in unleashed urgency. With a completely unconscious gesture, he rubbed his palm over himself as the yearning grew almost painful.

The captain slid on a silk shirt, catching Justin's lusting leer now and again, including that hand trying to deal with what was becoming, he obviously assumed, an unreasonable demand.

He chose a red velvet coat and white breeches, armed his new waistband with his cutlass, and laid his leather baldric with the three pistols across his chest. Next he tucked his dagger into his new high boot. Lifting his purse, he handed the men more than enough money for his and Justin's purchases. They nodded in appreciation, smiling as they bowed, leaving the men alone.

A deep exhale emerged from the captain's chest as he stood there, staring at Justin's wide-eyed gaze. "What is it, lad? Why do you look at me that way?"

Instantly Justin zeroed in on his serious expression. Stepping toward him slowly, pausing to quickly check around them first, Justin only heard voices speaking in foreign languages. They were alone in the room for the moment. "I am sorry, my Captain. Forgive me."

"For what, lad?" He tilted his head curiously.

Justin spied behind him before moving closer to stare up at his captain and feel his delicious heat. "I have never seen anything as beautiful as you, sir. I am very honored to be the one who serves you."

The captain took another glance around them. "I thank you, Justin Taylor." With a very devilish grin, the captain reached down and cupped his hand lightly over Justin's hardness, teasing him. "Now, are you ready for your lamb supper? Or are you too excited to eat?"

At the playful grope, Justin groaned in agony, reaching out to stroke the red velvet of his captain's lapel. "Aye, sir, both. But I know what I want for my dessert."

The captain tried to contain himself, but couldn't. He shook with laughter and got them moving on their way. "What a lad," he chuckled. "What a lad…"

* * * *

The multitude of ships in the harbor gave an indication of the number of men on the land: males hungry for food and women, eager to spend their ill-gotten gains at the gambling tables and on wine. The local church bells were silent, the customs house vacant, but the inns, pubs, and houses of ill repute, were overflowing. The noise of squabbling carried for miles in the still night air. It was mild and starlit as the pilot, the quartermaster, and the boatswain strolled around the town after buying new clothing, intent on finding their meal. They walked into a tavern and tried to locate a seat in the smoky, overcrowded room. Peckham nodded a greeting to the gunners, who were all seated around the gaming tables, cards in their fists, still dressed in their same salt-soaked rags. He could smell them from where he stood.

"Some men do not care of their condition," Peckham confided, watching as they scratched themselves like flea-bitten mongrels.

"I fear a bath meself, James," Tucker said. "I washed meself enough at the basin. A soak in water can't be healthy."

"Aye, John," Black spoke up, "they say it won't do ye no harm. And I like to think I've rid meself of the reek of a few months on board."

"There's Jack! Let's join him." Peckham waved and made his way over to their first mate.

They sat around the large table and eyed the bones picked clean on Cromwell's plate. "Ye took care of the first order of business, mate!" Tucker laughed.

"Aye! I fed me stomach first. The rest of the body can wait." He belched and lifted his wine goblet.

"How is the food? It smells divine." Peckham inhaled.

"Lovely. Don't speak up too loud though, Smithy's right behind us." He tilted his head to their cook and then roared in hilarity.

They spun to see Smithy with a plate piled high.

"Aye! Smithy!" Black teased. "Ye get sick of yer own salt pork!"

Smithy just narrowed his eyes, then waved the turkey leg he was gnawing on at them.

Laughing heartily, they turned back to face one another and inspect the bill of fare. They placed their orders and were served a round of wine.

"Where's Richard?" Peckham leaned up in his chair to scan the room.

"This isn't the only eatery on the street. He may or may not come here." Cromwell ate another morsel off a bone with greasy fingers. He had several pieces of food stuck in his beard.

"With our Justin? Or do I need to ask it?" Peckham chuckled.

Tucker bristled angrily. "Ye keep suggesting buggery! I think ye better stop!"

The pilot's posture stiffened. "Nay! Why does all I say come out wrong? I ne'er said naught," he whined.

Cromwell leaned closer to the other men over his plate to speak privately. "Look, maties, what our Captain and our Justin do behind the closed doors of that cabin is naught of our concern." He raised his hand to stop the interruption, then glared into their eyes in a challenge. "Ye tell me, after months asea you would turn down an offer from either?" His eyes circled the table of silent men. "Ye know those rules on sodomy don't apply asea. So why don't you leave it? If the captain and the lad have each other as comfort, what is it to anyone else's business? I ask ye?"

The men were quiet as they thought about it, and then a loud disturbance was heard from the gunner's table as they accused each other of hornswaggling. When the group of men took notice of the ruckus, they found their captain and Justin had just come in the front door, peering around curiously.

Peckham let out a loud exhale at the sight of the two of them, sparkling clean, freshly shaven, and dressed in royal splendor. "Aye, Jack, you have it right. Which one of us would say nay to that?"

They twisted over their shoulders to where he was gesturing.

"Not I, my boys, not I." Peckham's eyes misted over dreamily.

Tucker and Cromwell chuckled at their pilot's lovelorn expression, while puffing on their tobacco-filled clay pipes.

* * * *

Justin caught the tail end of the commotion at the gaming table and leaned against his large captain's side nervously, hiding himself. "Maybe there is a calmer place?"

The captain spoke softly, "Nay, lad, this one's got my

men in it. Believe it as not, it is the safest. I'd not want to be surrounded by the buccaneers with my pockets lined. Come, let's eat." He urged Justin out from behind him and kept a hand on his shoulder as he steered him along.

Tucker waved to them and shouted to the landlord to get more chairs. The captain acknowledged his greeting and made his way through the very packed pub.

Falling behind as his captain advanced to his crew's table, Justin flinched and gasped as every drunken sailor grabbed his rump as he passed. He twisted around and kept his back to his captain as he blazed the trail for him. There were no young men anywhere in sight, and the only women in the room were the serving girls who withstood similar abuse. Justin caught a glint in Will Davis' eye as he and the Captain found their table, then the gunner gave his attention back to his cards.

"Sit down, Captain. We just ordered up some food. Come and join us." Black made room for them as two chairs were shoved in.

Before the captain took his seat, he scanned the room carefully. With his back to the wall, he watched every movement with a soldier's alertness.

Justin squirmed in his chair, a big grin on his face. "It smells lovely! What kind of food do they serve?" He licked his chops hungrily.

Tucker leaned over the table to him and taunted, "Salt pork and hard tack."

"Oy?" Justin's lip pouted innocently in disappointment.

They laughed at him just as the plates were set before them. Justin's mouth watered at the rich variety of seafood and grains, fruits and vegetables. "Oh, blimey! I want one of each!" He pushed up his sleeves.

The captain chuckled with his men and put his arm around Justin's shoulders for an affectionate squeeze. "Eat until you fill, lad."

"I intend to." He sniffed at the food on Black's plate.

The boatswain smiled at him and offered a taste. Justin brightened up and was fed a mouthful from the man's fingertips. He moaned in delight and closed his eyes.

Justin and his captain sat so closely in the tight circle their sides were attached. They drank wine as the food was set before them. The plates were devoured with all speed. Justin slurped up his seafood paella and guzzled down wine to his heart's content, until he felt he would explode. All the while, his captain kept one wary eye on his surroundings.

Another roar rose up from the gaming table. Men jumped to their feet and made threatening gestures. At the chaos, Justin ducked under the furniture, peeking out sheepishly. The landlord, very timid in this rough, violent company, was hiding behind the plaster and stone of the kitchen walls. When cutlass steel was drawn, the captain stood tall in his red velvet coat to try and prevent the bloodshed.

"Settle it outdoors!" Captain Jones ordered his gunners.

The men were extremely drunk, and some had not eaten; none had bathed. Will Davis had his blade unsheathed and found his captain's well-dressed figure there, ever looming over him. He spat down on the floor and glared at him.

At the rude gesture, Peckham grabbed the captain's velvet sleeve to stay him. The room went cold suddenly as every man in it took notice of the challenge brewing.

"Ye don't order me on land," Davis growled. "I settle me own quarrels. Ye go back to yer pretty pet and let the gunners be!"

Everyone at the table felt the captain tense up in absolute fury to be humiliated this way in front of a hundred strong.

Tucker grasped his other sleeve. "Leave it, Richard. Leave it."

"Then settle it outdoors!" the captain thundered, refusing to let it go.

Everyone in the place was silent, staring at the two men. Goblets were left hovering over mouths, fingers stilled with morsels of food, tongues quieted from arguing.

Not caring what the captain did, Will raised his blade in a challenge.

It seemed to Justin that once again time was slowing. It was some trick, he was sure. How could he feel the tick of a clock with every pump of his heart? He couldn't believe Will would even consider pointing an edged weapon in a menacing way at the man they all loved and admired. It just didn't make any sense. With clenched teeth, he was biting the inside of his cheek, and his pulse rate skyrocketed.

Justin watched as Will's mates panicked when they realized what he was doing. They hurried him outside before he received the captain's long-bladed reach, his accurate pistol aim, or swiftly thrown dagger. Praying for peace, Justin took another peek over the edge of the table as the arguing receded into the night air.

"And see to it you are fit by daybreak for your careening task!" the captain yelled after them, as if to show all inside this establishment who was the master, be it land or sea.

Black tried to calm him down. "Sit, Richard, sit. Here, have more wine. Ye let me worry about the crew. *His Revenge* will be careened and tarred, ye let me worry."

Peckham and Tucker dragged him back to his seat by his sleeves. The captain would not relinquish his gaze on the door.

Justin almost crawled onto his lap in fear. "Don't get killed, sir. Please." He could feel an angry rumbling inside his captain's chest as he ran his trembling fingers over it.

The captain's right hand moved slowly to one of his firearms. Justin watched the captain's actions and shifted back to his own chair gradually. That hand drew the weapon and kept it concealed under the table. The captain pulled back the hammer, his index finger was on the trigger.

The men continued to carry on their conversation. The room once again came to life, the serving girls brought out plates of food and pitchers of grog. The murmur of voices overlapped in a noisy hum as they all discussed the scene to one another in muted tones, in a multitude of languages and dialects. Captain Jones' stare remained on the entrance.

Only a moment later, when things felt very calm and sane, and the chaos was over, Justin watched, as if in a dream, as the captain rose and took aim. A volatile blast echoed around the room, and Justin covered his ears from the deafening discharge and shock. Will Davis fell back, his flintlock dropping out of his dead hand. The captain's gun was smoking hot, powder spattered his fist. On his face was a look of complete resolve and indignation.

It had happened so quickly Justin couldn't catch up. He twisted to his captain who was standing still, expressing a look of pure defiance. The men at the table seemed to rise in unison when they suddenly realized what had occurred. A crowd of people leaned over the dead gunner's body. A bullet hole marked dead center on his forehead.

Justin attempted to reason with his thoughts. He knew what had happened, but he just could not believe he had witnessed it. With tremendous effort, he tried to get his vision and hearing back to normal. After the blast, he felt like he could not function or see properly. He gripped that red velvet coattail in a death lock, lest it be taken from him somehow.

Peckham hurried to the fallen gunner and checked

him over. He stood and relayed to his captain, "He's dead, Captain, sir!"

They all looked up at Captain Jones. Every soul in that smoke-filled room had locked eyes on the tall, handsome man.

"Did he say Will Davis is dead?" Justin asked, swallowing in a loud gulp.

Justin was ignored by everyone at the table as the captain's men tried to offer the captain comfort. Captain Jones shrugged off all their patting hands and comments and moved to the huddle around the dead man.

Justin got to his feet as the captain seemed to float away from him. The room was a blur of bulky bodies and cloudy smells. Only his captain's brilliant red coat and long brown ponytail were clear through the haze of his mind.

Captain Jones stood over the lifeless body, the empty, hot gun still in his hand. Everyone was staring at him in deathly silence. Perhaps the strangers were wondering who this man would kill next. The rest of his gunners were crowded at the door.

Justin was petrified one of them would avenge the death and murder his beloved.

The captain knelt down to the dirty plaster floor and ran his left hand over Will's tattered clothing. "We waited for this day, William, remember? This was our dream." He stroked Will's matted beard. "Aye, look at you now. Why, my friend? Why?" He reached up to his face and closed Will's eyelids over those blank, staring orbs.

Justin bit his lip as his tears flowed. *Why? I'll tell you why! Me!*

Peckham reached for his captain over the corpse. "You had to, Richard. He came at you. We all witnessed it."

"Aye, James, he did. We will give him a decent burial asea. You, men!" he addressed the remaining gunners.

"Swaddle up your mate and bring him on board. We will give him a last farewell."

They nodded and surrounded the dead gunner, lifting him up. His arms hung limply to his sides. The captain tucked his own gun away and raised those dead limbs to cross them over Will's chest. He picked up from the floor Will's still loaded pistol and gave it back to his lifeless hands, then he watched as they carried Will into the night.

Justin was struggling to get away from the table, clawing and climbing over chairs as it seemed everyone and everything got in his way. He felt very small as he tried to edge between broad, scratchy shoulders and wide, blocking backs. Half the room was on their feet to watch the spectacle and it was impossible for him to get free. When he made it to the doorway, his captain was gone. Like an eternal nightmare, he went into an icy panic and felt very faint. He called out repeatedly for him, then stopped when he realized he was inviting lascivious stares. Unwittingly, he had drawn all the attention to himself.

Justin assumed that several huge men leering at him were wondering if he was the reason for the row. They had seen him at the captain's side and heard the comment from the gunner referring to the "pretty pet." Justin fingered his cutlass as the viewing became more accusatory. Even worse, they were growing hungry, and not for the lamb stew.

"Oh, Lord...," he moaned. "Don't leave me, Captain. Please!" His lip quivered as he stared off into the blackened gloom, alone, in a foreign land, and feeling helpless.

When he remembered, he twisted back for the rest, for Peckham, Black, Tucker, Cromwell. They had all vanished into thin air. "Lord, help me." He gulped in fear. A few men were closing in on him. It was more a sense than a sight. They were tightening a circle around him, very slowly, like netting a butterfly. A slim opening

124

appeared between two men, and Justin rammed through. Their grimy hands tried to catch him and drag him back. He wrenched free and raced outside struggling to remember where *His Revenge* was docked. The waterfront was completely jammed with foul-smelling men and painted whores all wildly drunk, very boisterous, and extremely violent.

Justin endured many lecherous, lip-licking drools as he slid past in his fine coat and clean, light breeches. Trying to be strong and find his way, he merely wanted to survive. He hadn't paid any attention to his path, for he knew the captain knew the route. Punishing himself mentally for letting his mind wander and never bothering to check for landmarks, he swore it would never happen again.

A terrible smell wafted into his nostrils, excrement and decay. He twisted away from it involuntarily and bumped into someone. A foreign tongue lashed out at him in fury, threatening. He backed up, apologizing and nudged another. A hand grabbed his ponytail and urged him against a wall. A face tattooed with dots and lines loomed over him. A hand dug inside the front of his breeches, hunting for his cock.

He gasped and broke free, running away from the tattooed man, the ribbon falling from his hair. Panting to catch his breath, he leaned against a whitewashed stone building in the ever-creeping darkness. Nervously, he combed his fingers back through his long wild mane and tried to recognize his ship. There were so many masts, so many foreign flags.

He gasped in fear as someone trapped him against the mortar and brick. A woman was asking him if he wanted sex. She started pawing at him and touching his crotch and thighs. He didn't have to know the language to understand the offer. He shook his head no and tried to pry her groping hands off. The rushing memory of the wench in

Penzance and how she stole all his money overwhelmed him.

With a guttural growl, Justin shoved her away roughly, checking his pockets frantically. A Frenchman caught sight of his treatment of the woman and responded in a challenge, unsheathing his sword. Justin shook his head in terror and took off running. Those footfalls were right behind him. Every time he glanced back to see how close the attacker was, he bumped into another foreigner. He was about to break down in tears from all the groping and provocation. To his complete horror, he was swooped up by a very large male and lifted off his feet. He cried out in anguish and struggled, trying to wrench free.

"Justin! Justin!"

When he stopped battling, he found the handsome, sea-blue gaze he was searching for. As if he were the crashing tide, he burst into sobs of relief and clung to him.

Captain Jones hoisted him up higher into his arms and rocked him back and forth. "All right, lad, you're all right." He pressed his lips against his hair and nuzzled him gently.

When several men caught up with the mischievous imp, they halted in their tracks. He was in the arms of a huge guardian angel. One who had just killed a man with a deadly accurate aim. They lowered their heads and swords, then excused themselves before the captain's angry eyes found them. Justin was slow to calm down. He had never been so alone and terrified in his life. Like a babe, he hiccupped and sucked at the salty air. "You...you left me! I...I didn't know where I was!"

The captain set him on his shaking feet and leaned down to see his face. With his warm palms, he cupped Justin's wet cheeks and apologized, "I know. I am sorry. I just needed to get away after—"

"I am scared. They are all so foreign-looking and sounding. They keep touching me. I just wanted to be left

alone. Where is *His Revenge*? I crave her dank walls."
Like a steel trap, he gripped the captain's sleeves.

"Come, lad. I crave her solitude as well. She has a
skeleton crew on her whilst everyone shares their
pleasures in town." Reaching out to Justin with a
reassuring hand, the captain held him and led him to the
dock.

Justin spied her one-hundred-and-fifty-foot masts
with intense relief. They alerted the crew left on board
they were there and were allowed to pass over the
gangplank. The captain opened his cabin door for Justin
and then lit a small lantern. Justin sat down on the fresh,
clean bedding and tried to get his normal heart rate back.
"I am sorry. I didn't mean to panic. I just didn't know
what to do. How was I to defend myself against so many?"

"It is I who owe you the apology. I never should have
left you."

"Where are the others? Pilot? Tucker? I searched for
them."

The captain removed his new coat and placed it on a
chair. "They are bedding whores, my lovely. It will be the
last time for a long while for them."

"Oh." Justin bit his lip in fear of the answer to his
dreaded question. "Don't you want one?"

The captain removed his firearm-filled baldric, next
his cutlass and dagger, resting them gently on the desk.
"No, Justin. I do not."

"Oh…but…why not?" He caught sight of that bronze
chest as the cream-colored blouse was opened and slid off.

"Because they are filled with disease, lad. Disease to
which we have no cure."

"But don't you crave them?" With the lantern glow
glittering in his captain's light eyes, Justin watched as he
removed his tall leather boots.

"I do have cravings, Justin, just like the rest." Setting
them aside, he took the ribbon out of his hair and shook it

full. "What do you crave, my pretty?"

"Blimey," Justin moaned and started squirming out of his clothing at the sight of that more-than-obvious invitation.

The captain locked his cabin door for the first time. He obviously wanted privacy for this act. Dropping his breeches to the floor, the captain made his way to the bunk with a very slow strut and his eyes on fire.

Justin froze, his clothing part way off, staring at him in lust. With very confident yet patient fingers, the captain helped Justin remove the rest of his things. Then with the delicacy of someone cupping a flower, he held Justin's face in his strong hands and kissed his lips.

Anxiously, Justin got to his knees on the bunk, whilst his captain stooped before him. Justin wrapped his arms around his captain's neck and tasted his tongue and lips with unleashed hunger, swooning with the idea of possessing this man. In all his young life, Justin had never dreamed of this kind of passion, the sensation of flames that licked over his skin with every touch. His head fell back from the intensity. As if he were enduring agony, he groaned when the captain's lips kissed his neck and ear.

"Oh, Lord, I love you. I cannot contain the love, it is so great," Justin whimpered.

"All right, Justin. On your knees now, lad."

Justin moved quickly to his hands and knees, watching his captain as he did.

The captain found the liniment and coated himself efficiently, kneeling behind Justin.

Peeking over his shoulder, Justin found his captain admiring his rump before he impaled it, caressing it as if it were the object of his every desire. Justin shivered with anticipation and hung his head forward, then lowered to his elbows.

Captain Jones was given a grand view as he pushed in. "Oh, my Justin...my pretty, pretty boy...ahhhh..."

On penetration, Justin clenched his teeth at a ripple of boiling heat that was so amazing he could burst into flames from it. "I am yours, my Captain, yours to enjoy." Once the captain had slowly pushed in to the hilt, Justin felt him begin his deep thrusting. It sent waves of shivers over his skin. It didn't take long for the captain to reach his goal. Soon Justin was granted the sound of the captain's deep, throaty moans as he climaxed.

After some time, the captain stilled his hips, resting limply on Justin's back. Close to coming but not quite, Justin shivered in delight when the captain reached for his unsatisfied cock. Justin closed his eyes in ecstasy and pumped into that rough palm. In a split second he came, gasping at the intensity.

They separated gently, bathed in a light sweat, catching their breaths. High on the drug of orgasm, and totally sated, Justin wrapped his body around his captain to inhale the scent of him. With his numb fingers, he caressed his large biceps and shoulder gently. "What would I do without you? You are my world now. My protector. My lover."

The captain brushed the hair back from Justin's face as it crushed against his chest.

Exhausted from a night of stress and exhilaration, Justin was lulled to sleep by that powerful heartbeat. Right before he fell into a deep slumber, he whispered, "I love you."

* * * *

Justin awoke. It was still dark. With some effort to move his sleepy limbs, he leaned up to see the captain's face. It surprised him to find his eyes were open. Justin touched him gently and asked, "You do not sleep?"

"I cannot."

"Why? You need to rest, sir."

A grimace passed over the captain's fine features. "I have killed our gunner, Justin. A man I have sailed with thrice before. A man I had always seen as loyal. Now, he goes under the waves to Davy Jones's locker."

In response, Justin sat up and exclaimed, "No! You have not killed him! I have!"

"What nonsense is this?" The captain tried to hold him still as Justin flailed about.

As anxiety gripped him, Justin started gasping for breath, short bellow-bursts in the warm stuffy air. "It was his jealousy of me and you. Oh, my Captain, I have killed our gunner, not you!"

The captain tried to shush him and bring him down to his chest again to stroke and calm. "No, lad, it was a bullet from my flintlock, nothing more."

"I am a nervous wreck. I never should have come on board. What have I done?"

The captain squeezed him closer. "What have you done? Let us count, shall we? You have given Smithy a helping hand for which he is eternally grateful, you have made the journey lighthearted and easy for this wretched crew, you have never complained once, and you have saved your captain's life, and may I add, his mental stability, with your rich loving. What have you done, Justin?"

"And two dead! Two dead!"

"Yes, there are two dead. On my first voyage, we lost a dozen to typhoid. On my second, fifteen to the broadside battle, on my third, four in foolish skirmishes on land. So you see, we have done well." He dug his hands through Justin's long hair.

"But still you do not sleep, why?"

* * * *

"Why? I do not know, lad." But he did know. Deep

inside his heart, Captain Jones was wondering if his love for Justin was in any way affecting his love for Katherine. It was. And even with all his thinking and tossing, he just had no idea what to do about it.

* * * *

Justin nudged the captain to be allowed to sit up once more. If he concentrated, he could make out the captain's features and broad chest in the dim light. And if he strained and held his breath, he could still hear the noise from the waterfront. An occasional blast of a gun broke the steady stream of arguing. With immeasurable sadness at his captain's pain, he stared down at this man with the troubled expression, and smoothed his hands over that rounded pectoral muscle. "Tell me what to do to make you forget."

The captain smiled sweetly at him. "Of this you have already done, my pretty."

"Do you want it again?" With a mischievous giggle, Justin ran his hand into that forest of dark pubic hair.

At the touch, the captain appeared to consider the offer. "Yes, aye, lad. I do."

Justin scooted lower excitedly and clasped his hand around that cock, moving his palm up and down its length in delight as it hardened. Justin used one hand to stroke him, and the other caressing between those huge, muscular thighs. As he handled those large, heavy testicles, he lavished in their heat and size. When he heard the captain open his lips to a gasp, Justin stared at his face, hoping to see it in ecstasy. In moments, his wish was granted as the captain writhed in orgasm, gripping the bedding in powerful fists. Justin allowed him to recuperate, those muscular hips rocking side to side slowly. In the dimness, he extended his fingertips to the spill and touched it.

The captain leaned up to see him making swirling

patterns with the drops. "What a lad, what a lad..." he laughed. "If you are done amusing yourself, I am very thirsty, Justin. Let me get us some wine."

Justin nodded and sat back after wiping the remainder of the spent cum with his hand. As he watched the captain find his breeches in the dark, he said, "Be careful, sir. Hurry back."

With a smile and a nod from his captain, Justin was left in the silence. The stickiness of his fingers intrigued him. He stuck one into his mouth to taste. With that scent and flavor on his tongue, Justin spied down at his lap and examined his own hardness. After one last peek at the door, Justin wrapped his slick hand around his own hard cock, using it to pleasure himself, knowing he was coating his own length with the captain's seed. Just the very thought made him tingle.

"Captain?" Someone tapped the cabin door, then opened it.

Cursing at the timing, Justin had just finished pleasuring himself and jumped out of his skin, sitting up to cover up with the bedding. "Who's there?"

"Justin? It's your pilot. Where is the Captain? Is he with you?" Ducking his head to get through the doorway, he stepped in, to be able to make out the bunk in the low light.

"He went to get wine. He will be right back," Justin stated as a warning, as if being naked and vulnerable was something to fear around this ship.

"Did he? I've just been notified of the tide schedule. I wanted to let him know so he can plan our departure." Peckham loomed nearer. "Are you without clothing under there, lad?"

Justin curled the bedding closer. "No!" When Peckham slithered across the room, Justin flinched.

Instantly, it appeared as if Peckham knew what had gone on between he and the captain. "Oh, what I would give to crawl in there between the two of you," he hissed. "I can smell your sex." When he closed his eyes and inhaled it like an aroma of fine cuisine, Justin shivered in disgust. "Tell me, Justin, what is our Captain like as a lover? Can you describe his penis to me?"

"Oy?" Justin choked in shock. "I...We...I...haven't...we don't..." He shook his head in denial, stunned that the pilot would ask so direct a question of him.

As if sensing an opportunity, Peckham sat next to Justin on the bunk. "He is my dream man, Justin. The first moment I lay eyes on him, I loved him. I have never seen a man with such refined beauty."

"Please, don't be jealous and kill someone," Justin begged him, backing up, almost in tears.

Peckham laughed softly. "No, no one will die on my account. I am no William Davis."

"Are you a Ben Hornbolt?" Justin asked nervously, leaning further from him warily, the bedding in his clenched fist covering his chest.

As if he had to think about it, Peckham paused and then faced him full on. "My beautiful boy," he hissed as he caressed Justin's hair. "No, I would never force you. I may ask if you would come to me willingly. I have asked my captain, but he has you. Why would he need me?"

Disliking the contact, Justin gently nudged his hand away. "Do not ask me."

* * * *

Through the narrow passages, the captain made his way to the storeroom efficiently and found a bottle of wine left from the galleon. On his return to his cabin and Justin, a strange sound met his ears. Squinting into the darkness, he could see two of his crew members in a passionate embrace. They were kissing, each with a hand down the other's breeches. Holding back the sound of his surprised gasp, the captain backed away slowly.

When he swung open the door, Captain Jones found his pilot on the bunk with his naked Justin. In that moment, he caught Justin pushing away a caressing hand from his face.

"Pilot?"

At the sound of his master's voice, Peckham jumped off the bunk and faced him, the absolute picture of guilt. "I was merely looking for you to advise you of the tide."

"So, you have found me." Not convinced in the least, he set down the bottle and moved closer to the desk, which displayed his weapons. With a heavy heart, he was beginning to think he could trust no one.

Peckham watched him move his hand to the loaded firearms slowly. "Oh, no, Richard. Please, I came only under your command."

"Justin?" the captain asked. "What passed in my absence?"

As if catching his breath, Justin stammered as the pistol was now in his captain's hand. "No, don't kill anyone! Not our pilot!"

"*I asked what passed*!" Captain Jones growled louder as the very idea of someone handling his lover infuriated him.

"He...I...he asked me...I didn't..." Justin could not put words together any longer, for he was trembling in mortal terror.

Peckham swallowed nervously. "Richard, I merely told Justin that I would give up my pocketful of doubloons to be in that bunk with the two of you."

Justin hopped out of bed like a jackrabbit. He stood between the men, obviously trying to prevent any violence. "He's telling the truth! He never harmed me! Please!"

The captain's features softened instantly as he

enjoyed the fresh, young, naked man in front of him. With a soft chuckle, he set the pistol down and scolded, "You are giving my pilot some eyeful." He grabbed the bottle of wine and started to open it.

Peckham covered his relieved smile and shook his head at the view of Justin's slender back, long hair, narrow hips and very tight ass. "Oh, my Captain, you are one lucky man," he sighed.

Justin spun around in confusion. They were both laughing at him. "You don't want to kill each other any longer? Because I am naked?"

"Go get your breeches on, lad, for I fear even I would not blame our pilot for a straying hand." With a pop, the wine was opened. To sate his great thirst, the captain raised it and poured it down his throat.

Appearing flabbergasted, Justin turned from one to the other in total confusion, then gave up. In the dimness, he groped around the chair for his clothing and slipped on his breeches, buttoning up the front.

"Here, Pilot, you need this more than I." The captain handed him the bottle.

"You can be sure of that!" He took a long draught to calm his shaking limbs.

* * * *

With a thump, Justin sat down on the bunk and tried to conceive any of this. It was out of his league, as were most conversations he tried to understand. It was the month of June and soon he would be nineteen. Would he be wiser then? Would this all come to him? He rubbed his face at the frustration of never really fully fathoming what was going on around him.

The captain smiled endearingly at his quizzical pout. With his expression overflowing with affection, he sat next to Justin on the bunk and leaned on his shoulder. "Don't think too hard of it, my pretty boy."

"I am always the fool. I can never quite get things. Why? Why am I so dumb?"

The captain drew him to his chest and hugged him tightly. "You are far from dumb, Justin. You are merely young. Do not always take yourself so hard."

Closing his eyes, Justin sighed and felt his embrace in relief.

The pilot dragged over a stool and sat down in front of them, handing Justin the bottle. "My, you two are a pretty sight. The fantasies I have spun in me head would embarrass a whore." He grinned. "Aye! Now, to the business at hand. The tide. The locals say it will be high just at dusk tomorrow night. That should give us nine hours of sunlight to careen her."

"Good. Very good." The captain took the bottle from Justin and drank from it, then wrapped his arm around him and nudged him close once again.

Peckham sighed audibly while Justin purred as he snuggled against that solid chest. "Aye, it was inevitable between you two on this voyage. I knew that from the start."

"You know our secret, Pilot." The captain handed him back the bottle.

"Nay. Not I. Not even if they dragged me across the keel." Peckham laughed and took a drink.

"You're a good man." He winked at him. When Justin turned his face up to see his, the captain kissed him square on the lips. "Right, Justin, my lad?"

Justin was stunned he had kissed him in front of someone. "Aye, sir, whatever my Captain wishes."

Wiping his lip, Peckham handed off the bottle. "What of Katherine?"

Suddenly, the captain's smile vanished. "What of her?" he snarled.

Peckham cleared his throat nervously. "Naught, sir. It

is not my concern."

"No, she is not." With a very sharp tone of voice, he reinforced his thoughts.

"What about her?" Justin handed him the bottle and pushed his face into the captain's armpit to inhale his musky scent.

"Ne'er you mind, lad." The captain nudged him back out of his pit, then kissed his forehead.

Like a mole, Justin tried to burrow back under again. "Mm, you smell so good. Like the essence of masculinity," he groaned sensually.

With his mouth open and gaping at him, the captain shook his head at Justin's comment and lifted his arm up to get him back out again. "All right, lad, you're being daft, try and control yourself in front of our pilot."

Peckham couldn't stop squirming in his seat. "I should have found a whore."

Captain Jones grinned at him perceptively. "You don't like women, James."

"A male whore, then." He grimaced.

"I'll tell you another secret." The captain leaned over to him seductively.

In excitement, the pilot matched his movement. "You'll let me touch you?"

"No." The captain let out a low, amused laugh. "But if you head down to the storeroom, two of our own lads are in the midst of the act. I would wonder if they would mind three?"

As if the stool were on fire, Peckham stood instantly, trying not to run out of the cabin. "Thank you, sir. I shall be ready to set sail for you when the high tide floods the bay."

They witnessed him dash out and chuckled together over it. The captain quieted his laughter and then cupped Justin's face softly. "Oh, my lovely, what shall I do with you?"

"Sleep! I am exhausted."

"Right. I will try. Come on then." They doused the lantern and cuddled up on the bunk.

Chapter Nine

Every hand that was available scraped the hull of *His Revenge* of barnacles and worms. The carpenter was busy repairing broken boards and screwing down belaying pins. There were men climbing the ratlines to tend the shrouds. Justin was in the hold helping to organize the cargo. They were loaded once again with shot, ropes, spare parts, fresh water, beer, and food.

Smithy was with Justin stacking cages of hens and killing the rats that wanted to prey on their eggs. Crewmen checked on the ballast to make sure it wasn't too soaked with water. They pumped out the bilges and tarred any leaks.

Justin hated the smell of the bilge. Its moldy rot wafted up his nostrils. He dressed in tattered clothing for this detail for he didn't want to soil his expensive new garments. The stuffy heat made him give in to being shirtless, and on his legs, he wore a pair of his captain's baggy cotton breeches that were way too large for him. The folds of fabric created a pleated curtain as it was cinched at the waist with a rope to keep it from falling. His long shining locks of hair he had covered with a red printed bandana.

"Oy! It stinks to hell down here!" he moaned.

"That'll be yer gunner." Smithy hacked at a rat he had trapped.

"My gunner?" Justin tilted his head in confusion.

Smithy stood tall when he had finished the deed and wiped his sweaty brow. He tapped a large, wrapped bundle. "Our gunner."

At the realization, Justin gasped. "Will Davis is in there?"

Smithy laughed at his expression. "Aye, we'll take him out to open seas. He'd wash up on shore if we dumped him here, lad."

Stifling a gag, Justin tried not to inhale that sickly sweet odor of rotting human flesh. "Am I done here, Smithy?"

The cook shook his head at him sympathetically. "Aye, lad. Shove off."

Justin tried not to run. Like a monkey, he climbed the ladder to the deck for some fresh air and found some of the remaining gunners, fifteen left, cleaning their cannons. The guilt tore at him horribly. It was agony wanting to say something to them and not knowing what. But he did know. An apology. Will was the senior gunner, the one that made sure everyone else was properly loading. With a sadness he could not describe aching in his chest, he stared at them in their mismatched attire. Though he wore the same rough cotton trousers with button fronts that stopped to hang just before the ankle, his were rolled up to thick cuffs from the extra length. All had striped socks and buckled leather shoes. They were bare-chested in the heat, several with bandanas to hold back their matted hair.

They were young men. With Will gone, none over twenty-eight. Missing teeth left gaps in their sneers, digits were gone from most hands, scars crossed their tanned skin. Yet, none were minus an arm or leg. These men needed all their limbs for their job and were removed if they lost one. Justin knew they had the opportunity to get clean clothing and a bath. None chose to. Most had lost all their booty in the night of passion and play on the waterfront and had their sights on the next loaded galleon. Some were considering staying at Portobello and never seeing England's shores again.

Henry finally glanced up from his work to behold Justin.

"Ye hanging the jib whilst ye still have a pocket full of doubloons?" Henry called to him.

With some effort, Justin raised his chin to them while they were kneeling down next to their cannons as they worked.

Francis moved nearer to Henry and laughed at Justin's pout. "Argh! Ye has nothing to sob about! Ye pampered prince of *His Revenge*."

Oh, I deserve this. As if he were about to be smacked, he closed his eyes and withstood it.

"Will adored ye, ye scallywag," Samuel scolded him. "Would it a killed ye to show him some affection?"

"Aye!" Henry mocked. "He's too royal for the working crew! We knows whose pet he is!"

"Ye going to watch as our gunner meets Davy Jones?" Samuel asked cruelly. "It was ye what put 'im there."

Justin braved the insults like lashes from a whip. He felt infinitely guilty for the loss.

"Me pretty boy, ye come to our deck tonight and share that lovely white arse of yars. We'll show ye a night of good buggery," John piped up and moved closer to the other gunners, who were all crouching before Justin.

Justin raised his eyes up to them. Tears flowed like streams down his cheeks.

"Now ye made the lad cry!" Henry teased. "Ye think ye got something to cry about laddie? Ye cryin' from the sore arse from our captain's cock?"

"I'm sorry," Justin sobbed. "I know I killed our Will. I miss him something horrible. I didn't know how he felt. I didn't mean to make him die. He was a friend to me. He always looked after me."

The gunners exchanged guilty glances with one another.

Henry sighed. "Aye, lad, come 'ere with ye." He reached out his powder-stained hand.

In frustration, Justin tried to wipe his tears off and squat down near them. "Please forgive me. I never should have come on this ship. I have killed two of our men."

A smile curled their lips at Justin's comment.

Samuel gave in first and caressed the long, brown waves that spilled out from under Justin's bandana. "Nay, lad, we be just running a rig. Ye did not kill our William."

Justin could not be consoled. In his heart, he knew he would be eternally guilty. "I can never be like the rest of you. You all seem so confident. So sure of what you want in this life."

They grinned at one another in surprise and started laughing.

Justin stared at them in confusion. "Was it something I said?"

"Aye, lad. What would we do without our Justin Taylor?" Francis grabbed his arm and shook it affectionately.

"What we want?" Henry could not control his hilarity. "We want another galleon! Argh! That and a steady supply of whore meat."

At the blatant statement, Justin gaped at him.

"Look upon his face." John sighed. "Could ye blame our William?"

Justin swallowed down a dry throat as they all gave him very contented smiles. "Am I forgiven?" he whispered.

They laughed again and handled him playfully. "Aye, lad, ye be the one soul that goes up if ever this ship is doomed," Francis assured.

Thinking they were done, Justin attempted backing away from them to go and get cleaned up. When they would not let him stand, he stopped moving and started growing a little afraid. Hands ran over his arms and chest, up his neck and down his back.

"Ye be so very pretty, me lad," John hissed as he stroked Justin's hairless chest.

With stoic resignation, Justin closed his eyes and tried not to tremble, deciding he would let them do what they wanted. He owed them that.

One hand moved inside his thigh. "Come to the fo'c'sle and bunk with us tonight, me lovely." Francis touched Justin's crotch lightly. "We'll show ye a good time like naught you ever had," he crooned.

As his cock was stroked, Justin felt his skin prickle and clamped his eyes shut.

"Who did this to ye, lad?" Henry ran his fingers over the faded scars on his back. "Was this from Hornbolt?"

"Nay, me father," Justin admitted sadly.

All the hands released him suddenly. Astonished, Justin stared at them in total confusion.

"Off with ye, lad." Francis nodded.

"He's had enough punishment. I'd no notion he was beaten so," Samuel whispered.

"Aye, he's a good lad. Let him be." John nodded.

Stumbling back, Justin rose to his feet slowly, moving away from them, then went to find the captain.

With that task behind him, he headed to the bow and found what he was looking for. That sight was enough to clear his mind of any trouble. With unbridled enthusiasm, Justin straightened up his posture and stood next to the shirtless bronze man. "Ahoy, Captain!" For the first time, possibly because of the glaring bright sunlight, Justin noticed some very thin scarred lines on the captain's broad back, but said nothing.

"Ahoy, lad!" He received an affectionate smile in return. "You done helping our Smithy?"

"Aye, sir. What next do you have for me?"

"Go take a caulk. You've done enough." He patted his head.

143

"Will you join me?"

"Nay, lad. Not until we are well underway."

"When will that be?"

"Soon, very soon." He bit his lip anxiously. "Pilot!" he bellowed.

Peckham raised his head from his sextant. "Aye, Captain, sir?"

"How close to high tide?"

The pilot moved to the gunwale and squinted into the water. "Near! I'd make her fast!"

The captain thundered, "Black!"

The bearded man came scuttling up. "Aye, sir."

"Let's get a move on. The bay is flooding."

"Aye, sir."

"Black..."

"Aye, Captain, sir?" He stepped back again.

"How many men are sailing with us?"

"Forty-eight, sir. We lost eleven to the lure of Portobello and one—"

"Aye, I know how you lost one." The captain grimaced.

"Aye, sir."

"Off you go." He waved, pivoting around when he bumped into Justin who was standing there. "Oy! Lad. I thought you were taking a caulk."

"Nay, I like standing near you when you command." Justin grinned up at him wickedly.

The captain smiled and rubbed Justin's head, accidentally pulling his bandana off. With warmth, he laughed and apologized. "You look better without it. Less like these seadogs and more like my pretty boy."

"Aye! And I know that's how you like me."

The captain peeked around discreetly. "Come to the cabin, lad."

Hopping up in the air in pleasure, Justin bounded after him excitedly.

* * * *

Dusk brought a breeze to the sails, and the sunset was the pink hue of salmon flesh. A shipmate was hauling up the anchor from the capstan, and the pilot was shouting instructions to Tucker, who was on the rudder. They steered through the crowded port and into open seas. Captain Jones stood on the bow and gazed into the last of the sun's rays as it touched the distant horizon. Justin was at his side. The wind felt refreshing and cool after the stagnant atmosphere of the waterfront.

Having not even spent a piece of eight, Justin wondered what he would do with his small fortune once back in England. How does one go about spending Spanish booty when a single doubloon can buy a whole cow? Taking one out of his pocket, he admired it contentedly. The bust of the King of Spain on one side, and the Spanish coat of arms on the other. He slid it back into his pocket and gave himself a secret smile.

With the utmost love and affection, the captain rubbed Justin's back gently as they stared into the golden glow that was vanishing. They were clothed once again in their fine garments and cleaned up from their sweat. Smithy had just served a turtle soup and their storerooms were crammed with bounty. After four hours dead east, the captain called all the crew together.

Of the gunners, he requested they get the body of their William Davis. They wanted this task behind them.

Justin hid by the tall main mast as the linen-covered thing passed. The smell of that rotting flesh wafted in the air, and he was glad for the wind. Will was set on a plank and held level by some of his shipmates. The captain removed his hat and lowered his head.

"William Bartholemew Davis, born in the beloved land of Cornwall, Mother England," the captain began. "A brave seaman. No galleon was a match for his cannon. No enemy a match for his cutlass. His fellow gunners and the rest of the crew of *His Revenge* shall sorely miss him. Rest in peace, matey, rest in peace." With a nod of his head, the plank was lifted. Justin heard a faint splash over the noise of the wind, and the white linen, weighted with chain shot, sank into the black depths and entered oblivion.

There was a murmur of farewells as the men slowly dispersed to find their watered-down rum for consolation. Justin tried to hide in the shadows. A lump was in his throat he could not shed. The captain placed his hat back on his head and moved slowly to the quarterdeck to go over their course with his pilot.

When most of the men were in the galley and below deck, Justin walked to the bow of the ship. It felt very lonely there. How, he wondered, could he feel lonely on a ship so overcrowded with men? Sitting down on the bowsprit, he gazed out at the starlit night with its full moon, toying with one of the ropes that were used previously to secure them to a dock fingering it on his lap absently. With a dull ache inside his body, he remembered the first time he met Will when he shared the tack with him when he was hungry, how he helped him load all those flintlocks. Even teaching him to shoot one, laughing at him when he fell onto his butt from the recoil. Those memories made Justin cry. He cried for the loss of a friend and felt sorry for himself. He had very few friends in this life and treasured anyone who gave him time or a kind smile.

He raised his chin to the stiff breeze. It felt colder than it had a moment before, and the wind was blowing to starboard.

With a deep sea-born sigh, he lowered his head, knowing that when this trip ended, his beloved captain would go to his woman and he would never be near him again. How was he to deal with that loss? What path should he take? One thing he did know, he could not go home. He was very sure his father would beat him, literally, to death. There was no home any longer. The sea was his home. He would live and die on it, just like his friend, William Davis.

When he lowered his eyelashes, tears from his sorrow and the sting of the north wind overflowed down his face. Clenching the rope in his fist, he gazed out at the lapping whitecaps to say, "Good-bye, me friend, Will, I shall miss you."

* * * *

The captain met his men in the galley and shared a drink of beer as they crowded around the bench seats and tables. They debated quietly on what they would do if by chance they ran into another Spanish treasure ship. It was always possible on this course to spot another tall mast coming or going to the Spanish Main. The shipmates with empty pockets wanted another longside. The captain was trying to decide how many would vote aye when it was put to a count.

When the ship listed hard to the portside, the crew grabbed at the nailed-down tables for balance. There was a sound of breaking glass as bottles fell.

"Pilot!" Captain Jones solicited an explanation. They never expected the storm and could usually see it coming.

"A squall, sir! We need to ride her out!" The pilot gripped the table as they rode over another wave.

"Lower her sails!" the captain ordered, trying to keep from falling over. "We don't want the windstorm to capsize us." A few of the men scrambled to the deck.

The captain felt pale suddenly. "Where is Justin?"

Tucker, Black, Cromwell, and Peckham all stared at each other in bewilderment.

"Justin!" The captain rose up and rushed out to the

deck as fast as he could will himself there. Instantly he was pelted with sharp rain and cutting hail as the crew tried their best to tend the rigging and flatten the sails down without getting swept overboard. "Justin!" he cried. "Justin Taylor! Answer me!"

Peckham crawled part way out onto the slippery deck. "I remember him on the bow, sir! After Will's burial!" he cried out to be heard in the lashing winds.

The captain did hear it and screamed, "No! *No!*" Gripping the rigging in desperation, he narrowed his eyes into the blinding sheet of rain. The hailstones whipped his skin painfully like darning needles blown with amazing force. Dragging himself arm length by arm length to the bow, he screamed Justin's name. Clawing his way to the bowsprit, using every ounce of strength he could against the fierce winds, he tried to look out into the raging water. He sobbed in tortured agony, *"Justin!"* All he could see was the foaming tumult of black sea and white froth. Through stinging tears, he searched for even a glimpse of Justin in the waves, his white shirt or waving hand.

He cried out in grief at the image of that poor lad being swept over the side. *"Justin! Oh, my Justin!"* In an emotional tidal wave he could not control, he burst into wails as the ship moaned and swung underneath him, leaving him to cling onto the rigging with all his might as the angry squall sought to push him over and into the blackness.

The rest of the crew had done their job and scuttled under cover. As they all huddled together, only the captain was still hovering over hell. Peckham kept the hatch open and peered out into the blinding deluge.

The captain hung his head and cried as the wind and sleet crushed him in its powerful grip. Like a stone sentry, he stood impervious to the intense pain and discomfort.

For a single moment, he thought he heard a noise, then wondered if it was a siren's call and the wind merely playing tricks on his mind. Raising his head to strain to see, he roared with every ounce of vocal power he possessed. "*Justin?*"

He heard it again. It sounded very far away. Gripping the gunwale in two hands, he spied over the starboard side. Almost fainting from relief, he found Justin hanging from one of the ropes, swinging precariously over the raging sea. The captain tried to keep calm and kept hollering his name, trying to let Justin know he had found him and not to release his grip. With both his hands, the captain grabbed the rope, risking his balance and his life to try and get this young man back from the precipice of Hades.

His adrenalin was surging more now than in any broadside battle. Nothing meant more to him at this moment in time than that lad. Straining to hoist up the slippery line with pure brute force, he prayed he'd not shake Justin off if he tugged too hard. The hemp was slimy from algae and almost impossible to rely on the grip. He leaned over the side, keeping his eyes on Justin, and reached out to his extended arm as it clung to the rope over his head.

* * * *

Justin could not see. The salty waves and hail pummeled his face. He wondered if this is what it felt like right before death. In his mind's eye, he took heed to the angels' call. Their sweet, soft melody was telling him to relax his pain-stricken muscles and let go. To freefall into the abyss of sweet forgetfulness. It was too much anguish to hold on. He could hardly feel his hands and wasn't even sure they would obey his command as it was. His whole body felt like ice. It was as if he were undergoing a change, a deep freeze, starting with his fingertips and working its way to his torso and legs. Everything felt like it would shatter if something hit it. Crash like porcelain dropped down to stone, where he would burst into a million sharp slivers. All the King's horses and all the King's men would not be able to put him together again.

He smiled at the silliness of the nursery rhyme. Odd what the mind thinks of when it is through clinging on to life and accepting of death. Though he was trying very hard to just hang on as he was slammed against the ship's brown hardwood hull, he'd had enough of the battering. Did anyone look for him? Did anyone notice he was gone? *Done, I am done. I can hold this line no longer.*

Justin felt something through his numb limbs, an agonizing, crushing sensation on his right wrist. Was that what death feels like? He wondered why he hadn't hit the water. Something was happening to him yet he just could not comprehend what. Trying to see through the lashing bullets of ice, he found a very large, masculine hand clenched to his slender wrist. He gasped in absolute astonishment at that realization and started scrambling like a wildcat to climb up the slippery hull, his boot heels scraping and gouging the hardwood, his free hand grasping and clawing to get up. He heard his captain roar through his own pain as he brought Justin up towards the deck.

The ship listed to starboard sharply, and they almost both went into the murky depths. Justin dangled precariously by his one trapped arm. He caught a glimpse of the captain hanging onto the rigging on the fore-boom with one clenched hand whilst the other locked onto his wrist. Justin knew the captain would not release his grip on either, though judging by the captain's terrific, heart-wrenching growl, he wondered if the agony of fatigue had begun to seize him.

Waiting until the ship lay portside, Justin heard the captain let out a great thundering battle cry as he pulled him up over the gunwale. It seemed the captain was using every drop of strength he possessed.

Justin shimmied up the last edge and pushed himself

over. The captain clenched his shirt and urged him closer. With very little prodding, Justin wrapped around his captain's torso in a death grip, feeling some of the ice in him give way to that man's extraordinary heat. The captain seemed like he was on fire with a fever, he was pumping his muscles so hard to obey him. Justin kept his eyes shut and shivered in the wild wind, trying to turn his face from the sting when it kept changing direction on him. He burrowed into his captain's drenched shirt and just hung on. It was all he could do.

He had no way of functioning any longer and was totally dependent on this man to get him out of this alive. No resources did he have for this, no reserve of strength and will. He had never been brought up to think in an emergency. Pain he could deal with. He had a very high threshold. But, courage? Fortitude? Valor? He had given up! He was the weak one! It was the man he clung to with all his might that was the consummate hero. Not he. Not Justin Alexander Taylor.

No. This heroic act was solely the achievement of one man. The mighty Richard Cornell Jones. And mighty he was. Justin could not believe his toughness. The sheer tenacity of his will to not give in, never give up, and succeed against all odds. That was where this man performed his best. In a crisis, in adversity. Justin perceived him as nothing short of a god.

* * * *

Peckham peered out of the hold. No one dared step out onto the ship's slick-soaked surface now. The sails were loose and flapping like great white wings. Wings of the devil in the disguise of an angel in white. The sound they made added to the deafening clamor and belching of the storm. The sky was a sickly yellow color mixed with the blackness of the threatening clouds. Lightning bolts sizzled and crackled as thunder boomed like cannon over their heads. The pilot held out no hope. It had been too long. No one could survive on deck in that tempest. Peckham's heart sank with every passing minute. The water was splashing into the hull and he knew he couldn't keep the hatch up much longer or it would flood the hold and jeopardize the rest of the crew.

* * * *

Justin took a curious peek to see his beloved Captain Jones holding onto the main mast with his left hand and attempted to crawl them back inch by inch. The waves kept washing over them, and they struggled to keep their grip sure. It was up to the captain's brawn to get them back.

Justin assumed his life was over. The ship would go down and he would meet Will Davis under the currents. In his muddled mind, he imagined Will in that muslin shroud, weighted down by the ball and chain shot. His body would have floated so that he would appear to be upright. The shroud would flow back from his face. He would see that spot where an ear should have been. Maybe there would be little bright colored fishes eating at his other one. Justin imagined he was swimming with that thing. That dead thing that used to be Will Davis, now a stinking, rotting piece of cadaverous fish food. And there would be Ben Hornbolt, picked clean by the sharks. Just a bony skeleton with bits of rags hanging. How he would dance with him, clasp his emaciated claws and spin in the minuet.

* * * *

The captain lay still as a wave crashed over them, clutching Justin to him with his left arm, afraid Justin would weaken and release his grip and get washed overboard. This left him to fight the waves with only his right arm and his bruised knees. With gritted teeth, he made his way beyond the main mast, trying to hold on as the boat surged like a weightless log in the unforgiving sea. He knew of many a ship that had been lost. Crushed against rocks by a murderous storm. In all his journeys, he never thought this would be the way he would end. No, he thought he would die an old man on a farm. Who was he to decide his own fate? It was all in greater hands.

Sapped of strength, the captain rested a second, lying still and holding tightly to Justin as well as the wood planks of the deck. Finding more energy, Captain Jones inhaled and set out to crawl again without the mast as an anchor. When he released it, they slid along the slimy surface and into the iron cannons. He flinched at the pain the impact caused him when he took the full brunt of it. Battered and bruised like he had been beaten with a cudgel, the captain reached out his hand desperately to grab anything he could to stop them from sliding and slamming into the immoveable cannons once more. He almost died of shock when he felt fingers and then a hand. Clasping it in desperation, he managed to get to his knees as he was dragged to the safety of the hold.

Peckham gripped his shirt and succeeded in pulling him all the way in. They closed the hatch to the storm outdoors and caught their gasping, amazed breaths.

"Justin!" Peckham exclaimed when he realized he was there, clinging to the captain's chest. "We thought you were lost! Oh, lad, you are a sight for sore eyes," he cried with relief and looked around him. There was many a teary eye in that dimly lit hold, as the men fought the heartache at the thought of a loss, now regained.

Justin had not opened his eyes and still clung to his captain like a baby koala to its mother. Both men were soaked to the bone and black and blue. Blood seeped out slowly from slices where iron nails had penetrated the captain's skin.

Captain Jones sat with his back against one of the walls and managed to stretch out his long, aching legs. He cradled Justin on his lap, wrapping both his arms around him, lowering his head and sobbing quietly over how close he came to losing him. Though there were hardened seamen present, he permitted himself this weakness for once in his life; he allowed himself to be seen crying.

All the men crouched down around them in deathly silence, trying not to stare at them, giving them their moment to grieve at what might have been as the ship listed at forty-five-degree angles on that unrelenting sea. Peckham found a dry blanket and wrapped them in it as they both shivered from fear and shock. Tucker sat with a bottle of rum on his lap, ready for them when they asked it of him. They all knelt or sat together in silence, riding out the violence on the water.

After a long while, the ship felt more settled. The listing had lessened, and the sound of the wind and thunder had died back.

* * * *

Having been sound asleep, Justin opened his eyes. He pouted his bottom lip at his master and whispered, "Captain?" Justin tried to clear all his long soaked hair from the captain's face as it stuck to him from the wet wind.

The captain came aware slowly to connect with Justin's gaze. Wrapping himself around him tighter, the captain kissed him over and over again, trying not to cry.

Tucker tapped the first mate, and he and Cromwell raised the latch and took a peek at the deck. When they found all was calm, they climbed up to assess the damage.

Setting Justin back and pushing his damp locks from

his face, the captain gave him an adoring smile and said, "Ahoy, my Justin, you all right?"

"Aye, my Captain, a bit bruised from being battered against her hull."

"Aye. Me too, lad." When the captain smiled, tears of joy ran down his cheeks. "More liniment massages?"

"Oh, yes!" Justin brightened up. "You know, we are now even."

"Aye, we are now even. A life for a life." The captain wiped his eyes and face and nudged Justin to try and stand.

They followed everyone out onto the deck and looked around. The sea was completely calm. Not even a whitecap glistened on her slick, black surface. The moonlight was brilliant in the sky, an eerie torch to illuminate their way.

Boatswain Black met the captain. "We need some minor repairs, sir. Nothing the carpenter can't handle by light of day."

"Can we get her sails back up?"

"Aye, methinks we can." He nodded and touched one of the gently flapping sheets.

"All right. Pilot!" the captain yelled.

Peckham appeared.

"Can you get us back on course? We'll tend her better in the light of day. She's good for the time. We've still got her sails."

"Aye, Captain…and Captain…" He stopped the captain from rushing off.

"Aye, Pilot?"

"Thank you for saving our Justin." He laid his hand on that sinewy deltoid muscle as it peeked out from a torn sleeve.

The captain smiled and confided, "I would do it again and again, Pilot. Nothing would stop me."

"Aye, I know, Captain." He smiled in complete admiration. "There has never been another like you, sir."

"All right, Pilot. Flattery will not get you into my breeches."

Peckham's face lit up at the jest. He roared with laughter. When he gained control, he smiled sweetly and asked, "If you can tell me what would, I would be most appreciative."

The captain grinned at him and shook his head. "I'll have a think on that, Pilot. Now, back to your sextant."

"Aye, sir, I shall, sir." He beamed with affection as he walked with the captain to get their bearings.

* * * *

Justin found Smithy mopping up the galley. His kettle had tipped over and made a mess. He found a bucket and helped him out.

"No need, lad. After what ye been through. Go rest." Smithy nudged him.

"Nay, Smithy. I could not if I wanted to. Let me help you get her back in shipshape." With energy coming from his reserves, he started mopping and wringing it out into a bucket.

"Aye, whatever pleases ye, lad."

He worked tirelessly getting everything clean and set back in its place. When he was done, he sat down for a moment and started to feel the exhaustion and stress seeping into his bones. Smithy patted his head and told him, "Go and sleep, lad."

Needing no more prodding, Justine nodded and made his weary way to the captain's cabin.

* * * *

Captain Jones waited with his pilot until they found their way and were headed back in the right direction. As a true leader, he checked on all the sails and made a round on the deck to make sure everyone was all right before he bedded down for the night.

Tucker found him and squeezed his arm. "Argh! Richard, for pity's sake, get some rest!"

Though he was about to argue, Captain Jones paused before his quartermaster, and when he did, he felt it all catching up to him. The adrenalin was gone, and deep fatigue had arrived. "Aye, John. That's me done now."

"Good, man, sleep." Tucker nudged him along.

The captain came through his cabin door to see a lithe seraph. Justin had just washed himself and was standing in one of his oversized blouses. When he elevated his arms, it seemed as if Justin would fly away on wings.

"I need to grow into it, me thinks!" Justin giggled.

The captain covered his smile and shook his head. Then at that moment, he and Justin connected gazes and burst out into laughter from the relief. Crossing the floor to him, bent over from the low ceiling, the captain knelt down and held Justin's handsome face in his hands. Justin hugged him, wrapping his long sleeves around his back. The captain loved the heat and energy that passed between them.

* * * *

They rocked together and tried not to cry. Justin leaned back to contemplate this man's beauty. His cheeks were red from windburn and his arms were covered in scrapes and bruises. "I think it is I who shall medicate you tonight," Justin warned.

"Nay, not tonight. Leave it for the morrow. Come, my lovely. Come to bed with your weary captain."

Releasing his embrace, Justin crawled onto the bunk.

As the poor man teetered on fatigue, Justin watched the captain strip off his torn blouse, breeches, and boots, then make his way over to him after dousing the lamp.

When he reached the bunk, the captain raised the satiny shirt over his head and wrapped around him as if he yearned Justin's nakedness.

"Thank you, my Captain. Thank you for looking after me. Where would I be now if—"

With a light touch of his index finger to his lips, he silenced them.

Justin moaned softly as that sensuous mouth licked his skin. Releasing himself completely, Justin lay back and floated above the tall masts, as he was the one receiving for a change. As a warm tongue tickled his neck and ran down his shoulder, a shiver of pleasure raced through him. Groaning and wrapping his legs around those massive tree-trunk thighs as hands found him in the dark and clasped him tight, it took nothing for Justin to climax as the captain's hands moved him to delirium. Like a puppet, he seemed weightless and pliable. His legs were spread and elevated to rest on very muscular shoulders. A soft sound escaped his lips as he was penetrated. So overtired was he, he felt he was high on opium. His head had a light, giddy quality he had never felt before. Maybe it was the stress, the relief, or just the plain old burnout from too much exertion, but the way he was being touched and handled was like nothing he had ever felt before. He was alive with it. The sensations were intensified and rebounded on his skin. Maybe that was the answer. He was alive. So very much alive, and now very well indeed.

Reaching for those solid forearms as strong hips thrust into him, a grunting sound Justin knew very well reached his ears. Justin smiled in pure delight when he heard it. The weight that rest on him felt delicious and welcome. He wrapped around his beloved captain and fell asleep.

Chapter Ten

By light of day, the carpenter was rapping his hammer into a broken boom. A replacement sail was attached, the bilge pumped free of water, and *His Revenge* was good as new. There was a sense of calm over the crew. They had no urgency to their voyage. They were almost restful after that devastating squall.

Justin, dressed in his breeches and blouse, his hair tied back in a ribbon, was about to find Smithy when he paused and glanced down at the logbook. After a peek up at the door first, he opened its cover. The account of his near-death experience during the squall had been entered. He read it with great interest.

'*...it had not occurred to me before now what this lad meant to me. The thought of him lost asea was like a poker through my chest. I haven't had an attachment such as this since I left my Katherine. I adore that lad and he will never stray from my heart...*'

Justin's skin broke out in hot chills. *Blimey! I knew it! He loves me too!* Oh, sweet mother of God, his dreams had come true. When they reached England, he and the captain would be lovers. That lovely man would kindly explain to his lady that he no longer wished her company. That he had found a partner to share his life with. Of course! He knew what he meant to that man!

Justin's heart burst with joy. Closing the cover, he hummed to himself as he went to attend to his chores. When he climbed to the main deck, he heard some cheerful shouting. Hurrying to the noise, he found his

159

shipmates fishing. They had cast their lines in excitement as they hunted a school of tuna riding the bow. Justin leaned over the gunwale and gaped in amazement at the shear size and number of them. Dolphins leaped into the air in acrobatic displays of strength and agility. He had never seen anything like it in his life.

John exclaimed, "Something's biting the end of me line!"

The rest of the gunners handed off their rods to help him with the fight. And a battle it was. Four gunners against one fish. The line was pulled taut and bent the rod almost in two. It appeared likely it would snap. They heaved and groaned and grew weary. Henry joined in for the struggle, relieving an exhausted John. He, Samuel, Moses, and Francis grunted and strained to get this tuna on board.

Justin bent over the side to see the enormous fish leap out of the sea and slap down with a cannonball splash. "Blimey! It's a whale of a thing!"

Peckham stood next to him and rested against his side as he watched. "Aye! A devil of a creature. I think our gunners are a bit on the runt side, lad. They could use the bulk of our Tucker or captain to help even the odds."

"You want I should get our captain?"

"Nay, lad, the boys would be too embarrassed to admit a blasted fish outfoxed them. You let 'em go and see what comes of it."

They twisted back to witness the gunners sweating profusely from the strain. Henry started getting tired and glanced around to judge who he could get to replace him. "I don't give up easy, mind ye!" he grunted, "It's just me arms be tired from me chores!"

"Argh! Shut yar gob and keep pullin'!" Moses growled. "Ye won't let some scale-covered rat beat ye?"

Henry gripped the pole over Moses' head, and they made a plan to all pull as one. They asked someone to count, since none of them knew how, and on the count of three, they all leaned back with everything they had.

They managed to wrestle the fish all the way up the hull. Several of the crew reached over to try and net it. It was flailing so powerfully, no one could get close to it.

"Bring her on deck!" John yelled, his cutlass ready.

"That's easy fer ye to say!" Samuel puffed at the effort.

"Lads! Someone count again, and we'll get her up!" Henry roared against the strain.

Justin counted to three, and they heaved once again. They managed to get it over the side of the gunwale. It slapped about in jerking spasms, slamming into the cannon and mast. At first, everyone backed away from it in fear, then they tackled it and hacked at it with their cutlasses.

Justin went from watching it with a thrill to revulsion at the redness of its blood. "Blimey! What a fray!" He shivered in disgust.

Peckham rested his hand on Justin's shoulder as he observed. "Aye! Some battle. But the gunners won that one."

Captain Jones came up from the hull and stood over the slaughter, grinning in delight. "Ah! Tuna for dinner. Well done, lads! I wish I had been here for the battle."

"Aye, Captain, sir. So do we." Henry wiped his sweat soaked brow. "We coulda used yar weight to reel her in. Aye, but we got her in the end." He bent over and put his hands on his knees to try to stop gasping and breathe normally.

Tucker smiled when he found the fish as well. "Argh! Smithy! No stew this time! Make something else in yar blasted pot."

Justin cracked up with laughter at the teasing. When the enormous fish had finally laid still the gunners stood back and wiped their dripping faces.

"That was a tougher battle than the galleon." Henry

panted to catch his breath. "What a she-devil! Who'd have thought that thing would put up such a fight?"

Smithy heard his name and came on deck. He stretched over Justin's shoulder to see the fish. "Aye! Fish stew. Best I can do with one kettle."

They all moaned and then went about cutting it up. When they threw the head overboard, Justin watched it bob and disappear. "Me mum used to roast fish over an open grill."

A loud chorus of anguish surrounded him.

"Don't rub salt in the wound, lad." The captain nudged him.

Justin tilted his head in confusion, then got it. "Oh, right, Captain, sir."

"Swab up the deck of blood, Justin, before she dries. She'll bring flies and disease, so do a good job."

"Aye, Captain, sir." Justin went for the mop and pail. He worked very hard making sure it was spit-spot. After he was done swabbing, Justin peeled some potatoes for the meal. The aroma of the fish cooking was rather pleasant. He felt his stomach grumble and didn't think he could wait too long as dinner wouldn't be done for some time. After doing what he could to get Smithy set up for the meal, he headed to the hold to get a few biscuits for his gurgling belly.

With his hands full of tack, he sat down on the deck in the shade and munched on a biscuit, relaxing with the other crackers on his lap.

The captain walked by him and seemed about to commend him on a job well done. The captain smiled sweetly as he passed, then backed up and stopped, looking down at him. "Justin?"

"Yes, Captain?" He grinned up at his handsome face knowing he was pleased with the mopping job, waiting for some wonderful words of praise.

"Spit out the tack."

"Oy?" Justin tilted his head curiously. It wasn't what he expected him to say, and it dumbfounded him.

"Spit it out."

Justin did, emptying his mouth of it and wiped his lip. "Why?" He took a look at his lap. The other biscuits had maggots in them. In complete horror, Justin let out a gasp and stood up, brushing them off his legs in dismay, then went on spitting and spitting again until he could no longer develop saliva for the task.

Captain Jones turned his back and covered his mouth as he tried very hard not to laugh. The other men weren't as polite. When they realized what had happened, there was an uproar of laughter from the crew.

In agony, Justin was searching for something to wash out his mouth with. Anything. He rushed around reaching his fingers out in desperation, begging for some help.

Through his absolute hilarity, Peckham found him a jug of rum. Justin grabbed it frantically and took a huge mouthful, gargling and spitting it out over the side. When he felt he had cleansed his tongue enough, he stood still catching his heaving breath. "Aaagh!" he shouted. "That was *horrid!* I et a worm! I et a worm!"

Doubled over with laughter, Captain Jones wiped the tears from his eyes. "Justin, lad, you have to inspect the food first. It doesn't stay well in the damp hull."

"Argh!" Justin still felt sick. "I cannot believe I et a worm!" He guzzled the rum and then choked on it.

"Aye! I've eaten worse!" Tucker warned, "And so will ye if ye be at sea long enough."

Justin swiped at his tongue with his hand. The sensations would not disappear.

Peckham glanced over at his captain, and they shook their heads as they covered their smiles.

"What a lad, what a lad." The captain sighed and went back to his task, stopping short when he remembered something. "Oh, good job on the swabbing, Justin."

Justin answered with his mouth open and his fingers still mopping his tongue. "Aww, thwanks, therrr." He stopped spitting and rubbing his mouth finally and collapsed down on the deck to sulk, the rum bottle in his fist.

Peckham sat down near him and pressed against his shoulder. "Don't worry your pretty head about it. It ain't naught. You'd be amazed what the crew will eat to stay alive, Justin. A small worm is nothing, believe me."

Justin's pout didn't fade. "The bloody fool. Always the bloody court jester." He swigged the rum angrily.

"You be finishing that, and you will be the jester!" Peckham pointed to the bottle.

"Aye, I know." He handed it to his pilot to stop himself from drinking it.

Peckham smiled kindly at him and stared at his profile. "You worry yourself too much. No need. Just go on, lad."

"Aye, Pilot. It was just the shock. I should be used to being the laughingstock." He ran his hand back through his hair. "At least my hunger is gone. I am now nauseated."

Peckham sipped the rum and sighed, gazing out at the other men on the deck who were all resting in the hot sun.

"Pilot?"

"Yes, Justin?"

"How long have you liked men?"

Peckham blinked in surprise at the blunt question and checked around them quickly. "Justin, lad, save conversations like that for in private."

"Oh, sorry. Is it a secret?" Justin scanned around. No one seemed interested in the least. Everyone was busy working, daydreaming, or sleeping.

Peckham toyed with the bottle of rum. "Nay, not a secret anymore, lad. I gave up trying to hide my true feelings on this little ship. I felt this way all me life, lad.

That's one of the reasons I came here to sea. No one cares about that buggery law out here. I feel lucky to be here where I am able to act on my impulses."

"Have you ever been with a woman?"

"Yes. I've had several whores." His eyes misted over as he lowered his voice to a whisper. "None can make me feel anything but hollow, Justin. They leave me lacking. I feel no passion for them."

"I never thought of loving men, Pilot. I am surprised at myself for falling in love with Captain Jones."

"Really, lad?" He shifted to face Justin. "Why?"

"I don't know. I suppose when one is growing up one thinks of whom he will marry and of children. You know? But now, I'm not as certain. I have never been with a woman. Oh, once, right before I boarded *His Revenge*. A whore did a naughty deed to me. That's it."

"And? You think your path is with men now?"

"I don't know. What do you think, Pilot?" Justin asked.

Peckham replied, "Justin, I cannot decide for you. You must go with what is deep in your heart. If you love a man, then you love a man." He shrugged. "It is really not that complicated. At least not for a sailor."

"Aye, here on board it is all right to be that way." Justin stared at Peckham's fine features and fair blond hair. "How did you learn so much about being a pilot?"

With his new avid listener, Peckham told Justin about a man he once knew and sailed with who took him on as an apprentice. "You learn after years asea and a good teacher. Do you want to learn, lad?"

Justin touched his lip as he thought about it. "I don't rightly know. The captain and I may settle down after this."

Peckham's eyes widened. "You...you think you and the captain—"

"Aye! He loves me, you know."

165

Peckham smiled sadly. "Aye, well, if you ever decide to come back to us, you'd be welcome. I know no one here would have any objections to you sailing with us again. Now that you're an old sea dog." He winked.

Justin beamed in pride. "Thank you, Pilot! That made me proud."

Peckham stared at Justin as he rose up and tucked himself in. "Off to eat, lad?"

"Yes, I think I can manage real food now. And not worms!" He laughed at himself. "...then off to bed, my favorite part of the day." He grinned slyly.

"I'll bet it is, lad, I'll bet it is." Rising up, Peckham craned his neck to the stars as they just started to shine in the evening sky.

* * * *

Justin slurped the fish soup hungrily and enjoyed the company of the men around him. He'd gotten used to their smell and rough ways, the eternal scratching they did and the snorting and spitting.

He leaned over to Henry and asked, "Do you ever want to settle down and have a family?"

Henry's face was tanned. He had a pockmarked complexion covered by his fuzzy chin hair and long sideburns. A scar ran over the bridge of his nose where a cutlass had come too close to its mark. His teeth were rotting and his hair was tied back in a blue and white bandana. He was very thin and wiry, no fat on his bones.

As he thought of his answer, Henry looked around first at his gunner mates and then shook his head. "Nay, lad. Not I. A woman is like a chain shot, she'll drag ye down."

Justin searched around the table at the men seated on that bench. They were all shaking their heads no. "Not one of you?"

Henry laughed at Justin's curiosity. "Nay, my pretty. Naught a one."

"Huh." Justin rubbed his chin.

"Ye fancy a female gibbet cage, our fair Justin?" Francis asked.

"Me? Nay, I think naught. I'm too young to die."

A low laugh rumbled around the table. "Why ye be askin' us then, lad?" Samuel leaned over to him.

"Well, I was just thinking about our Captain Jones. You know, his plan."

They exchanged glances with one another. Henry put his arm around Justin's shoulder and gave him a squeeze. "Ye be welcome to come with us for as long as ye wants. Ye need never see yar bastard father again."

It stung. He didn't know why, but it did. Whether it was that they knew he had no one and the captain would not want him, or the mention of the father he left back home, he wasn't sure. But something made his chest ache in longing.

John tried to catch his gaze. "Ye miss yar mum?"

"Huh?" Justin caught his one good eye, the other was covered by a patch. "No, not really. I think I'm a bit tired, that's all."

"Off with ye then." Henry patted his back.

Justin rose up and left with a heavy heart.

When he opened the captain's cabin door, he expected to see his lover. He wasn't there.

Justin removed his boots and filled a basin with fresh water. He caught sight of the logbook again and wondered if there was a new entry. Setting the pitcher down, he moved to it slowly. When the door swung open, he gasped and stuck his hands behind his back, the picture of guilt.

Captain Jones smiled at him, then appeared to notice his odd expression. When Justin's eyes darted to the logbook, the captain sat down at his desk. "You all right, lad?"

"Aye, sir. I was just about to rinse the salt off me."
He started stripping.

Captain Jones opened the log and inspected it, then
turned over his shoulder to Justin. "Do you know how to
read, Justin?"

"Aye, sir." Justin answered in a mumble.

"You do?"

"Aye, sir." He stepped out of his breeches and lay
them aside.

The captain folded up the logbook and appeared deep
in thought.

The jingling of keys made Justin feel horrible. He
knew that the captain had suspected he had read his private
journal, and he was even more miserable that he needed to
hide it from him. He pouted out his lower lip as he wiped
the watery rag over his arms and chest.

The captain secured the lock of his cabinet and
pocketed the key, sitting back down to remove his boots.
There was an awkward silence between them when
previously there never was.

"Captain," Justin whispered.

The captain raised his weary eyes. Justin was hoping
his nakedness would calm and soothe him. Setting down
the rag, he floated seductively across the room. Captain
Jones sighed loudly and leaned back as he approached.

Yearning to entice, Justin pushed against his captain's
knees and stroked the captain's long hair, which was
falling out of its ribbon. "Forgive me."

The captain softened up considerably and held
Justin's narrow waist. "They say curiosity killed the cat,
Justin."

"Aye, yes, I have heard that one." Justin tried to crawl
onto the captain's muscular lap.

The captain allowed it and positioned him across his
knees. "You are a very naughty lad for invading my
privacy."

Justin laid his head on that rounded shoulder and kissed the captain's jaw and ear. "Forgiveness, I beg it of you."

The captain moaned softly and pulled Justin's legs closer to him. With little effort, the captain found his mouth, and they kissed passionately. Justin moved his hand up to that long brown hair, tugging it free of its ribbon.

The captain's palm smoothed its way across Justin's slender thighs to his hip. They were exchanging little noises as they kissed, tiny grunts and miniature whimpers to show each other the anticipation of sharing the act together. Justin reached into the captain's shirt and caressed his chest. As he did, the kissing seemed to intensify. They were both piqued with excitement.

Justin's thrill was clearly visible, protruding from between his thighs whilst the captain's could be felt throbbing under his naked legs.

When the door opened suddenly they parted mouths, but it was too late to separate bodies. Justin hid his face over the captain's shoulder as the captain tried to cover Justin with his embrace. When Justin peered up, he found his first mate's wide brown astonished eyes.

"Argh! Sorry, Captain, sir!" The door was quickly shut.

"Is it urgent, Jack?" the captain shouted after him.

"Nay, nay!" came the fading reply as he hurried away.

The captain paused a moment to think, then nudged Justin and found his mouth once more. Justin was elated with his priorities in life.

The captain parted from Justin's lips with a soft breath. With a quick glance down at his lap, Justin watched the captain finger his hardness before he stared once again into his eyes.

"Are you not hiding us any longer?" Justin asked as

he squirmed in delight at the handling.

"Nay, lad, there should be no secrets on board. And everyone knows by now as it is. So, why bother?"

"No secrets?" Justin nibbled his earlobe and breathed those words in his ear.

The captain sighed. "No, not the log. That is me own private journal." He leaned his head away in irritation.

"Eh, don't stop what you are doing to me." Justin urged the captain to continue playing with him. "I'll end upsetting you now. No more mention of it."

"Good lad. Go get onto the bunk on your knees." The captain gestured to the bed.

Justin kissed him and scrambled to the bunk. Getting in position, he waited, watching the captain take off the remainder of his clothing.

The captain's dick was very large and hard after the foreplay. Justin shivered at the sight of him coating himself with the liniment. As the captain strut towards the bed, his big cock bobbed and swayed deliciously on top of his long hanging sack.

Closing his eyes as the warmth entered from behind, Justin groaned in pleasure and wanted only to please this man, never to upset him. He gasped as that hand clasped hold of his cock and handled it roughly. The sensation of being filled, the captain's body deeply connected to his own brought Justin so much joy he was in tears.

With the heat stroking him inside and out, Justin felt the surge to his groin overwhelm him. Jamming his cock into the captain's tight palm, Justin came. As his body shot out cum in pulsating beats that kept time with his racing heart, the captain did the same behind him, pumping his seed into him.

Justin's head drooped as he shivered with the aftershocks. The captain pulled out slowly, and they lay side by side as they recuperated. Coated in dewy sweat, Justin cuddled into the nook of his captain's shoulder and petted his chest softly, whilst the captain nuzzled into Justin's hair.

Justin wanted to ask if he loved him. He wanted to hear his captain say those three words to him. Opening his mouth to actually form the request, Justin could hear the captain's breath softening into slumber. He sealed his lips and reconsidered.

Chapter Eleven

After weeks on the Atlantic Ocean with nothing for the eyes but water and sky, the men caught sight of land. Peckham clung to the main mast with his telescope.

Justin was mixed with emotions at the sight of the tiny spot of green and brown visible between sea and air. He didn't want it to end. It was perfect as it was. But their provisions were running low, and the men were getting hungry for food and women once again. Captain Jones reached for the telescope and gazed out at the speck of earth ahead. "England, Pilot?"

"Should be, sir!"

"Good! Good man! Come in by night only. I don't want to be at port in broad daylight whilst we dock."

"Aye, sir!" Peckham took back the telescope and stared through it again.

Justin sighed and tried not to get emotional as he tugged the captain's sleeve when he walked by.

"Not now, lad." The captain smiled patiently and passed him.

Remember what is written in the log. The last thing he read was the expression of the captain's love for him. He shouldn't be nervous. They were bonded, soul to soul. Weren't they?

"Pilot?" Justin called up to him.

"Aye, lad?"

"How long now?"

"Dusk tonight. You'll be happy to get your feet on England's soil again?"

With growing dread and remorse, he bit his lip. *No, most unhappy.*

Leaning on rail at the bow, Justin stared at that spit of land as it grew. Soon only the sparkling firelights could be seen as twilight deepened. His eyes kept welling with tears at the thought of the changes that were coming.

The corvette glided silently into the bay they had left so long ago. The sails were lowered, and the men worked in the silence to tie her up to a dock.

Justin was shaking with anxiety as the waterfront of his home came into focus. Recognizing every shop, every pub, every tree, the church steeple, all of it was very familiar to him. He knew it like the back of his hand.

On returning to the cabin, Justin found the captain packing his clothing. "Captain, sir."

He raised his head and gave Justin a sad smile. "Aye, lad?"

"Should I take my things as well?"

"I cannot decide your fate, Justin." His voice was no more than a whisper as he lowered his lashes.

"Is it with you?" Justin stood behind his captain and felt the coldness of his back.

"Me? Nay, lad. My fate is with Kath." He continued his task.

"But your log. You wrote—" Justin was about to burst.

Captain Jones sighed and sat down on the bunk, waving Justin over to him and urging him close so he was leaning against his knees.

Rivers of tears were streaming down Justin's face. The captain brushed them off with his thumbs. "Oh, my sweet lover, you have no idea what you mean to me."

Justin was trying to stop the incredible urge he had to wail in agony. The captain kissed and embraced him, rocking him in his arms.

"No...no...no...," Justin moaned. "You cannot do

this. You cannot just leave me so I may never see you again. No."

"Justin, lad." The captain urged Justin back and connected to his liquid-filled eyes. "You knew I had this plan. I never hid it from you." He reached up and brushed more tears away as they fell.

"But, you love me," Justin cried in anguish.

"I need to settle down. I need sons," the captain explained.

"How can you do this to me?" Justin sobbed, his body convulsing with the torment.

"You need to go your own way." The captain's voice faded out.

"Oh, Lord, you have killed me! I am dead. You should have just allowed me to perish in the sea. It'd been quicker than this death you have sentenced me to."

"Justin, please." With an effort, the captain rose up. Without looking back, he tried to continue gathering his belongings and seemed to be having a tough time concentrating.

Justin was numb. This couldn't be happening to him. With clumsy fingers, he found his own things and wrapped them up in a bundle. His pockets were overflowing with coins, but he didn't care. Silently he followed the captain onto the main deck as he shook the line of hands that bid him good luck. Justin felt sick. He'd no idea what to do. He walked as if he were a dead man, passed all the crew. The pilot stopped him when he spotted those tears running down his cheeks. "Justin," he whispered kindly and reached out to him.

Though he could neither see nor hear clearly through the fog in his head, he heard his pilot tell him they would be in port for three days and then set sail. That he was welcome. Justin nodded, hurrying behind that tall man before he vanished from his vision and out of his life forever. Heavy boot heels trod on the dock in front of him as he was dwarfed by his enormous shadow.

Captain Jones stopped and turned around with a sigh. "Justin."

"I've nowhere to go. What am I to do? I cannot live without you," Justin cried, wiping his eyes with the back of his hand.

The captain scanned around the area, then brought Justin to the side of the narrow lane. Justin immediately recognized the spot where the whore picked his pockets. That felt like so very long ago.

"Look, lad, you cannot just follow me." The captain dabbed at another flowing tear.

"I must." Justin would not look him in the eye.

"No, go back on board then. All your mates are there."

"How can I? You are not among them," he wept and did finally find that lovely set of baby blue eyes.

"Justin," the captain admonished.

"Fine! Go! Shove off!" He pushed the captain away. "You're rid of me now. Rid of the pest!"

Captain Jones stood tall and lowered his head, walking back down the cobblestone street.

Unable to watch, Justin turned away in complete misery. Dropping his kit, he covered his face, crying in the dark. He had no idea it would hurt this badly. No one in his life had ever meant anything to him before, but he now understood the pain of a broken heart. It was like someone close to him had died and he was destined never to see them again except maybe in his dreams. It devastated him, and he knew he could not function any longer. As if a chasm opened, he envisioned the darkness of a long depression covering over him and then finally killing himself from the loneliness.

A drunken sod was thrown out of a tavern and rolled onto the pavement to the water-filled gutter. He got to his knees and swore in slurred vulgar blasts of words.

Through his inebriation, he stared at Justin's tear-stained face and recognized him. "Oy! That be Justin Taylor?"

Justin gasped in horror, and his first impulse was to run, but instead he froze in fear. "Father!"

The ragged, filthy man got to his feet and staggered over to him with a great effort. "Yer in for the whipping of yer life, ye little maggot! Ye left yer mother to tend all the work!"

"No, Father. Let me explain." Justin backed away from him in terror.

Samuel John Taylor grabbed his son's hair and started beating his head and face with raging violence.

Justin tried to turn away, covering himself. "Please! Father! Let me be!" he cried out, just when he thought he could not feel any more pain and misery.

Samuel John kept pounding away relentlessly, as if all his hatred and frustration could be suddenly unloaded on someone else. He pummeled and slapped Justin trying to do serious damage to him until a very large shadow loomed over them. In the pause, Justin looked at his father and then the man who was standing near.

Justin watched as his father found a set of furious eyes the color of blue steel, glaring at him with intense hatred. He released Justin from the fright and backed away.

Trying to get over the assault, Justin gasped as his captain grabbed his father by the throat.

* * * *

Captain Jones could hear the beating from two streets away. When he realized it was Justin being abused, he rushed back as quickly as he could. The moment he laid eyes on this drunken beggar, he knew exactly who it was. The sight of the attack on Justin brought out a ferocious reaction in him. He knew Justin had tolerated nothing but thrashings from this creature. Now he wanted to kill him for it. As he choked this man, he raised him off the ground, his teeth clenched in anger. "How *dare* you punish the lad that way! How dare you inflict those whipping scars on such a boy? Who in blazes do you think you are to abuse the lad this way?" he thundered.

"Who the devil are you?" Samuel John panicked and wheezed in fear. His face beaded with sweat and turned snow white.

"Ne'er you mind! But you best be ne'er setting hand nor crop to that lad again, or you will find me to reckon with. And I shall not be as merciful as you have been to our Justin. Do not tempt me. I should kill you for what you did to him. And I shall, if I ever hear of you touching the lad again. Am I understood, you filthy bilge rat?" He tightened his grip on his neck.

Samuel John urinated on himself in mortal terror. "Aye! Whoever you are! I'll not touch the boy again. I...I promise you that!"

"You see to it. I will be watching. And you will not want to die from my hand. It will be slow and painful, I assure you."

"Yes, sir! Your grace, sir. Never again, sir. Just spare me life, sir!" he whined.

Captain Jones threw Samuel John off the dock and into the shallow water, where he landed with a splash and flailed around until he found his feet. "Filthy scum!" the captain sneered and tried to wipe his hands off on his breeches.

* * * *

Justin's mouth hung open as his captain passed him with a wink. He could not get over what had just happened. Stepping to the end of the dock to gaze down into the bay, he found his father sputtering and choking out salty water. Justin laughed to himself and tilted his head up to see that broad back making its way down the dimly lit street. "Blimey!" he chuckled. He simply adored that man.

* * * *

The captain could not get over the fact that he was home. It was like some vision he'd seen in a dream. The house was a gift from him to Katherine. He wanted to assure her of his intentions when he returned. Walking up the front stoop, he used his own key in the lock. When he pushed open the door he could smell the day's baking in the air. It was quiet in the interior, and several lamps were lit. He set his kit down and peered into the reception room. A fire was burning in the hearth, and Katherine was seated in front of it, catching up on her sewing. When she raised her head at the sound, it took a moment for her to register what she was seeing. When she did, her eyes lit up with amazement. Rising up, Katherine dropped everything on her lap and ran to him.

He opened his arms wide for the woman he cherished.

"Richard!" She embraced him, tears of joy running down her cheeks.

He set her back on her feet and gazed into her eyes. "Katherine, my lovely Katherine," he sighed, unable to believe the day had come and he was touching her once again. Stepping aside from her, he scanned around the interior of the house. Though the rooms felt large compared to the compartments of the corvette, it had a sense of claustrophobia to him. A dark contrast to the vastness of the open sea.

"Richard. It's been an eternity." She touched his smooth jaw.

"Yes, it felt as if it was forever. Did you miss me, my darling?" He reached out to her again and held her at arm's length. Her ginger hair seemed to glow with the fiery embers behind it. He loved the light freckles on her nose and cheeks.

"Of course I have. How can you say that?" She lowered her green eyes and placed her hand on his solid chest as it peeked from out of his opened blouse.

"Good, my love. It is music to my ears. Did you wait for me, Kath?" He embraced her again and rocked her slowly, staring at the flames licking the ashen log.

She paused, and he felt her shiver against him.

"Kath?"

As if in pain, she moved away, lowered her head and stepped to the window to stare out the leaded glass. It had started to rain. The water pellets struck the panes noisily.

"I asked you a direct question." Unable to understand her hesitation, he stood in the middle of the room, waiting, watching her back rise and fall with deep breaths.

She sighed and appeared to take heed of something. Suddenly she exclaimed, "There is a boy out there. He is sitting out in the rain. How queer." She tilted her head curiously.

"*Katherine Ann!*" he implored. "*Answer me!*"

At his tone of voice, she inhaled sharply in surprise and twisted to face him, trembling visibly.

By her expression and the lack of a reply, he knew very well his answer. "What have you done? You have betrayed me? You have broken your vow? With whom?" He moved closer to her, looming over her. "I demand you tell me!" He was about to explode.

She raised her hand to her forehead and didn't meet his eye. Stepping back from him hesitantly, she stared into the depth of the hearth. "I heard news you were lost at sea," she answered weakly. "Word came to me you were gone."

"News from whom? Words? Whose words?" he growled, towering over her. His body felt like cold stone from the anxiety this was causing him. He could not believe his own ears.

"From Charles Collins. Your old shipmate from the Royal Navy," she answered quickly, as if it was too noxious to swallow down.

When he heard that name, he felt like he had indeed swallowed poison. His veins went black, and it seeped into his bones. "When the devil did you see him? Has he come calling on you? Tell me! You believed that lying, spineless braggart?"

"Richard! I had no way of knowing if it was the truth. You were gone for so long. I thought my life was passing by me, and I would be alone. I am getting older, my love. I want children. What was I to do? Mother and Father were pressuring me to make a decision. You are always away, and I had no idea you would return to me."

As if stabbed repeatedly, he covered his ears to try and stop the words from entering, shaking his head in denial. "No! Not Charles Collins! Tell me you are lying. Not that hornswaggling bastard! Did you already marry him?" he thundered in rage and twisted around like he expected that fiend to materialize from a darkened room.

"No! I have not married him." She started crying.

In growing despair, Richard ran his hand back through his long hair and faced her. "For weeks I fought and died for you. I brought back a fortune to shower you with. I bled and starved for you. Now I ask you. Did you marry that dog?"

"Did you not hear? I did not marry him yet. Calm down, Richard! You must believe me." She clasped her hands together.

"*Yet?*" he roared. "Then, have you lain with him? Have you slept with that filthy yellow coward?" he snarled and thought he would literally implode from the shock.

"I...I...," she stammered, as if she were trying to get out what she went through.

He could imagine her excuses. The months of worry

and waiting. He'd heard all that before.

"Wait, Richard, let me explain—"

"Where is he? I shall murder him." He clenched his fists and searched the rooms. "Please, tell me you are making this horrible tale up. Tell me it is anyone but that bloodsucking bastard." His muscles felt so tense he thought he would tear himself apart.

As he darted in and out of rooms, she ran to him and tried to stop him, touching him. "I don't know where he is now. He is not here, Richard. He means nothing to me. It is you that I love. It can be as we dreamed. Let us put the past behind us. You are home. All is well." She grabbed at his arms to try and keep him still.

In disgust, he spun away from her. "I told you this last trip would be almost four months asea. Now, here it is, exactly as I said. And you did not wait? Why? Why, Katherine, when you know what you mean to me? When you know we made a plan...all our plans...of a house, a farm, of children," he moaned in agony.

As if in frustration, she sighed loudly and moved to the window once again. "The boy is still out there. Surely it is getting very wet and cold."

"Katherine!" he shouted in fury. "I am talking to you. I demand answers!"

She gasped at the volume and force of his words and faced him once more, but this time it appeared with complete resignation. "I am sorry, Richard. I cannot change things. You do not know how I suffered for you. Lived in fear for you. Even now, I am being honest with you. I have not lied."

"You think you know what suffering is?" He could not catch his breath. "Oh, but Katherine you have lied. You have lied *and* deceived me. Both. Do you know the risk I take? Do you know the amount of blood on my hands?" He held them out to her. "For you. For you. All this for you!" He reached into his pockets and dumped out some doubloons. They showered the carpet in a shimmering golden waterfall. "For you I bled. For you I murdered. For you I starved," he cried as his heart broke.

"Richard, shh, we will be all right. Please, calm down." She crossed the room and reached for him.

"No! Get away from me, you whore!" He wrenched out of her reach.

"Richard, please!"

"You can have Charles-the Dandy-Collins. Take him with my blessing." He got ready to leave, searching for the kit he dropped when he first came in.

"No! Richard, not this way. Let's talk this out. Sit. You are weary. You are hungry and dirty. After a meal. After a bath. Then you will see the sense in it. You will not want to end it."

He stopped his progress to the door and faced her once again. "Talk? You think mere talk will make it all right? Do you have any idea what you have done to my heart?" Before he could prevent it, he broke down into tears. "What you have done to me?"

Cringing, she cried, "Richard, I love you. Please! Let us take some time. We will get over this. You must allow some time to pass."

"No! Do you know what will happen? Let me inform you, my dear lady. I know Charles Stratford Collins very well. He is a liar and a traitor. He has had you in mind as a means to destroy me ever since he laid eyes on you. And this comes after he has been after my cock for more than over just a year's time. He told me of the jealousy he felt over my loving you. It is my guess he will summon the authorities and see me hanged. Anything to seek vengeance against me. He'll have waited. He'll wait to see if I return. When he sees I have, it'll be the hangman's noose for me. He is that treacherous. That is what you have done to me, Katherine. You have killed me."

She choked, shivering with strong tremors. "Oh, for

the love of mercy, what have I done? No! You are wrong. He is not that way. Do not go."

Captain Jones took one last look at her. "What choice have I?" he snapped. "My dreams are shattered. A life of leisure, a farm, sons. Vanished! All gone because of your filthy indiscretion with one dangerous fiend. How could you? How could you do this to me?"

She burst into tears. "Richard! I didn't know. Please, I beg of you to forgive me. Let me talk to him. Let me reason with him. He'll listen to me."

"Reason with him? That will give him time. He knows not I am here now. You *reason* with him, and I am doomed. Hanged!" He waved his arms around in frustration.

"Why did you choose that life? Surely the Royal Navy was enough."

"Are you mad? Do you have any idea the harsh punishment they inflicted on me? The beatings that I endured? At the hand of your 'lover'?" he spat out the word venomously. "Because I rebuffed his advances, he found joy in beating me. I was publicly flogged by that man. Do you realize what he has done to me in the past? I am better off with the scum on *His Revenge*."

"No! I do not believe Charles is capable of that. He is too kind. Too much a refined gentleman. Richard, wait. Where are you going?" She panicked and reached out to him. "No! Richard, do not leave me again. I cannot live without you. We shall run away together then. Let me pack. Wait for me!"

"Get away from me!" He jerked back from her. "You have shown me you lived very well without me thus far. Your talk defending that beast is a slap in the face to me. You know of nothing. You have no idea what he is. But soon you will learn. Go! Marry that monster. It will be the fate you deserve." He pointed to the coins on the carpet. "Keep that. That is what I owe you for the few months of heaven we shared."

"No! No! Richard, I won't believe this is it for us. Of all our dreams." She clawed at his shirt.

He twisted away and showed his teeth in his rage. "I am dead to you. Do you understand? Dead. When your Charles returns and asks if you have heard news of me, you say I am dead. That is the only way I shall be allowed to live. Do you see?"

She covered her ears and sobbed, shaking her head in denial.

Richard smashed through the door and never turned back.

* * * *

At the noise, Justin raised his head. The door had opened, and the sound of quarreling found him. He stood. The rain had stopped, and his captain was moving with great speed, his long stride like a marching infantry soldier. Gathering his things, Justin ran after him, trying to catch up.

They ended back at the waterfront. The captain pushed through the doors of a pub and found a seat, collapsing onto the hardwood chair and throwing his kit down at his feet in defeat. Justin crept in warily and hid in a corner.

Captain Jones ordered a bottle of rum and an ale. When they were set before him, he lifted the rum and drank it like water, wiping tears from his eyes.

From the shadows, Justin studied him closely as he finished the bottle and then tankard after tankard of ale. He felt so much agony for him knowing his heart was broken. The woman had betrayed him. It was very plain.

When his captain lay his head down on his arms, across that scarred table and cried, Justin could not sit by any longer. He stood up slowly and tiptoed his way to him.

Shoving a chair right up next to him, Justin sat on it.

In sympathy, he heard the captain's soft whimpering and watched his large fists ball up into a clenched knot. Justin petted his hair softly and whispered, "My Captain?" He did not respond, almost seeming to twist further away in his shame. Justin leaned on his captain's side and wrapped his arm around his back trying to comfort him. When he did, Justin scanned the room mechanically and knew some men were staring at them.

He tried to forget how it appeared to others and thought only of his captain. When he found his ear, Justin brushed his lips over it to whisper, "When I was in misery and lonely, you were there for me. You were my rock, my savior. I will never forget you for it. Let me be that for you. Let me help you forget and move on." Again, he felt no movement, no response. Justin sighed and tried to squeeze his lover, laying his head on his shoulder. Justin's eyes misted over as he gazed into that smoky room. He didn't know what the others were thinking. He wasn't sure he cared. Once again he faced his captain, and crooned, "I love you, my Captain. Please don't be sad."

Very slowly, the captain raised his head off his arms. His hair had fallen out of its ribbon and was in wild waves around his face. The captain almost knocked over the empty bottle, but managed to grab it before it rolled to the floor. Justin reached for it at the same time, and they ended up clutching it and each other's hand. Captain Jones first stared at Justin's fingers as they held his own, then he turned to see his face.

In agony, Justin shook his head at the state he was in. He'd never seen him this drunk and forlorn. It almost made him seem more human, more vulnerable. Never had he imagined his captain weak or in need in any way. He felt so much pity for him. "My poor captain, do not do this to yourself. Come. Come with me to our ship's cabin and let me serve you." He smoothed his fingers down his arm and squeezed his captain's wrist. Sliding his hand off the table, Justin located that huge thigh under it to massage warmly.

The captain sighed loudly, trying to get the long hair back from his eyes. When he did, he found Justin studying him with unmatched intensity. He exhaled tiredly and said, "She betrayed me, Justin. Deceived me."

"Aye, I figured." He nodded sympathetically. "I am so sorry, my Captain. I know what that dream meant to you, sir." He rubbed that large quadriceps muscle lovingly. "Tell me what I can do to help you forget?"

The captain let out a sad laugh. "Forget? I will never get over what she did to me, Justin. She has lain with a snake. One who was guilty of atrocity. How could she do this to me?" He choked up and tried to swallow it back.

"Shush, sir, please." Justin peered around as it seemed the crowd grew unfriendly. Englishmen didn't cry in public. This display was upsetting them. "Come on, sir. Come with me to the ship." Justin nudged him.

Captain Jones didn't budge. "Nay, lad. I need more rum." He attempted to wave at the bartender.

"That is the one thing you do not need." Justin caught his hand and flattened it out to the table before it was spied. "Sir, please, not here. I can tend you better in private."

The captain gave him a wry smile. "Tend me?" He tried to laugh. "I should be grateful of one who wants me. One who is loyal to me. Shouldn't I, Justin, lad?"

"Aye, sir, you should. I would never disappoint you," he assured him.

"Can you give me sons?"

Justin felt his face break out in a hot blush. He peeked around the crowded room again. "Sir."

"No, you cannot. Well, my Justin, that is what I crave. No, lad. It is finished. I am finished."

"Stop. Do not say this. She is just a wench. She is not

worthy of you." He rubbed the captain's thigh briskly under the table, feeling its heat.

Captain Jones sat up taller and stared at Justin's moving hand. "Not worthy of me?" He shook his head at the irony. "She is like a queen, and I am but a pauper. It is I who has failed her. I promised her I would not go out again, and I did. Do I blame her for finding another? Nay."

"Yes! No!" Justin tried to think straight. "I do not know. But I know one thing. We need you. Come back to *His Revenge* and stay with us."

The captain jumped when Justin's fingers brushed over his crotch. He tilted his head to him, trying to see though all his long hair. "What do you do to me? We are not on board, lad."

"Sorry." Justin's cheeks grew hotter. "I just want to remind you of what we had."

The captain rubbed his face tiredly. "Maybe you are right. It is useless here. I am now an outcast like the rest of her crew. I have brought this fate upon myself."

"Shh, Captain, please." Justin pushed his hair back from his face.

The captain looked around the room. "Lad, I am in no shape for a battle."

"Oy?" He widened his eyes curiously. "Battle?"

"Aye. You caress me once more, and I will have a fight on me hands."

Justin lurched up quickly and scanned the crowd. He did indeed find several intimidating snarls. "Blimey!" In fear, he rose off the chair and nudged his captain. "Off we go, come then."

The captain stood and swayed unsteadily. Justin grabbed both their kits and had a devil of a time keeping the man steady with his arms fully loaded. They made their way to the dock as Justin endured the weight of a very large, muscular man leaning on him for support. He strained and led him to the ship's deck. "Pilot!" he called out. "Tucker!"

Only a few had remained on board. Two of the gunners found them. They helped Justin escort a very drunk man to his cabin, laying him back on the bunk. The captain closed his eyes and twisted away from their examining gaze.

"She didn't wait for 'im then?" Henry whispered to Justin.

"Nay, Henry, she did not." Justin shook his head.

"Aye, typical wench. He's better off with our lot. Ye look after him, mate." Henry patted Justin's head.

"I will, Henry. I will." Justin waited until they left, then brought over the wooden stool to sit and watch his captain. The tears had dried on his handsome face, and his eyes were glazed as they dazed off at nothing. "I will look after you, sir. I will see to it you are well again," Justin whispered, petting his hair.

The captain bit his lip and hid his face away.

Justin leaned closer. His captain's teeth were showing as his ire and fury grew. Justin realized the captain had time to think about it suddenly. And that was not a good thing.

"Captain?" Justin touched him. The man was burning up, like a raging fire was growing inside him. "Sir?" Justin studied him as if he were a volcano about to blow. The amount of seething lava in him was growing uncontainable. "Oh, Lord. Stop thinking about it! Stop!" Justin shook him violently.

It started deep inside his chest and moved up like rushing magma. A roar of complete hostility and deep pain erupted from Captain Jones. Justin covered his ears to try and stop the anguish it inflicted on him. He loved this man most in the world and to see him like this was pure agony.

He stood and threw himself on his captain, laying his body over the top of that writhing, suffering soul. Gripping him with clenched arms around his neck and wrapping his legs around his hips, Justin squeezed with every ounce of strength he could muster and closed his eyes as he pushed his face deep under that long, wild head of hair.

Captain Jones enveloped that body on top of his and drew out deep heaving sobs of agony.

Justin only squeezed harder, trying to help him ride out the torture.

Chapter Twelve

Charles Collins entered Katherine's home and removed his tri-cornered hat. At the sight of him in his blue uniform, her smile fell.

"My dear lady, I expected a warmer welcome than that. You behave this way to your own betrothed?" He handed her his hat and searched around the room mechanically.

"Please forgive me. I had a terrible sleep last night." She set his hat on a hook in the hall and hurried into her sitting room. "Shall I get you some tea?"

"Yes, that would be lovely." He smiled tightly and waited for her to leave. When she had, he strutted to the hearth which was unlit in the warmth of the day. Finding himself in a mirror that was hanging over the mantel, he attended to his black hair, all in perfect ringlets, and then his embroidered frock and cuffs. Pausing to inspect something on the mantel, he lifted it into his hand and realized it was a golden Spanish coin. He spun around quickly to make sure he was still alone and tried to think of the implications. It could only mean one thing. He rubbed it between his fingers before slipping it into his pocket.

A moment later, Katherine returned with his tea on a tray. She set it down gracefully and filled two cups. "Please have a seat, Charles."

Like a servant, she stood waiting as he found a chair and crossed his legs comfortably. "Any news from our dear Richard?" he asked slyly.

She grew very pale. Her green eyes seemed to gray as he studied them. She sat down across from him and lifted a porcelain cup with trembling fingers. "No. How would I hear from him? You said yourself he is lost at sea. Do you not remember?"

He knew she was lying. If there was one thing a trickster could do, it was recognize another. Calmly he slurped his tea, his pinky finger raised high like a stiff mast. A long moment passed before he placed his cup down. Smiling with self-satisfaction, he boasted, "Yes, that he is. Lost. So let us plan our wedding, dear lady. Your father tells me we should not delay. Your mother begs me to make you a permanent home. And we need sell this house. It is unsuitable."

Flinching at first, she replied, "Yes. We must sell it."

"Good. I am sure we could get a few bits for it. Then you will come and live with me in my manor. You shall be my lady of the house. Does this please you?"

He could read her tension easily. "Yes, Charles, this pleases me."

"Good." He let his lips curl into a wicked grin.

As soon as he could, he made his excuses and left her to walk briskly to the docks. Standing at the first slip, he inspected the flag and crew, carefully gazing down the line of masts, intent on scrutinizing each one. Yes, he knew he was here. He could almost smell him.

With delight, he envisioned that handsome male in perfect clarity. He grew an erection every time he relived the lashing he delivered to him. That broad, muscular back, flinching in pain with every lick of the leather. What he would have given to mount that man after the punishment, to taste his sweat. He would have sold his soul. *Ah, no bother now, I have stolen his woman. Given him the pain, he has given me. An eye for an eye? A heart for a heart.*

He felt a grin spread over his mouth. It will do. Once

191

she was his showpiece wife, he could disregard her and go back to his male lovers. She would be a fine breeder for his sons, a perfect hostess for his affairs, a cover for his real sexual identity, and subservient to him in all ways. Now, if he could just set eyes on that virile man again, know he is really in port, that would be the ultimate pleasure. See the pain he created in that flawless face. Then his revenge would be complete. No one said no to Charles Stratford Collins! No one!

* * * *

Justin was awakened out of a deep slumber.

His pilot was shaking his captain. "Wake up, Captain! Justin!"

Captain Jones raised his head off his arms sluggishly and stared at his pilot.

"Men! Officials! Snooping about!" Peckham panicked.

Reluctantly, Captain Jones sat up and tried to tame his wild hair as he thought things through. "Have they boarded?"

"Nay, Captain. They are just on the docks looking at the ships."

"Damn to all hellfire!" The captain clenched his fists.

Feeling ill, Justin grabbed onto his captain. "No, they are not after you, no!"

With an effort, the captain straightened himself up and climbed out onto the main deck warily. His pilot pointed them out. They were checking documents. The captain held onto the mizzenmast and studied them. Justin stood near him, touching his back as he peered out from behind.

"Go get our papers, Pilot, and some gold. You know where I keep it?" The captain pushed him off.

Peckham nodded and hurried to the cabin.

Justin was trembling in terror. "What's happening, sir? Are we in any sort of trouble?"

"She couldn't have betrayed me. She couldn't," he mumbled to himself.

When the two men strode up the dock, Peckham met them with their paperwork. It stated they were a merchant vessel, privateers. They had a forged letter of marque. The officials nodded, and Peckham handed them a purse of coins.

Justin held his breath as the officials raised their stares to the tall man with his chest bared and his hair loose from its ribbon. Captain Jones never flinched at the inspection, but Justin could see his fingers clench as he held the wooden mast.

The officials saluted the captain, and when he returned it, they headed back down the dock. Justin was panting in fear when Peckham returned.

"All went well, Pilot?" the captain asked calmly.

"Aye, sir, no problems." He held the document in his hand.

"Good. Put that away." The captain nudged him.

Peckham nodded and went to replace it.

"Are we all right now, Captain? Are we all right?" Justin asked.

"For now, lad. For now."

"We need to leave here and never return," Justin said anxiously.

"Aye, lad, we do. And ne'er return."

Justin stared after the two officials as they boarded the next ship. As his captain did the same, scrutinizing everything silently, Justin scanned the dock and locked his focus onto another man; one who was in a Royal Navy land uniform, appearing immaculate.

About to ask the captain who he was, Justin could immediately see the captain's blood boil in rage at the sight. Justin watched every move both men made.

"Captain? Captain, where are you going?" Justin shouted after him.

* * * *

Charles Stratford Collins smirked in amusement as he waited for the approach of that half-naked stallion. He fingered his flintlock and could see very clearly the captain was unarmed. Charles stuck out his white-embroidery-covered chest and felt very powerful in his perfect uniform, complete with gun and sword. When he was face to face with that marvelous looking man he couldn't help but delight at the attraction he felt. He took a moment to enjoy the spectacular sight, inspecting Richard with the slow deliberation of a painter. "My word, Richard, you haven't changed a bit."

"I should kill you." Richard's teeth showed from under his snarled lip.

"Should you?" Charles' laugh mocked him. "Kill a man who hasn't even turned you in to the authorities...yet? Why, my beautiful Richard, would you want to kill me?"

"Don't play those games with me." Richard placed his hands on his hips as he towered over him.

"Are you referring to *my* Katherine?" Charles sneered.

Richard flinched.

"Too bad you won't be in port long enough to attend our wedding." He pursed his lips in a tease.

At the baiting, Richard started seething with anger, his fists clenching in his growing rage. "Why have you always tormented me?" Richard growled through grinding teeth.

As delicately as a ballet dancer, Charles spied around them first before stepping close enough to kiss him. "You know why, my love," he breathed, "You have known why since we first met."

Leaning away in revulsion, Richard raised his hand to Charles' chest and pressed his palm to it, backing him up to give him space.

His sharp eyes flickering down at the act, Charles trapped Richard's hand quickly under his own, squeezing it mercilessly as he begged, "Give me what I want and I will let you live."

"Give you?" Richard choked at the absurdity. "What is it you need from me that you have not already taken?" Advancing step by step, his hand still on Charles' chest, he began moving them out of the steady flow of the cobblestones where they could speak privately. Richard continued in a measured voice, "You have taken my career. You have taken my self-esteem." He pressed Charles back further behind the tall, white-washed buildings. "Now you have taken my woman." He ground his jaw in agony. "And still you ask me for more?"

When his back hit the wall, Charles relaxed against the stone structure he was pressed upon. Lovingly stroking that large, callused, masculine hand with his soft, manicured one as it continued to rest on top of his chest, he purred, "You see how foolish you are, Richard. If you had given me what I wanted all those years ago, I would not have taken anything else from you." Charles made sure a venomous grin spread across his lips.

Richard moaned in frustration. "What is it you want from me? You want my flamin' arse, Collins?" Moving even closer, Richard hissed into his smirk. "You want to stick your cock up my arse? Can it all really be all about that? That one act of submission you have been yearning for ever since we met on board?"

Charles smiled in complete satisfaction, caressing Richard's hand like it was a cat lulled to sleep. "Did it truly take you all this time to unravel that mystery? Oh, Richard, dear, I thought you were cleverer than that."

Charles batted his eyelashes at him in a mock flirtatious tease.

Richard's eyes darted from that pale, white, skinny hand that caressed his tanned one, to Charles' stare. Richard glared at him with intense hatred. Finally, he sighed as if resigned, but that blazing fire remained in his hot gaze. "If I give it to you, am I through with you once and for all? Will you end being a plague on my life?"

Astonished that he might get what he had been after for so long, Charles stood up off the wall and brightened at the possibility of the union. "Why, of course, Richard dear. It was all I ever wanted from you. You have my word, I will never turn you in to the authorities," he lied. "And as far as our Katherine is concerned, I will treat her as a queen. She will never want for a thing. I promise you."

Charles could see Richard trying to contain his rage. As if finally resigned to get this done, Richard stared at the fabric of Charles' Royal Navy uniform as it rose and fell under his palm. After what appeared to be a moment of contemplation, Richard scanned the area quickly. "Fine. Go. Go somewhere private."

Hearing that heavy footfall behind him, Charles grinned in absolute victory. He led Richard to a farmer's field, gripping Richard's hand like they were a couple of lovers skipping in glee to a picnic outing.

* * * *

About to combust, Richard bit the inside of his cheek trying to contain his anger and frustration. The years of torment and agony washed over him; images of standing on deck, his uniform thrown at his feet while his hands were bound over his head. His crewmates all looking on as this villain--this demon--Major Charles Stratford Collins, lavished in the whipping. A vicious beating, simply for rebuking his advances.

And while all these thoughts were running through Richard's mind, Charles brought them to a small stand of dark secluded trees and made a good appraisal of the area first. Seeing they were completely alone, Richard witnessed Charles panting to catch his wind, always the soft, pampered, weak brat.

Like a prim dandy, he took a small kerchief out of his pocket to dab his lip, then set his lascivious eyes him.

Wanting to get this finished, never releasing his gaze, Richard backed a step away from him, then very slowly started to open the brass buttons of his breeches.

* * * *

Trembling in anticipation, Charles was riveted to the movement, holding his breath, his own body already up for the task. Here it was. A gift from God. He knew the day would come when the one he so longed to have would give in. It was only a matter of time.

With both thumbs in his waistband, Richard lowered his britches to the ground, leaning over to fold them down to his high black leather boots. Then he smoothed his hands back up his bare thighs seductively and waited.

Salivating at the sight, Charles was glowing radiantly as he eyed that naked beauty in absolute wonderment. "Oh, Richard, you have surpassed my wildest dreams of you."

In a gesture completely out of character for him, Richard pushed out his pelvis to him and purred. "It is yours. Take what you've been after for forever."

He could not believe his own senses. Why had he waited so long? They could have been lovers on board. Shared this delight night after night. All he had asked was his submission. His complete compliance as a sexual plaything. Why was that so hard to do when here- here it was! That fantastic male anatomy bared and willing.

Charles took a moment to just stare at him, admiring this treat before he devoured it. He shook out the kerchief and lay it on the soil in front of him, then sank to his knees slowly before him. "First, my dear, I will savor you, then I shall have your tight, scrumptious virgin ass."

"As you wish."

With an air of ceremony, Charles set his hat aside and sat back on his heels. He raised his hand to that soft package and cupped it lightly, feeling the weight of Richard's balls in his palm. "You are too handsome, Richard. That was why you were given so much misery in the Royal Navy. The crew hated you for that height and beauty of yours, especially when you refused to share it." Charles toyed with him lightly. "And now you are mine at last, sweet victory." He sighed and caressed his testicles lovingly, kissing them as if they were sacks of pure gold.

* * * *

In what he hoped appeared to be prayer, Richard raised his eyes through the stand of tall trees to the brilliant brightness above them. Secretly, he fingered the dagger he had slid out of his boot in his right hand. As Charles leaned forward to take him into his mouth, Richard gripped the knife in two hands and jammed it down into Charles' back.

* * * *

Charles was completely astonished. He was untouchable; able to get everything he desired with his money, his influence, his sexual favors and his power. Just when he thought he had gotten everything he dreamed of, even when this beautiful cock was being handed to him on a silver platter, it had ended. This man, the one who had been a bane of his will his entire career, had finally given in to him, dropped his breeches for him, been beaten down so far he was willing to reveal himself and be devoured and penetrated by him. But it was not to be.

Richard heaved the blade out of his back and readied for the next strike. He came crashing down again with all his brute force, and the thud and crunch of bone and lung echoed in the quiet. Once more, he unveiled the blade and raised it yet again. Richard waited, staring down at him as his blue uniform started to seep red.

Still suffering from the shock, Charles staggered back and collapsed onto the dirt. He stared up at this naked vision with its huge muscular arms raised to heaven, a small-bladed dagger dripping with his 'blue' blood. Helplessly, Charles held up his hand, as if staving off another blow.

Richard stared down at him with so much hatred, he was blind with it. Violently, he came down on him once again and penetrated Charles' chest with so much force he broke ribs. Richard stood again and waited, arms raised for another strike.

But it was unnecessary. Charles lay bleeding, totally stunned it had ended this way. He was to marry, inherit a fortune, gain wealth, title, flaunt Katherine around to his contemporaries. He wasn't supposed to lie dying in a farmer's field. Not murdered by this man! The man who he had made a mockery of his whole life. The man he had intended on getting hanged once he had his way with him.

* * * *

Richard watched as the snake closed his eyes and went into a death spasm. Lowering his arms gradually and staring down at him, he hung his head and tried to get his mind and body back under control. Bending over slowly, he tugged up his breeches, tucked the blade back into his boot, then knelt down to make sure the fiend was dead.

When he searched his pockets, he found a gold Spanish doubloon and was very surprised. He held it tight and took what he could to make it appear as if Charles were a victim of a robbery. Tossing his valuables and weapons into the woods, Richard stood over him and reached into his breeches. With complete disdain, he took himself out and urinated on his dead body. "Rot in hell, you maggot."

* * * *

Justin was biting his nails to the quick. The noon sun was high in the sky and he could not see a sign of his captain. He paced and groaned until Peckham was about to lock him in the hull.

At the moment when he thought he would go mad, he caught sight of naked bronze flesh approaching.

"Oh, thank heavens, thank heavens!" Justin wrung his hands in nervous agony. He and several other crew members stood by as the captain walked the gangway to the deck. Justin rushed him and wanted answers.

"Everything all right, Captain?" Peckham asked.

"Aye, Pilot." He walked right by him to his cabin, Justin at his heels.

When they were both inside the cabin, Justin stood there, arms crossed, tapping his foot. "Well? Sir?" he demanded.

"Leave it, lad." The captain collapsed onto the chair at his desk.

"Leave it? How can I? You went off with some man in uniform." He flailed his arms in exasperation.

Captain Jones peered up at him from under his long hair. "Not jealous again?"

"Oy? Jealous? Should I be?" Justin gaped in shock. That was one thing he wasn't. Worried, panicked, and terrified, yes. Jealous?

"No, no, you should not be." The captain's eyes were

vacant and hollow.

"There is blood on your hands." Justin moved closer and raised one up to inspect. "And on your breeches."

Appearing numb, Captain Jones studied Justin's reactions with what appeared to be idle curiosity.

"Have you killed someone, sir?" Justin whispered nervously.

"Get me some fresh water, Justin."

"Aye, Captain." Justin lowered his head.

"And a bottle of rum."

He nodded, frowning, and left to go down to the hull. Justin wondered what on earth was going on. As fast as he could, he brought a pitcher of water and a bottle of alcohol up from the storeroom. Coming through the door again, he found his captain staring off into space.

"Sir, you really need to slow down. You've been through some very bad things lately." He knelt beside him after setting the bottle and pitcher on the desk. Ignoring him, the captain opened the rum and guzzled it down.

Justin unbuckled his boot and slid it off. A bloody dagger fell out onto the floor. He stared down at it and then up at his captain. "Did you need to kill him, sir?"

"Yes, Justin."

Justin went for his other boot and almost expected another concealed weapon. He set them aside and leaned on the captain's lap. "You've blood on your breeches."

"I know, lad, you've said." His voice was patient and calm.

Trying not to shake from his anxiety, Justin filled a basin and dipped in a rag. He started scrubbing the captain's bloody hands. When he was done, he nudged the captain to stand so he could unfasten his breeches. Complying tiredly, the captain stepped out of them and dropped them to the floor before moving to find another pair out of his storage chest.

"Ah, sir."

"Yes, Justin."

"There is…ah, blood, on your…," he pointed.

The captain peeked down at himself and sighed. He stood before Justin patiently.

Justin rinsed the rag and washed him clean. "Can I ask?"

"No, lad."

Feeling defeated, Justin lowered his head and pushed out his lower lip.

Completely spent, Captain Jones dropped down heavily on the bunk, naked, and drank his rum.

Knowing his captain was going through so much chaos in his mind he couldn't think straight, Justin spied over at him and whispered, "Will you be all right, Captain?"

Hunched over his knees, the captain let out a long exhaled breath. Then he smiled and started to laugh sadly. "No, Justin, I don't think I will ever be all right again."

Seeing pain written all over him, Justin crawled across the floor and lay his head down on his bare legs. The captain stroked his hair softly as he finished the rum.

"Poor captain," Justin sighed. "I wish I could make you happy once again."

"It's all right, Justin," the captain breathed quietly. "Some things are just meant to be."

Raising his head off those warm thighs, Justin knelt up and pushed his way between them forcefully. After the captain had spread his legs, Justin reached around his waist and embraced him tightly. Captain Jones set the bottle down and returned the embrace, burrowing his nose into Justin's soft, long hair.

As they rocked together, Justin tried not to grow excited at the nakedness of this man and just allow him to rest, but in his mind, he kept imagining pleasuring him. Though he tried to prevent himself, he couldn't. Slowly, he moved his hand down between the captain's legs.

When the captain felt the contact, he flinched.

Getting a good grip on him, Justin worked the captain's cock until it was rock hard. Still embracing him, continuing to lean his head against his captain's chest, Justin heard his lover's breathing quicken, and then his gasping grunt as he came, sending ropes of cream in a fountain into the air.

Petting him lovingly, peering down at Justin as he did, the captain mumbled softly, "Thank you, lad."

"My pleasure, sir."

Chapter Thirteen

The next day, the September sun shone brightly, and the waterfront was awash with pedestrians and horses.

The crew repaired anything that needed tending, and the hull was loaded once again with fresh water, beer, tack, and as much food as they could store. Peckham viewed the activity in the port with interest until he found a lone female figure standing in the chaos. White gloves covered her dainty little hands, her peach-toned dress a light silk, ruffled at the sleeve and hem. Long, flowing, ginger hair was pinned up on her head, leaving a slender neck exposed. He sighed and bit his lip, knowing precisely who it was. The men did their best to ignore her and continued to get ready to sail. No one wanted to return to the rain-soaked cold of the British Isles again. The Caribbean coast was their new destination. And after the next loaded galleon, the warmth of Madagascar.

* * * *

Justin mopped the deck and noticed his pilot staring out at the land. Moving near to lean on him, he inquired, "Daydreaming, Pilot?"

"Nay, lad. Kath is there."

Stunned at the news, Justin dropped the mop and leaned hard against him. "Where? Point her out to me, Pilot."

"You merely have to look, lad."

Scanning the dock with sharp eyes, his vision stopped

on that peach-colored image of femininity. "Blimey!"

"Aye, lad, that's what our captain's dreams were made of."

"She's just standing there? Does he know?"

"Aye. She's been there since morn. He knows."

"What's he doing about it?"

"Naught."

Justin narrowed his eyes at her. The distance between them was about forty meters from where they stood on the main deck. "Why is she doing that, Pilot?"

"She has nothing else now. So, she stares at her beloved's ship until it leaves her forever."

Justin moaned at the pain of that reality. "Poor lass. I cannot imagine losing a man such as our Captain Jones."

"Aye, but you can, lad," he replied. "But you can."

With his youthful exuberance, Justin met his eye and returned his smile. "Yes. I can. But now he is mine again."

* * * *

The captain was in the hull counting barrels of stock with his cook. "Aye, Smithy, you have enough to get the men through?"

"Aye, Captain. We're bound to catch some fish as well, and turtles once we get nearer."

"And another galleon of plenty, with luck." The captain patted his back.

"Aye, sir." He smiled.

"Good man. You let me know if we're in need. Tonight we sail."

"Aye, sir."

The captain climbed through the main hatch to the deck and checked around for his boatswain. Another half-dozen men were lined up to replace the few that had left him in Portobello. Busy with other things, the captain had not met these men yet and wanted to discuss the next voyage with each of them and have them sign the articles as they came on account.

As he scanned around for them, he caught sight of that peach blur. Turning his face away abruptly, he continued his task. "Black!" he called.

"Aye, sir!" The boatswain hurried to meet him.

Rubbing his jaw tiredly, Captain Jones kept his back to the dock, losing his train of thought completely with the sight on land.

Patiently, Black waited before him. "Sir?"

Becoming lucid once more, Captain Jones raised his head instantly to meet his eye. "Where are the new crewmen?"

"I can round them up for ye immediately, sir."

"Good. Send them to my cabin."

"Aye, sir."

* * * *

Justin leaned on his mop as he watched that tall man's posture sink along with his heart. Furious, Justin turned to the shore and snarled at that woman. Why did she have to be there? Why did she have to rub it in? Twisting around to watch him, he waited until the captain vanished into his quarters, threw his mop down and stormed toward the dock. A hand on his shoulder held him back.

"Argh! Where ye off to, laddie?" Cromwell asked.

Justin fumed. "Why is she torturing him? I must tell her to go. He cannot abide her there. Someone must make her leave."

Cromwell held his arms and forced Justin to look into his face. "Nay. Don't involve yarself in that tangle. We'll shove off, and she will be a memory. Leave it, lad."

He bit his lip and spun around to sneer at her once more. "I hate her."

"Go and find Smithy. Enough swabbing for now." He

nudged Justin to get off the deck.

Justin huffed and pouted like a spoiled child, picking up his mop and heading into the hull. He found Smithy trying to kill rats. Unsheathing his cutlass, Justin chopped away at them violently, attempting to get rid of some of his pent-up rage.

* * * *

The ropes were dragged on deck. The anchor was raised. A crewman pushed back from the dock and leapt on board. The pilot guided *His Revenge* out to the wide-open sea.

Justin held the telescope in his hand and turned it to stern. He found that woman there, standing alone. He inspected her face and expected tears. No tears were there. Perhaps she had cried them dry. Thankfully, she grew smaller and smaller as they left. Curious to see what else he would leave behind, he continued to scan the docks, then caught sight of his mother. She was trying to find him on the remaining boats, too late.

Not feeling any remorse, for he cared not about his mother, he was very glad he did not have to face her whilst they were at port. *Goodbye, I am through with you forever.*

He beheld one last time the land where he was born, then thought he spotted some more men in blue uniforms snooping around. They had approached the captain's woman and were acting very strangely. "What does it matter now?" he mumbled to himself. Then he found his pilot and handed back the telescope. "Thank you, Pilot."

"You see what you had hoped?"

"Aye, more than enough. Me mum came a-looking finally, too late."

"Oh, sorry, Justin."

"No need. I'm not bothered." He shrugged. "I did see a strange sight though." Peckham urged him to continue.

"Men in uniform, the same uniform as that man the captain confronted. They seemed to be contacting that woman. The captain's wench."

"Oh?" Peckham grabbed Justin and made him search his eyes. "What did you see?"

"What?" Justin startled at his urgency. "Just the men in uniform. Like the one that dandy fellow wore. That's the Royal Navy uniform. Right?"

Taking off like a jackrabbit, he left Justin spinning in his wake. When Justin realized he had just sprinted off to inform the captain of the news, he tried to catch up to him.

When Justin got to that cabin, he heard the tail end of what he had just told the pilot. With his stomach in a knot, he studied the captain's reaction.

"Sir, we should go to her full eleven knots. We should take no chances."

Captain Jones set his pen down and raised his weary eyes to his pilot. He seemed so lifeless now. So spent. "They may be merely enquiring of her of his whereabouts," the captain sighed tiredly.

In reflex to try and comfort him, Justin moved towards him and climbed onto his large lap, laying his head on his shoulder. Lovingly, the captain kissed his hair.

"Maybe, Captain, maybe not." Peckham prodded, "Sir, please, in case the authorities have figured it out."

"Aye, Pilot. You do what you think is best."

"Thank you, Captain." He hurried out to advise the crew.

Justin nuzzled his captain and wrapped his arms around him. There was little, if any, response. After a moment, Justin set back to see his devastated face. "You will get over her. You will find happiness in a wonderful new home. One where you will be safe."

Biting his lip, appearing to hold back his emotions, the captain turned his face away.

Justin could not stand to see him in so much pain.

"Please," he begged. "Please forget her."

The captain tilted his chin aside from his light kisses. "Not now, lad. I have work to do."

Very reluctantly, Justin slid off his lap to stand, leaning against him. As he caressed that rough face with the back of his hand, Justin whispered, "Let me shave it for you. I know how intolerable it is for you when it grows."

Raising his light blue eyes to Justin, the captain answered, "Perhaps I shall let you. The way the boat lists, with hope, you will cut my throat."

"Captain!" he exclaimed. "Why do you say such things?" Justin panicked and reached out for him.

"Shove off, lad." The captain nudged him gently.

"I cannot stand this," Justin cried.

The captain stared at the maps, but Justin knew by the blank look on his face he was not really seeing the drawn ridges of land and seas.

Getting nowhere, Justin backed to the edge of the bunk and collapsed down onto it. Hanging his head, he sobbed to himself. As if the captain could not tolerate the sound of it, he rose up in irritation, and left him there alone. Justin assumed he was headed to the hull for another bottle of ale.

Justin was miserable. Nothing he did was right. Nothing he said made any difference.

Soon after, Peckham tapped the door lightly and called out to the captain. When he opened it, he found Justin in tears all by himself. Releasing a great, heaving sigh, Peckham sat next to him, putting his arm around his shoulder. "All right, lad. All right. Give him some time. Give him a chance to forget."

"He wants to die, Pilot," Justin sobbed.

"Nay, he is just hurt. The sight of a laden galleon's mast will cheer him up."

Justin tilted his head to see those light eyes. "Really,

Pilot?"

"Aye, lad. Come, let me show you how to read the sextant." Peckham rose up and held out his hand. Wiping his teary face with the back of his sleeve, Justin took it and followed him out.

Sensing someone's eyes on him, Justin turned his gaze from his lesson to a hungry leer. The replacement gunner for Will Davis was ogling him. Just as everyone had grown used to him, new shipmates appeared. Justin shivered, as the man hardly hid his attraction. Shaking off the effect, Justin gave his pilot back his attention and tried to ignore the intrusion.

After he completed his chores cleaning up the galley with Smithy, he headed to the cabin to rest for the night. On his way, he passed most of the crew moving in the opposite direction after getting their ale. Growling in rage when a hand got too friendly with him, Justin spun around and couldn't make out who it was in the line of bodies. Reluctantly, he continued on his way, now in a foul mood. With uncapped hatred, he pushed through the door angrily and surprised his captain, who had been writing in his log.

"Sorry, sir," he mumbled.

Getting over the scare, the captain lowered his eyes and continued to document their location. In a huff, Justin sat on the bunk and took off his boots and his shirt while staring at this man, completely disgusted with his attitude. He was sick of the captain moping about. Justin wanted it as it had been. Rising off the bed, he stepped carefully out of his breeches, approaching that impossible man with yet another effort at snapping him out of his mood.

* * * *

The captain tried to continue, but he knew Justin was standing naked next to him. Pausing in his train of thought, for he could not remember the next thing he wanted to record, he faced him and sighed, "Not now, Justin, lad."

Appearing stubborn and indignant, Justin would not budge.

Struggling to remember what he was about to document, the captain wrote one more word, then stopped. "Justin, look, I cannot—"

Like lightning, Justin grabbed the captain's hair in his right hand and twisted his face up to him. With unrestrained passion, Justin connected to his mouth and sucked at it hungrily. His eyes springing open in surprise, the captain held his quill suspended and tried to end the kiss tactfully. Squeezing Justin's arm gently, he attempted to move his face aside. "Justin, lad, just let me finish my task."

Ignoring him completely, Justin slid the pen out of his fingers and set it carefully down. Then like a worshiper before an altar, Justin settled to his knees and started to open the brass buttons of his captain's breeches.

Knowing he meant well, the captain sighed in irritation and glanced over at the half-done entry. He gasped in astonishment as a hot mouth found him. It was something he had never experienced before in his life.

Stretching out his long legs, spreading them wide, the captain watched Justin absolutely amazed. He had no idea where the lad had picked up this new trick. "Oh, Lord! Justin Taylor!" he exclaimed in awe as the lewd act brought him to the edge of orgasm instantly. "Ah!" Clenching his teeth, he grunted at the sensations that were too intense to contain. His flaccid cock became a hard rod as Justin sucked and drew on his length with hard, deep tugs.

Getting over the shock of the deed, the captain soon was overwhelmed with unbelievable pleasure. Unable to stop himself, he cupped Justin's head and began fucking his mouth. At Justin's zeal, and hearing the young man's whimpering moans, the captain's body responded. A thrill of lustful urgency washed over his skin. "Justin! Ah! My Justin!" The captain thrust harder and felt his entire length being consumed in a hot, wet, sucking hole.

The captain closed his eyes and came in a rushing blaze of fire, shocked and in total disbelief at how unbelievably powerful the climax was.

When he had recovered, he blinked and caught his gasping breath. "My Lord...Justin Taylor!"

* * * *

Success at last! Sitting back on his heels, Justin shivered and groaned in delight. He adored this man and would do anything to make him happy. Folding his arms over his chest proudly, he grinned at his accomplishment, waiting as the captain recuperated, gazing at his stunned expression with pure pleasure.

"How did you like that, Captain?" Justin giggled. "Something new we can do together?" He leaned over and sucked the tip of his captain's semi-erect cock lightly for his own pleasure.

"What a lad, what a lad," the captain groaned, his head tilted back, his eyes closed.

* * * *

With a load on his mind, Cromwell stepped into the cabin without a second thought. "Aye, Captain, sir," he mumbled under his breath as he considered the discussion he had planned. When he found a naked, fully aroused Justin on his knees in front of his captain--whose breeches were wide open, exposing himself--sucking on his cock, Cromwell rubbed his face in disbelief. "Argh! Methinks I have the worst timing on the ship!"

Hearing an unexpected voice inside the cabin, the captain sat up in panic and tried to tuck himself in whilst

Justin turned his face and body aside modestly. "I'm sorry, Jack...I...it..." the captain stammered miserably.

"Ne'er, ye mind, sir! Carry on! Carry on!" Cromwell left, shaking his head at that unbelievable sight. He headed to the storeroom to find some ale to get over the shock to his system.

Pilot Peckham caught his odd state. "Jack? You all right?"

"No! You don't want to hear this one, James!" He held up his hand in denial.

"Our captain and Justin? At it again?" Peckham laughed in amazement.

"An act such as that I ne'er witnessed before!" He kept moving to the hull, leaving a bewildered pilot behind.

* * * *

Captain Jones rubbed his face from the embarrassment. "Are you getting lessons from the whores, lad? Where the devil did you learn that trick?"

Justin caught the twinkle in his eye and was very relieved to see it. He purred, "As long as it pleased you."

"Pleased me? I'll be asking you to do it from now on! Now, get yer rump on that bed and let me finish my work." Laughing in delight, he pointed his finger.

"Aye, sir." Justin stood up and touched the captain's furry face first, kissing it. "Shave, sir."

"Aye, lad, I may find the strength soon." He tilted his head to the bunk and lifted his pen once more.

Justin sat on it and waited for him to finish, fingering himself whilst he stared at his captain.

Chapter 14

The next morning, Justin found someone else helping Smithy in the galley. Watching in surprise, he stood idly for something to do.

Smithy greeted him, "Ahoy, Justin. Ye no longer be the lowliest creature on board any longer, lad. The new recruits have ta climb up the ladder as well, all but the trained gunner."

Justin was stunned.

"Go report to our boatswain, my pretty."

"Aye, Smithy." He nodded and went on deck.

Peckham found him first and waved him over. Patiently, with Justin's full attention, Peckham went through reading a map and setting a course using the sun and stars as well as the bits of visible land, to guide them.

* * * *

After a decent night's rest and more of Justin's talented mouth and tongue, Captain Jones stared at his gaunt face in the mirror. Exhaling heavily, he raised a shaving razor to the dark growth on his jaw. Just as he started, he heard a rapping at his door and called, "Come in."

Cromwell took a good gaze around the cabin first before he entered.

And knowing exactly what he expected, the captain smiled to himself. "It's all right, Jack, I'm alone."

Sighing with relief, Cromwell stepped in and sat at

the desk watching the captain shave. "Good to see ye up and about."

"Aye, Jack. What have you got for me?" The captain went back to his shaving.

* * * *

Justin turned to glimpse over his shoulder when a very tall, clean-shaven man, with his chest bare and his hair pulled back in a ponytail, came on deck.

Peckham noticed he'd lost the lad's attention and checked to see why. "Ah! He looks much like his old self, my Justin."

"Aye, he does, Pilot." He sighed dreamily.

"He still may fall back on occasion, lad. Remember to give it time."

"Aye, time and rich loving, that is my recipe."

"Aye, lad! That'd work for me!"

Licking his lips seductively at the memory of their sex, Justin smiled sweetly at his lover before he returned his focus to the maps.

After the captain made his rounds, he stood behind Justin to look at what they were doing. "Pilot, you think our Justin will be able to guide us soon?"

"Aye, Captain, sir. He's a very quick learner."

In complete adoration, Justin beamed up at the handsome man, his cheeks warming at the very sight of him. The captain caressed Justin's face lovingly and then went back to his chores.

Reliving the night of bliss, Justin was set on fire as he thought about their contact. Unexpectedly, he noticed a few of the envious sneers of the new crew and looked away from them to stare out to sea.

Having caught the exchange, Peckham touched his back. "Not to worry, lad. No one will harm you again."

Trying to smile and find faith in that statement,

though he doubted it, Justin bit his lip and nodded.

* * * *

A few days out of the Cuban coast, Peckham spotted a mast from his perch aloft. Everyone stood on deck portside. Captain Jones climbed up and reached out for the telescope.

"Captain?" Peckham asked his opinion.

Black and Tucker stood shoulder to shoulder under their leader. When he lowered the telescope, the captain said, loud enough for them all to hear, "Spanish man o'war."

It was very silent. Justin tiptoed to his quartermaster. "What'd he say?"

"A war ship, lad. She may have up to one hundred forty-four cannon on her."

"Augh! Turn away! Turn away!" Justin panicked.

The captain climbed down and stood with his boatswain and quartermaster. They stared at the horizon as three masts appeared clearly.

"Ship of the line," Tucker said.

"Aye. She'll be laden," the captain whispered almost to himself.

"Maybe not," Black said. "Maybe just a war ship."

The captain's mouth appeared to water at the sight. "Nay, not just a war ship. Not coming out of the Caribbean. We can try and bluff her."

"Bluff her?" Justin moaned. "With one hundred cannons aimed at our broadside?"

When Peckham climbed down, he nudged Justin's shoulder to quiet him.

"She could have almost three hundred men on board, sir." Tucker never took his eyes from the war ship.

"Or she could have a skeleton crew," Captain Jones muttered softly.

"Are you mad?" Justin could not contain himself. Again, he felt his pilot's squeeze on his arm.

"We've fear on our side, lad," the captain said, "fear and the devil. She may give up."

"We can test her," Black suggested.

"Aye. We move just out of her range. She keeps her flag up, no test, in we go," the captain announced.

Justin geared up for another comment. But Peckham warned him, shaking his head.

"Raise the white jolly!"

"Aye, Captain!"

Justin craned his neck as the British flag came down and the white went up. "No...no...it's a death wish, no...no," he moaned.

"We can out maneuver her easily. She's large and sluggish. If she unloads her cannon, we'll retreat out of range." The captain eyed the enormous ship. To Justin, it seemed terrifying merely by virtue of its size and number of gun decks.

"Aye, Captain." Black ordered the men to man the sails.

"To the guns, lads! Load and ready!" the captain commanded.

"No...no...," Justin whined. "I am having a nightmare."

"Get my flintlocks, lad." The captain shoved Justin.

Obediently, Justin hurried to the cabin and trembled as he grabbed them, trying not to drop them. This time, there was no mate Will there to help. Maybe his ghost was laughing at the folly.

When Justin came back to his captain, he handed him all three guns with his baldric, then he spun around to see that menacing ship. The corvette looked like a dinghy in comparison. This was sheer madness.

"Pilot!"

"Aye, Captain!" He lowered the telescope.

"Where are her men?"

"On deck and with the cannons, sir!"

"Run a shot across the bow!"

"Aye, Captain!" Black shouted back.

Seconds later, Justin heard the sound of one of their own cannons booming. He gasped and spotted the ball as it splashed into the sea, sending up a plume of white spraying water. They were still too far away to reach the massive hull from where they were. It was a mere sign, that was all.

"Pilot?" the captain asked.

"Nothing yet, sir. She's still flying her colors!" He gazed through the telescope as he answered.

"Hoist the red jolly roger!" the captain thundered. "No quarter, lads!"

"Aye, Captain!" Black responded.

Intense terror had set in as Justin backed away instinctively. It was not possible to win this war. This was a suicide mission of a very distraught man. Surely, they would not live to see the next sunrise. They would be overrun, outnumbered, and outgunned. He would be cut up. Killed. Or even worse! Gang raped!

The sound of thunder reached Justin's ears. He peered up at the sky. It was crystal clear. Then the water churned with huge towering fountains. He choked in horror as he realized they were being shot at. "Oy! I knew it!"

"Bring her aft! Stern side!" the captain ordered.

The amount of shot was amazing. The blasts came one after another after another. The corvette rocked with the power of its own cannons and the churning of the waves. Ten guns on starboard side were spewing twelve-pounders in a barrage of explosions. Black smoke billowed up from the gunpowder as the red flames of the blasts lit up the deck. The sea was suddenly a bed of turmoil. Whitecaps of foam bubbled and spouted like a boiling, angry kettle.

At the tilting of the hull, Justin held onto the gunwale in fear. They were still just out of range. Neither cannon had reached its target. Searching through the running men, Justin spotted his captain standing mid-ship; his eyes were on fire like he was possessed. Making his way to him, Justin begged him to halt this madness. He grabbed his captain's arm and wrenched him around. "Stop! You will kill us all! And all this for a broken heart? It is foolhardy!"

At those mutinous words, the captain's fury uncorked. Shoving Justin back roughly, he ordered the men, "Closer to the stern of the beast!"

"Aye, Captain!"

The bow groaned as it rubbed the taffrail of the Spanish man o'war. The men scuttled up her with their boarding axes, around the thick netting. The sound of flintlocks blasted and white plumes rose. A rope was secured to one of her masts as the men from *His Revenge* boarded like ants over a hill. Justin followed this captain's suicidal lunacy as he climbed up onto the ship. When he stood on the deck of the battle rig, Justin was stunned. There was hardly any enemy on board. He could not believe it.

His crew hewed and severed everything in their way, mechanically making their path to each new level to clean out the inhabitants. How could there be so few on board? It didn't make sense to him.

Trying to find some inner strength, Justin had his cutlass raised and rushed behind his captain as he went wild, slashing and hacking at everything in his path, like he was rabid.

Justin stood behind him on the ship's quarterdeck. There were several enemy men still fighting, cornered, but unwilling to admit defeat.

Justin stared in horror at the sad, violent scene. One of the Spanish crewmen caught sight of his handsome captain. The hatred burned like death in his eyes. The

Spaniard wanted to take this English monarch with him to Hades. The Spanish sailor raised his pistol to aim it at the captain's exposed bronze chest.

Justin screamed in disbelief when he realized the captain was purposely letting down his guard. Captain Jones lowered his cutlass and pistol and widened his stance to receive the sorrow-ending bullet.

Justin lunged at his captain, pushing him out of the line of fire. The bullet grazed Justin's back, cutting a swath through his blouse. Flinching in agony, Justin shouted out in pain and then twisted back to the gunman just as Tucker cut him in half with his powerful stroke. When Justin's vision and hearing returned to him, he found his captain back on his feet leading the charge once more. Was he searching for another suicide attempt? Not allowing himself to think, Justin scrambled to his feet and hurried after him.

When they reached the hold, they found a ghastly prison. Men were lying everywhere, rotting in decay in the dank filth. The stench was so overpowering it felt like an impenetrable wall of noxious gases. The captain abruptly halted his crew and thundered for them to retreat, shoving and rushing them back from fear of disease. He made them get onto the deck and into fresh air, to avoid breathing that toxic atmosphere.

"Aye! Men! This is a boat of plague!" he roared for all to hear. "That is why she is so sparse of crew. Stay out of her hull and none of her food or water touch. Bottled wine and beer with unbroken seals, and her booty. Then get off her as fast as you can scuttle. Strip and throw your clothing overboard! That's a direct order!"

"Aye! Captain!" they shouted.

He waved to Tucker, who hurried to his side, and said, "See if she has a treasure, my friend, but cover your face, do not breathe her poisonous air."

Tucker removed the bandana from his head and

wrapped it around his nose and mouth.

"Good man." The captain nodded to him and allowed him to pass, then he walked up to the bow of the enormous ship and stared out at the horizon.

The pain in Justin's back began to grow and throb, and it only fed the infuriation he felt with his captain. That man had tried to get himself killed. They were very lucky most of this slave crew had died before they had met it. Now Justin wanted to get off the disease-ridden thing before one of them caught the plague and they became another dying group of sinners.

There was a load of treasure once again. The ship was heavy with it. And this time as well as gold and silver, they took porcelain made in Italy, fine wine casks, olive oil jars, salt holders, goblets and bowls, all colorfully adorned with yellows and blues painted on white backgrounds.

They set up a line and unloaded what they could safely. The corvette was laden as it was with most of their own store. Some enormous gilded sculptures they had to leave behind reluctantly. They pushed back from that colossal monster and left the sick and dying alone. They would not set fire to her. The whole feat left Justin in a foul, dark mood. Storming through the captain's cabin door, he found him alone, staring at his hands. He was covered in blood up to his elbows.

It deflated Justin's fury instantly. With a sigh, he poured some fresh water into a basin, approaching his captain and getting him out of his blood-soaked breeches. He took them and his own clothing and bundled them up into a pile. Quickly, he scooted out onto the deck, without a stitch on his frame, and tossed them overboard as the other crew members did the same. The ocean was speckled with fabric trailing in her wake. He hurried back to the cabin to tend his captain before the crew's hungry catcalls reached his ears.

It was as if Captain Jones could not see or perhaps he hardly felt the water cleansing his skin; the oatmeal soap washing his hair and face. Justin combed out his tresses for him, the water running from it in slow, lazy drops. Again Justin noticed very light, thin lines, as if from a whipping that may have occurred ages ago. Never once did he mention them to his captain. And never he would.

When he was through, Justin attempted to tend himself. As he washed up, he felt a stinging that was intense and painful. He tried to look over his shoulder, but could not glimpse the injury to his back.

The captain came out of his dream slowly and found Justin's cringe of pain. "Come here, lad." His voice was weak and exhausted. It was so faint Justin almost didn't hear it. He drew closer to him as the captain sat naked in his chair.

The captain turned him around gently. Justin's posture slouched from weariness, he waited for a moment that felt like hours long, then spied over his shoulder. He was stunned to see the captain's face running with tears. Yearning to hold him, Justin crawled onto his naked lap and held him tight. "I need you alive, please, don't have a death wish now. I cannot stand the thought of you perishing."

"It is because of me you have this wound." He tried to contain his sobs. "You almost got yourself killed because of me."

"Yes! I would die to keep you alive! Do you get it now? I need you alive!" Justin admonished in frustration, hoping to be heard and understood. He exhaled tiredly at the idea of yet another scar on his back. "It is nothing. I have endured many wounds, my Captain. Please don't bother about it."

"Yes, but wounds become infected here on board. We need to get you cleaned up and that liniment applied." He wiped his eyes and searched for a clean rag.

Justin smiled at him sweetly. "A liniment rub. Yes, that would be delightful."

The captain caught Justin's impish grin and could not help but smile. He embraced Justin warmly, then nudged him off his lap. Finding clean breeches and sliding them on, he said, "Let me get some for you, lad."

"Thank you, my Captain."

* * * *

After giving him an affectionate wink, the captain went on deck and met with his quartermaster and first mate before searching for the doctor. He made sure the crew stripped their clothing, no exceptions, and ordered these two men to see that it was done immediately. They nodded and made the rounds once more to stand by as each man obeyed. Most did without hesitation, fearing the threat of a slow, painful death by plague.

When he returned, he found Justin had bathed himself as best he could and was lying face down, naked on the bunk. The captain brought over the pitcher of fresh water and soaked a clean cloth with it. He dabbed it over the burn and then patted it dry. Justin moaned as the salve cooled his angry skin.

The band of merry sailors came into the cabin to share the victory, each with a bottle. They appeared better for the change of clothing. Some had clean reserves but just never bothered to change into them. They found their captain medicating the lad and took a seat to talk of their luck and share a toast.

Cromwell smiled at the sight he was once again enjoying. "Aye, Captain, methinks I'm getting used to ye and the lad. And ye be used to me intrusions!"

"Aye, Jack. I think Justin and I have finally gotten over the shyness." He smiled sweetly at him while he massaged the liniment over his tight rump in a playful tease.

Justin turned his head to face the room of men. "He speaks for himself!"

They all roared with laughter as the captain spanked Justin's naked bottom playfully and told him, "Find a pair of breeches, lad."

Rising off the bunk to allow Justin to get his things, the captain sat down on his chair and thanked his boatswain for the wine. "How many men did we lose, Thomas?"

"Five, sir."

"Who?"

After he changed into clean clothing, Justin buttoned his breeches and sat on the floor near his captain's feet to lean against his legs.

"Samuel Stone and Francis McCoy, two of yer gunners. Then three we picked up at port. They were green, sir, and too quick to move in."

The captain was handed a bottle of rum as he thought about the loss.

"I reckon we be riding high on lady luck with that empty ship," Tucker muttered as rum dribbled down his beard.

"I'll drink to that!" Peckham raised his bottle.

Captain Jones lowered his eyes. "I must apologize, men. I took a big chance with your lives." When Justin's soft hair brushed against his knee as he leaned on him, the captain caressed him lovingly.

"Argh!" his first mate grunted, "What else do these scurvy dogs have to do?"

"Thank you, Jack." The captain smiled at him for the supporting words.

"Naught one of us would have had the devil to do it." Black wiped his lip.

"No? Not a one? Am I the only one mad enough?" The captain winked at Justin as he tilted up to see his face.

"Ye ne'er used to be!" Cromwell scoffed. "Me thinks retiring is last on yer mind now!"

As if he thought the words would upset him, reminding him of his shattered dreams, Justin leaned across his captain's lap and tried to squeeze him close.

"Aye, Jack, last on me mind." He stroked Justin's hair and face gently.

"What do you think about the plague on board?" Peckham sat up and combed his fingers through his blond hair. His skin was bright red as if he had scrubbed himself raw at the fear of infection.

They all waited quietly until the captain spoke up. "I don't think we need worry. But if so, within a week we'll have sickness."

Justin shivered and gripped the captain's thighs tighter. Feeling his fright, the captain touched his hair lovingly to calm him.

"No one et a thing, no one touched naught," Tucker announced, "And ye turned us back before we shared the air with that lot, Richard. We rid the clothes, cleaned up. I think we did more than most scurvy dogs."

"Let's hope so, John." The captain reached out for the offered bottle.

Suddenly, they heard a terrible, painful screaming. They all paused until it died out. Not knowing why someone was in agony, Justin raised his head off the captain's lap and gazed at him in fright. Mechanically, the captain checked with his boatswain for the explanation.

"Argh, that'd be Thomas Moore, sir. He suffered a wound on his leg."

The captain nodded. "Right or left?"

Black thought first, then answered, "Right, sir."

"See to it he gets his extra five hundred pieces of eight."

"Aye, Captain."

After cringing with disgust, Justin asked, "You get

paid for losing your limbs?"

A rumbling laughter surrounded him.

Captain Jones dug his fingers through Justin's long, damp locks. "Nay, not quite like that, lad. It's compensation."

Laying his cheek back on the captain's legs, Justin shuddered. "Aye, nothing could compensate me."

"If ye had to sacrifice a piece of yarself, laddie, ye'd be singing a different tune!" Cromwell informed him, waving his rum bottle at him.

As if the very thought horrified him, Justin quivered with a chill. The captain rubbed his back softly, avoiding the line of liniment over the burn. "Are you cold, lad?"

"Nay, Captain, just shivering me timbers of the idea of the doc chopping at me bones."

Another ring of laughter surrounded him.

"Ye keep out of harm's way, lad," Tucker warned him.

"Oy! Tell him that!" Justin pointed an accusing finger at his captain.

The captain was embarrassed by it and lowered his head. "I need go see Thomas Moore and offer what comfort I can." Wanting to escape, he tapped Justin and was allowed to stand.

* * * *

Yearning for him to come back, so they could lean against each other again, Justin watched him leave the cabin and sighed sadly. When he felt a light caress on his shoulder, he raised his long lashes to his pilot.

"You all right, lad?"

"Nay, Pilot. I am not."

The other men took an interest and leaned forward. Justin met their curious eyes. "My captain tried to take a bullet whilst on board that man o'war. Our quartermaster,

Tucker, blew the man down after he unloaded his flintlock at the captain's chest."

The quartermaster lowered his eyes sadly. It was obviously no surprise to the men. Peckham smiled gently at Justin. "Aye, lad. We knew his whole mission was one of suicide."

"And you allowed it? You followed him?" he gasped in fury.

"Ye would rather see a mutiny?" Cromwell replied.

"No!" Justin shouted but was terribly confused.

"Lad." Peckham tried to calm him down. "We go to battle this way. This is what we do. Everyone was with the captain in his choice. Believe me, Justin. We would not have left the Spanish ship unchallenged."

"But!" He sat up and tried to explain that they would eventually lose. They could not keep it up against the odds. The ships were getting larger and carrying more men, that they were lucky this time because half the crew had died of disease.

His gaze made the round of worn, battle-scarred faces. He knew they would continue to fight and challenge enemy ships. It's what they did. Only his captain had dreams of leaving it all behind for a life of calm and peace. And that had ended in a shattered mess. What was there now? Madagascar?

He sighed. "Ne'er mind."

* * * *

Avoiding Justin's recount of his suicidal tale, Captain Jones strut across the main deck to the fo'c's'le. He met with several tired men and tried to thank them as best as he could. Making his way to the doctor's tiny room, he found him burning the stump of Thomas Moore's leg at the knee with a hot iron. There were men holding him down and giving him strong rum. He was white, covered in sweat, and near passing out. The smell of burning skin was sickening.

The captain knelt down by him and held his hand. Thomas barely opened an eye.

"You'll be all right, Thomas; this is the worst of it." He combed back his sweat-soaked hair from his face. "Five hundred pieces of eight for you, mate. You dream of spending her."

Captain Jones caught a very slight nod, and it seemed as if Thomas lost consciousness from the shock. The captain stood and touched all the men who were around him to thank them for supporting the wounded man while he underwent this painful surgery.

Making his way back out, he ducked into the crew's cabin. The gunners were seated in silence with their bottles. The captain sat down among them and gave them his condolences, "Sorry, mates, that you had to lose two of the best gunners on the open seas."

They wiped their red eyes. "Thank you, Captain."

"All remaining gunners will get another quarter share in the booty. I'll see to it Tucker is advised."

"Aye, thank ye, Captain, sir." Henry grabbed his hand.

"Nay, Henry. Do not thank me. It is you men who made the day."

When he finally made his way back to the cabin, only Peckham was left to keep Justin company. Standing when his captain returned, Peckham smiled gently into his face. "I'll leave you be, sir."

With a gentle hand, the captain stopped him. "Set sail for the coast of Africa."

"Aye, Captain, I take it you mean around the Horn."

"Aye, Pilot."

He nodded and closed the door behind him.

* * * *

Shaking his head, Justin exhaled tiredly at the sight of that man who was now dragging himself around, he was so exhausted. "My Captain," he sighed. "Come to bed."

"Aye, Justin. I just can't even see my way there."

Justin climbed off the bunk and helped him with his boots and breeches. He led him to the bed and crawled in beside him, leaning up next to him to stare at his noble profile in the dimness. Wondering what thoughts were going on in his mind, Justin rested against him and listened to the beat of his heart.

After a long moment, Justin found he could not sleep. Moving to lie on his stomach, he noticed the captain's eyes were open as well. He kissed his cheek and asked, "Why do you not rest?"

"I cannot, lad. Too much on me mind."

"Talk to me." He smoothed the captain's dark hair back from his face.

The captain let out a long exhaled breath. "I've ne'er been very good at talking about my feelings, Justin. It was one of Kath's complaints."

"Is it her then? Why you cannot sleep?"

"Aye."

Justin sat up and found the captain's arm in the darkness. He lifted it to his chest and ran his hand down its length. "You miss her?"

"Aye."

"Even after what she did to you?"

"You don't see it, lad, 'tis what I did to her. I left her again though I promised her otherwise. I didn't want this life asea for a lifetime. I wanted to be done with it. Done with the blood on my hands. I'm a simple man, Justin. I only wanted a farm and a son."

"Can you get that in Madagascar?"

"Aye, I will try. But with a native girl, lad. Not my lovely princess."

"Then, it is really the same. You will leave us again. I mean, leave me again."

The captain gently took his arm back and rolled to his side to face him. "Justin, you talk to me as if we are like a couple. How can I settle down with you and have a family? You know this isn't possible."

Biting his lip in pain, Justin was trying not to get upset. "Then... then, what do I mean to you? You...you wrote that you loved me...in your log."

"I do love you, Justin. But it is not the same kind of love. Not the love I would have for a wife." He reached out and caressed his soft cheek.

"Then you used me? You used me to keep you sexually sound?"

"Nay, lad. You know as I that was never the reason. And let's not forget to mention, 'twas you, lad, that seduced me."

Justin remembered. Yes, it had been he that started this whole relationship. He had no reason to complain. It had been heaven on the sea.

"Justin, we each find our own way in this world. Our paths have crossed and I am glad to have met and fought with you. But inevitably, we go our own way. It has to be this way, lad. Do you see?"

"You are through. Through with life as a pirate and with me." A tear rolled down Justin's cheek.

"Not like the way you say. Tired of this life, aye, I am. I wanted that bullet in my heart. I won't deny it. I am too weary to start again with another woman. A woman I cannot cherish, one who will not speak my language, one with strange ways and customs. But I have no choice. Charles Collins' death may have stirred the authorities in England. You have seen them speaking with Katherine on the dock. Possibly, they were just there to inform her of his passing. More likely, it was to question her. And what will she do in her grief? Will she reveal her secret to them?

Tell them it was I? I do not want to hang, lad. The bullet would have been quicker and more my liking."

Justin ground his teeth. "Argh! Stop! Stop this self-pity talk. I cannot abide it. You are still a free man. They will never find you."

"Justin. Lad." The captain reached out to quiet him. "You are so young. What? Seventeen?"

Breathing fire, Justin panted in his frustration. Why could he not change anything? Why was he so powerless? He sighed and answered him. "Eighteen last July, sir."

"Eighteen then. You have it all ahead. This is not a lifelong career, lad. Many of us die very quickly. You look around you, all the crew are only in their twenties. Just a few are in their thirties. We play heartily, and die off. We are a scourge to mankind, lad. We are no heroes. We are villains, thieves, ruffians. Deserving of the hempen halter." The captain paused as if to gain his thoughts before he continued. "So very many before us have been caught and publicly hanged, lad. I don't choose to die that way. So, the coast of Madagascar I go. There I will live out my days. You cannot think of coming with me. No. You will go mad there. You need more under your belt first, lad. Then, if you live, you too will yearn to settle and get away from this life."

Justin's lip was quivering, as tears were rolling down his cheeks. "How will I live without you?"

"You simply shall. Soon I will pass to a memory and with luck, a legend to tell." His eyes twinkled with his smile.

As his heart ripped open, Justin wrapped around him in the pitch dark and cried against his chest.

"Do not be sad, Justin. It is the way of things. I am just glad I had the honor of loving you. Without you, I surely would have gone mad. You have saved my life in many ways. I will never forget you for that. I owe you so much, Justin. More than mere doubloons can ever pay."

It was of no consolation. Justin sobbed from his very soul. This was his best friend, his lover, his truest companion. He knew there would be no replacement for him in this lifetime. "I will come to you. When I am older and ready to leave this behind, I will find you. And we will be together as we were meant to be."

The captain laughed softly. "Fine, lad. Fine. If and when that day comes, I shall be there with open arms."

Chapter Fifteen

Too soon for Justin's liking, Peckham announced they had come to the east coast of the great red island. The port was overloaded with pirate ships; English, French, Portuguese, all based there to attack the merchant ships that were rounding the Cape of Good Hope.

In his last act as captain, Richard Jones ordered his men to drop sail and anchor. The place had a lush, tropical feel to it and smelled fresh and wholesome. Soon it would be home to Richard Cornell Jones, retired seaman.

Unwilling to admit this was the end, Justin held him one last time in his arms. He raised his light eyes to that handsome face and whispered to him, "I will never love another soul the way I love you. I will come to you again one day. This I promise."

His captain could only smile adoringly, as if he could not say a word from the pain in his heart at their parting. Perhaps he wondered how life would be without his Justin to hold in the night. Surely, it would be misery. Justin knew it would be for him.

"I love you, Justin, with all my heart. But I cannot ask you to come live with me yet, lad. You need to grow up on your own first. Yet I know what the pain of separation will be like for the both of us."

With a mixture of pride and sorrow, Justin watched him go. He was very glad he had stowed away on *His Revenge* and had the luck of meeting the finest man he knew existed. Gazing over at that tall, muscular body and strikingly handsome face, he tried to sear it into his memory forever.

The captain had his kit on his back and his treasure of gold in his arms. Taking one last look over his shoulder, he caught the tears flowing from Justin's eyes. He smiled sadly at him before raised his chin to his future home, deciding on which path to take.

Epilogue

When they first set sail that fateful day from Madagascar and away from his Captain Jones, Pilot Peckham approached him to comfort him. And as if Peckham were a mother hushing her son, Justin held onto him tightly and cried like a babe.

The pilot kissed his hair. "You are welcome to share my bunk now, sweet Justin."

Justin raised his eyes to his and informed his fair pilot, "Solely to sleep, nothing more."

His pilot understood.

So, it was agreed. Though Peckham tried to seduce him, he could never succeed. Instead, in the dark of night, they would talk about that legend of a man they both missed dearly. Justin shed a sea of tears over him and felt his heart was so damaged it would never recover.

As the years passed by, the crashing of the waves was the only thing ageless and eternal. Many had perished and more had come aboard, as the crew was renewed and recycled. Soon *His Revenge* had a shipload of fresh faces, all wild young men out to find fortune and fame in a culture that was fast becoming out of fashion.

Justin had seen many things in the last five years. He had been learning and absorbing everything he could, like a student at university. An expert seamen, he knew how to set a course and sail guided by the stars. One of the best pilots on the ocean waves, though he would blush modestly when accused of that fact, he could sense a squall approaching, smell that scent and feel that cold wind, never letting one of those killer storms come again without warning. Developing sharp eyes and ears, he could spot a mast as it first broke the horizon. With the experience of a seasoned seadog, he was fast becoming irreplaceable to his crew. He honed his skill with the cutlass and flintlock until he no longer paled at the idea of battle. Growing taller, five feet ten inches, and filling out his lithe frame with his daily work of climbing the ratlines and mock fighting with his crewmates to keep proficient with the cutlass, he was both muscular and strong.

His face he kept clean-shaven, his hair, long and always scrubbed. At times, he had knelt at the side of dying men and killed a few in duels on land, but at others, he had become frighteningly intimidating and had no idea of the effect his stern, angry gaze had on his fellow pirates. He was brooding and preoccupied, never smiled, never laughed. He had become a man without a soul. Long ago, his had died when the love of his life left to find his happiness elsewhere. What had he to fear? He'd been to hell. It didn't scare him anymore.

When he was finally voted captain of his own ship, his chest swelled in pride. He modeled himself after his hero, and in his mind, he imagined over and over again that he was Captain Richard Jones when it came time to make a decision. "What would my beloved do?" he would ask himself. It was how he made all of his choices, and he made them wisely.

He never touched another soul the way he touched that man. The whores he ignored, the invitations from the men on board he avoided. No more did a hand dare to caress him uninvited. Justin would have cut it off in fury. He was no longer the weak young lad to be taken advantage of and his temper would boil quickly with any violation to his person. Those days were gone. Justin had experienced enough exploitation in his past to last a lifetime. Never again would he withstand a forced advance or a groping paw.

His wealth was assured, for he mastered the broadside and counted his luck as well as his doubloons. He had a cache of booty, for he spent hardly a silver piece of eight at any port. Simply he had his bath and meal, and a new suit of clothing. That was enough. His mind was of his future and of never working again. A wise man had followed that path. He intended to as well. Insisting no quarter be given his foes, he knew no one knew his name.

Hating the enemies of England and gladly murdering any in cold blood, he was awarded a letter of marque from the government and felt the protection of international law. It was the reassurance they needed to port at Mount's Bay without a worry. That was what a hefty payoff of gold had bought him. Once again, lessons learned by his mentor had saved him dearly.

It didn't take long before he felt it was time to quit this life of filth and blood. He was twenty-three, and the weight on his shoulders made him feel years older. Knowing he was growing wretched and vile inside like a decaying spirit, for it was the murdering, the company he kept, and the hollowness of his heart that rotted him. He'd had enough. Enough of this misery, the hardship, the violence, the stinking reek of the bilge, and the eternal scratching and stench of his crew. In complete frustration, he couldn't face another year at sea. He would rather die. He was empty enough as it was without a partner to share his life with. Why continue this career whilst his pockets are bulging full? Only one thing was on his mind. One handsome, six-foot, four-inch thing.

As he stared out at the mass of land approaching, it was with anxiety and yearning, but most of all hope. He had something he needed to do. A promise he had made to himself and to one he loved most in the world. A love that did not fade, but seemed to become enlarged and more intensified over time. No matter how he tried to extinguish it, he could not ignore the erotic craving in his loins.

But, what if? What if he found his beloved and was shunned? What if he had married and didn't want anything more to do with his ex-lover? These were the questions burning in Justin's mind. He knew he could face devastating rejection yet again. But he just had to lay eyes on that man once more in this lifetime. If he was rejected by him, so be it. And that was only if he could find him. He was wondering on the odds of even that.

The wind stinging his eyes, he stood at the bow at many a sunset reliving his kindness, his heroics, and most of all, his loving caress. Who could replace that for him? No cabin boy, no crewmate. No one. He dared not look for a substitute. It would only disappoint him.

An ironic smile spread over his mouth when he thought of how often men had tried to bed him. Late one evening, on open seas, after a broadside and some rum, his cabin door opened. One of his handsome crew members was smiling in just the right way, gesturing to himself at how exciting the idea was to touch his captain, to serve him.

"George? Again you try?" Justin laughed, pausing as he wrote in his log.

"I shall try, me captain, until you allow me to show you what a night it will be!" He closed the cabin door behind him, and strutted over like a gamecock.

"Aye, matey, though it is mighty flattering, I must refuse." Setting down his pen, Justin gave his gunner his complete attention.

"Why, Captain? Why do you stand alone, no whore, no companion? The men, they tell me ye have no lady awaiting on England's shores. How starved for contact you must be." He caressed Justin's long hair.

Closing his eyes, imagining a different man's touch, Justin groaned softly.

Moving closer, George stood before him, cupping his

face in both hands. "Ye celibacy is fer naught. So much beauty in ye, I cannot stay me lips." Kissing Justin's mouth gently, he set back to see if there was a reaction.

And though this man was incredible-looking, clean and polished, Justin could not seem to motivate himself. "It is no use, my pretty."

"Talk is that you've gone impotent. But I see that's not so." He caressed the mound between Justin's legs.

"Nay. Hardly." Justin laughed sadly at the never-ending spate of rumors about his love life.

"Come. Come to the bunk with your matey." Coaxing him up from his chair, George drew him to the bed.

Images were flashing through Justin's mind like cannon blasts, his lover naked on the bunk asking him to assume the position, liniment rubs turning into sexual bouts, and holding that hot flesh next to his as he slept.

George moved slowly. "Ye lay back and let me do you proud."

Resting with his eyes closed, Justin tried to imagine another time and place. His hair was caressed gently, his blouse opened slowly.

Peeling back his white britches, George took him out gently and admired him. "Lovely—yer a lovely thing to behold, Captain. Such a shame we could not have made the effort when I first met ye three years ago."

About to shove him back in irritation, Justin knew this would only disappoint in the end. As if feeling that hesitation pending, George made for his lips and kissed him passionately while he gripped his cock.

It was too much. Justin pushed him away and cried, "No!"

Rejected and scorned in a painful way, George closed his mouth on his pleading and sat on the floor near him, trying to touch him in comfort.

As his emotions overwhelmed him, Justin covered his face and sobbed miserably. "Please! I know you mean well. But—leave me. God. Please. Leave me be."

Struggling to speak, George managed to say, "Whosoever he was—this lover of yers, he had better be worth all this torture, Captain."

Hiding his face and curling his knees up into a fetal position, Justin cried deep, heaving sobs.

"Aye, I'll leave ye then, sir." Hearing the door close and the silence that followed, Justin tried to stop crying. But it was obviously useless. No one would touch him that way again.

* * * *

His crew shouted out that they were closing in on the dock. Justin came on deck after writing his thoughts in his log book and felt his heart quicken at the sight. After ordering the sails lowered, the anchor was tossed overboard.

The day had come. He was finally on the shores of Madagascar. How would he even begin to find him? Was he alive or dead?

The gangplank was lowered, and as Justin stepped onto it, his crew watched with troubled expressions. Justin knew they loved their captain and didn't want to lose him. Not yet. Not whilst he was still so young and capable.

"Ye be coming back to us, Captain?" his quartermaster enquired.

"Aye, Jason! You wait for me. I'll come back either way. Meanwhile, you get her stores filled and clean her bilge of water." He waited for his nod, then waved to them.

Trying to find some hidden strength, Justin fingered the three flintlocks in his baldric and the cutlass on his hip, carrying a dagger in his boot as well, taught to him by a very savvy captain. He was prepared for anything, be it a fight, or a helping hand. Making his way to an inn at Ile

Sainte Marie, he spied the landlord. "Do you speak English?" Justin asked.

He shook his head and pointed to another man. Justin approached and addressed the stranger, standing before him, feeling proud and brave in his clean frock and white breeches. "Do you speak English, mate?"

The man nodded and waited to see what he wanted.

"I am looking for an Englishman. Richard Jones. Have you heard of him by any chance?"

Rubbing his bearded jaw, the man searched over the crowd, then he shouted out in Malagasy the question he was asked, repeating it in English.

Justin braced himself and eyed the mob, his hand on the hilt of his sword. After a moment, someone waved in acknowledgement.

Justin's heart pumped in excitement. He tried to keep still as the man made his way across the smoky room. Trying to read his face, Justin inspected him carefully. By his appearance, he expected him to be French or English. He had a fair complexion and dressed as a European would dress, in mismatched attire with filth on his skin.

"Aye, who's looking fer me mate, Richard Jones?"

Justin was about to explode with joy. "A fellow Englishman! My luck is riding high."

The Englishman thanked the interpreter and took Justin aside from the prying ears and eyes. "Who be ye then?"

"I'm Justin Taylor, Captain of *His Revenge*. I need to see Richard. Please, can you take me to him?"

"Ye a friend or foe? I won't be bringing someone who's got a score to settle." He narrowed his eyes at Justin. "The man just wants to live in peace."

"Aye, that I know. I am a friend. A very good friend. I assure you." Justin reached into his pocket and handed him a golden doubloon. The man's eyes widened at the sight. Justin could see he was not yet convinced. "Look, you take me part way. Then you tell Richard I am here. Will you do that, me matey? There is one more doubloon for you if you do."

The man considered Justin's offer, eyeing his clean expensive clothing with the baldric loaded with a trio of pistols. "Aye, fair enough."

Justin couldn't move fast enough. He was trying to keep behind this sluggish fellow and not shove him to hurry up. It seemed island tempo was a bit slower than the pace he had been used to on his ship.

"Ye wait here."

"Yes, I will. Please hurry." Justin wrung his hands nervously.

He received another slant-eyed stare as the man sauntered off. Justin waited, tapping his foot, biting his lip, and wondered what he would see when he finally laid eyes on him again. It was only five years. What would he look like? Had he found a woman to settle with? Had he any children? What would they say to one another? Had he been missed? He was in agony with too many thoughts on his mind and no answers. Hopefully, all his answers were just moments away.

An image flashed upon him of kneeling before his lover, smoothing his hands up those enormous thighs and opening those brass buttons of his breeches. Like a rush of orgasmic sensation, he remembered the day he had taken him into his mouth for the first time. Uncontrollably, Justin moaned to himself. What he would give to kneel before him again. Every coin he owned and more.

What felt like an eternity had passed. Justin started to wonder whether this was some kind of set up. Touching his pistol, he kept alert to his surroundings. With a few golden coins in his pockets, he would be an easy target for an ambush. Swallowing his nerves, he tried to prepare himself for a fight if it came to that. Would it be his luck that this man knew nothing of his lover and was bringing his mates along for a mugging? Justin grew more nervous with these new suspicions in his head. He wondered how he would deal with a fight of more than three foes.

When something caught his eye, he raised his head and found the Englishman rounding the bend alone. He was horribly disappointed, yet relieved to see he wasn't betrayed. In defeat, Justin sighed sadly.

Then, after a moment, another man emerged from the trees. When they met astonished eyes, Richard beckoned to him with outstretched arms. Justin handed the Englishman his promised coin and shoved past him without taking his gaze off that vision. The Englishman made a sound of disgust at their embrace before he left them alone.

Tears ran down Justin's cheeks as he took in that image before him for the first time in what felt like a lifetime. "Oh, blimey! Look at you!" Justin cried.

* * * *

Richard was stunned; Justin had not only found him, but had returned as he had promised. Richard had done nothing else but think of him. Not a day would pass when he wouldn't remember their closeness, their passion.

When the Englishman had initially contacted him, Richard was seated in his courtyard, enjoying the cool breeze. After the man had explained that there was a tall, handsome captain of a ship asking about him, he rose up in excitement and asked who it was. That name shot through him with so much pleasure he thought he might faint. Racing to meet Justin, Richard had expected an eighteen-year-old lad. He was overwhelmed at this tall, twenty-three-year-old man.

* * * *

Their embrace felt so familiar, so satisfying, that neither could let go. Justin rocked in his arms, inhaling his scent, loving the surges it brought to his loins and the flames it ignited in his chest. Choking with his emotions, he said, "My God! I am touching you again!" Then he ran his hands into Richard's long, thick, dark hair and down his neck to his shoulders and arms. He yearned to whisper in his ear that he had touched no other since.

Richard set back to stare into his face. "Justin, you are a fine man."

Smiling in pure pleasure, Justin responded, "And you are so beautiful, my Captain. You have not changed." That wonderful square jaw was still clean-shaven. He was slender and fit, with a tropical tan.

"No? Oh, I am getting gray, my pretty." He pointed to his temples and smiled. "Come, let me take you to my home." Wrapping his arm around his waist, they moved down the packed red clay lanes in excitement.

The sounds were so strange to Justin's ears. The birdcalls were exotic and unfamiliar, the flora and fauna were like nothing he had ever seen. They were both quiet during their stroll, just content to be in physical contact with each other. Justin was completely overwhelmed that he was once again in his company. It was as if he were floating above the clouds in a dream. In some odd way, Justin started to wonder if perhaps he was really lying in his bunk and soon he would be awakened for the sight of a mast on the horizon.

When Justin was brought up to a front garden with a long, white pavement leading to a grand front entranceway, he gasped in amazement, whispering, "Blimey!"

Richard opened the door of his stately home.

"What a lovely place." Justin craned his neck at the high ceilings and light, bright windows.

"Yes, it is amazing what Spanish gold will buy out

here." He winked. "So, tell me, what has passed? Are you still in the same line of work?" Richard asked excitedly. "What happened to our crew?"

"Aye, sir, still in the business, but with a letter of marque. Yet, like you, I am growing weary of it. And of the tale of our crew, it will take time to tell you what has happened to them all."

"We have time. Are you not staying?" He reached out for Justin's hand, and Justin caught his affectionate smile.

Justin nodded shyly. "I have some time." He was brought over to a settee and sat down on it, his hand still being held tightly.

"Yes, it is a very hard life, Justin. One most of us die of. If the hangman does not get you, then surely the storms or disease will. Will you leave it then? Are you truly fed up with it, Justin?" Richard studied Justin closely.

Justin considered the motive for the question carefully. The only thing keeping him at sea at the moment was the lack of belonging anywhere else. On *His Revenge* he was needed, wanted, and adored. Where else could he find those essential emotions? He had cut ties with the world.

"Justin?" Richard tilted his head as Justin struggled to find a way to answer that impossible question. "What is it? What more do you want from the sea?"

"From the sea?" Justin was confused. "I want nothing more of it. Even now, the rocking from it, though I am sitting still, sickens me. Though I no longer topple over." He smiled.

"Then you are ready to give it all up? Truly?"

Almost rising and throwing up his hands in frustration, Justin didn't know what answer Richard wanted to hear. When Richard grabbed his arm to stop him from that gesture, Justin exhaled a deep breath and said, "What am I to do? I am not wanted back in England, nor do I crave her damp shores. I have no lady in waiting—no yearning for a wife and sons. I am a bastard son. I wander where I feel I can be of some use."

Cupping Justin's callused hands in his, Richard drew him closer to speak quietly. "Am I getting this straight?" Richard whispered, "You don't want to go to England, and you do not want a wife."

"Yes." Justin nodded, still trying to determine the significance of this conversation and why expressing his pathetic state was of so much interest.

"And—sweet lover—you do not long the sea and the treasures any longer?" He tightened his grip on Justin's hands.

Pausing, trying to read that expression and failing, Justin shook his head. "I've more than enough treasure."

Richard's face lit up. He moved to lean against Justin's length, his hand squeezing Justin's tightly. "Then, will you consider staying here?"

Justin felt his skin prickle at the sensuousness of his tone. "I...I...," he mumbled, shaking his head again. Unsure what kind of invitation it was. He knew what he was hoping for. Did the captain mean stay for the night? A week holiday? Or a lifetime? "I...I do not understand." Justin tried to clarify.

"Are you ready to settle down?" Richard asked seriously.

Blushing shyly and lowering his gaze, Justin replied, "My Captain, you know I have had enough of the sea and the battles."

"And on board—" Richard whispered. "Have you a new man to share with?"

In what was akin to rage, Justin met his eyes quickly and growled, "I've no other. I've touched no one since we parted."

Letting that comment sink in first, Richard gazed at him in astonishment. "Justin! No other? How could this be? It is five years."

"Do not remind me!" Justin growled. In anger, he cupped Richard's face and whispered, "I tried. Of course I did. I was not without my admirers, Captain. The boys, they came to me, offered their kindness. But they left me cold, my love. How—" he stopped his lip from trembling before he continued, "How, sweet blessed virgin, was I to touch another after you?"

"Oh, Lord," Richard gasped.

"But I am a fool." Justin lowered his hand and his eyes.

"No," Richard breathed.

"No?" Justin jumped in surprise as Richard grabbed his face this time in both hands, to make him focus on his words.

"I am asking you to stay," he repeated. Tightening his grip on Justin's jaw, he kissed him, slowly, languidly.

Tears immediately filled Justin's eyes, and a sob of relief sought to overwhelm him. He gripped both of Richard's hands and massaged his fingers as he devoured lips that he had been missing for so long.

After kissing passionately, Richard stood from the couch, held Justin's hand and led him into his bedroom. Once he closed the door, he began removing Justin's pistol-loaded baldric.

"What are you doing? My Captain? I do not understand?" Justin tilted his head, bewildered at the action until his breeches were popped open. "Are you serious?" Justin laughed, amazed this was happening.

"More than you can imagine." Laying the weapons down, Richard went to work on Justin's blouse.

"You still want me?" Justin kept laughing in disbelief as those fingers quickly worked on disrobing him.

"If you only knew how lonely it is living here without you. I love you, my beautiful Justin Taylor. You and I are well matched."

"Me? Oh, I could never hold a candle to you, Captain,

sir." He started trembling as those hands moved on him. He was rock hard.

When Richard peeled back Justin's blouse to his bronze muscular chest, he moaned and ran his hands over it. "You are a man now. Not my cabin boy any longer."

Justin laughed again. He was so giddy he was light-headed. "I can be your cabin boy, sir. I will be anything you want me to be." Gently, lovingly, Justin rested his hands on Richard's shoulders.

At the wonderful offer, Richard's handsome face lit up with delight. Wrapping around Justin like a coil of rope, Richard kissed him passionately, moaning in pleasure as he pushed his tongue into Justin's mouth.

In some small place in his mind, Justin thought he must be dreaming. "I love you, my Captain, I always have," he gasped between kisses.

"Justin, my pretty Justin," he groaned and inhaled him as he led him to the bed anxiously.

Savoring every touch every breath, Justin allowed his captain to do as he wished with him. It wasn't an illusion; it was reality. He had found him. Now he could have him once again, the way he had dreamed of having him on some very lonely nights with only his right hand for relief.

Lying back on the bed, he stared up at his handsome captain as he disrobed, their eyes never leaving their contact with each other.

"Am I being rude to you? You must be hungry or thirsty; would you rather eat first?" Richard asked.

Justin broke up laughing. "Nay, sir, I would not. This hunger is far greater than any other."

Richard smiled sweetly, dropping his last item of clothing with great ceremony, and crawled over the bed to him. When their naked lengths met and the heat of their skin was exchanged, they groaned in ecstasy at the sensation.

Even after telling himself, he was really there and

actually caressing his beloved, Justin kept wondering if he was hallucinating. Having fantasized about this meeting over and over in his head, Justin had always thought it was just a farfetched notion to actually think he could make love to this man again. The fact that he was in his arms, his lips were connected to his, that tongue was in his mouth, and those hands were on him, was almost too much to bear.

Richard set back from him with a breath. The excitement was causing him to pant. Gazing down at Justin as he lay over him, he stared into Justin's eyes to find tears rolling down his face. He smiled sweetly and whispered, "Are you sad, my Justin?"

At the inaccurate appraisal, Justin purred, "Nay, sir. They are tears of pure joy. I love you. I love you with all my heart."

Richard leaned up on his elbows to see him more clearly. "And I must love you too, Justin. For I have thought of nothing else since we parted."

"You…you still do?" Justin gasped.

Richard grinned broadly. "Oh, my beautiful lad…aye, I still do. I never stopped loving you."

As if he were a child on Christmas morning, Justin squirmed under Richard in joy. Justin was so hard he thought he might come just rubbing against that solid body on top of his. Uttering a masculine groan, Richard seemed to be savoring that heated friction as well.

When his captain hopped off the bed to get something, Justin moaned in frustration. Running his hand over his length, he had never felt himself so hard before. When Richard returned with a jar of liniment, Justin laughed and said, "Assume the position, sir?"

Richard's smile turned sensuously wicked. "Aye, lad! On your knees!" he shouted in a mock order.

Biting his lip at the hilarity, Justin tried not to go into a fit of hysterical laughter. Like an obedient soldier, Justin got to his hands and knees and stretched back to peer over his shoulder.

Richard stopped in his tracks and just admired him. "Oh, Justin Taylor, look at you. You are magnificent."

Hiding his grin against his right shoulder, Justin blushed to the ears. Slowly, Richard crawled behind him and ran his hands over his tight rump and waist, groaning as he pushed the tip of himself inside his body.

As Justin expected, his skin raced with hot chills. He hissed through his closed teeth and knew as soon as that large hand caressed his cock, he would explode. It was his captain! His beloved Captain Jones' cock that was once again at one with him. Justin knew it was right. No one meant more to him than his captain, and the love they shared both spiritually and physically could never be duplicated with another.

It seemed as if Richard was having the same reaction. Holding Justin's waist, Richard pushed in deeper, pausing as if trying to hold back and still his hips. The moment he produced a rhythm thrusting deeply inside, Richard came quickly with a deep masculine grunt, burrowing his length deeper inside him.

Shivering from head to toe, Justin heard his cries of pleasure. He savored that heat as it shot inside him and tried to catch his breath as his body tingled, and his love grew stronger.

When Richard recovered, he wrapped around Justin's back and found him with his hands, squeezing his hard cock and running his palm along its shaft.

Justin felt his body almost convulse with the power of the climax. He clenched his teeth and eyes and came with so much force he collapsed to the bed.

Completely sated, Richard rested on top of his back as Justin gasped for air, trying to get his breathing under control. Richard pulled out of him gently and dropped down beside him, staring at him from along his side.

Taking in the entire experience, Justin was still recuperating. When he felt a gentle touch on his arm, Justin moaned, "Blimey."

Richard tried to keep a straight face, but couldn't. He burst out laughing and tears ran from his eyes. Like a young pup, Justin jumped on top of him and buried his face into the pillow of Richard's long hair. Needing no urging to reciprocate, Richard wrapped around him and held him tight. "No one will separate us again, lad. It is up to you to choose."

Justin exhaled a long sigh and luxuriated in the affection from the one he adored most in the world.

* * * *

They had made love for almost two hours, feeling free and at ease as they never had in the cramped cabin on the corvette. In between coupling, they rested in each other's arms.

Still sparkling with sweat, Richard brushed the long hair back from Justin's tired eyes. "Now that we are very satisfied, my love, tell me, what of my crew?"

After pecking his lips quickly, Justin sighed. "It is not all good news, my Captain. Not all good to report."

"It never is, lad. But I am ready to hear it." Richard supported his head on his palm and kept in contact with Justin's body as he nodded for him to continue.

"Aye, your Quartermaster Tucker, next time we stayed on at Portobello, he requested permanent leave. I think he fancied a whore there and had designs on keeping her."

Richard smiled softly. "Aye, yes, I could imagine that. He was getting long in the tooth for the trade, though a better man you could not sail with."

"Boatswain Black," Justin continued, adjusting his body to a more relaxed position, inviting Richard's hands to rest on his chest. "He had taken ill while we were asea. We kept him in quarantine, Captain, though it pained me to do so. We knew not what he had, so we couldn't take any chances. Jason thought it was infection, but with the plague so rampant, what were we to do? Two days he slept in the bilge. Didn't do him any good, sir. He made it back to port but died soon after. At least he was back in England and could be buried proper like."

As if knowing the tales would get worse instead of better, Richard nodded silently for him to go on.

"And our best mate, First-mate Cromwell," Justin muttered, "Well, sir, he lost an arm in a broadside and gave up the dream as well. He's living in the wilds of the Americas. I was stunned, sir, he wanted to be left off in a place where he was unknown and a bit helpless. But there you have it, Captain. We gave him what he wanted. We couldn't dock near enough, so we sent him on a dinghy craft with someone to paddle for him. They saw to it he was set up on land, then came back. I heard terrible tales of wild men living there. I'd not chosen that meself, sir."

Richard rubbed Justin's skin at his pelvis, just dipping his fingertips into his pubic hair as he spoke. "Nor I. But I know Cromwell. He's not one to feel comfortable without a limb. My guess is he ne'er wanted to bump into a man he knows again from the shame."

"Aye, maybe so, sir."

"What of our pilot, Justin?"

His face darkened.

"No! Not a sad tale of James!" Richard's hand paused in its stroking momentarily.

"Aye, sir. The worst." Justin bit his lip on his misery.

Pausing to prepare himself, Richard finally nodded. "All right, lad. I'm ready."

"We left Tucker off at Portobello, right, sir? Only two years after your departure from our crew. Well, of course we spent two nights there, getting her stores filled and her boards repaired." Justin's eyes flickered down as Richard's hand moved lower into his dark pubic hair. Finding his train of thought, he continued. "Right, well, while we're in town, Pilot goes looking for a male whore. I'd not thought twice about it, sir, or I would have discouraged him. Honest!"

"It's okay, lad." Richard slid his fingers between Justin's thighs.

"He ends up propositioning a buccaneer, sir. One who gives him the impression he's interested. But it was a nasty trick, sir. The buccaneer, he had some mates waiting. They ended up gang raping poor ol' Pilot, sir. Then—" Justin's eyes watered.

"Oh, lad..." Richard reached to push his hair back from his face gently.

"Then they murdered our pilot, sir. And not in a pleasant way. I'm loath to speak of it, sir."

Seeing Justin was on the verge of tears, Richard curled him into his embrace and held him close. "You could do nothing to prevent it, lad."

"We found him, me and the gunners. It was in an alley. A terrible sight, sir." He bit his lip as he remembered it.

"There, there..." Richard kissed Justin's neck and cheek in comfort. "It's a dangerous place, that. Pilot should have known better."

"Aye, sir. And he had a lover on board who committed suicide once he heard the news, sir. It was a very tough spot for the crew. We tried to get a posse together and seek revenge, but no one knew who had done the deed, and no one was talking."

Richard exhaled sadly. "I hate to think all that you had to witness and bear. I should have been beside you. I should have been there."

As if preventing himself from agreeing wholeheartedly, Justin bit his lip.

Richard could only shake his head in wonder at the news. "All right, lad. Enough reminiscing. It was just idle curiosity that made me ask. The important thing to me is that you are whole and well."

"Aye, sir. I have managed to make it through. Though during some brutal broadsides, I came closer than I'd like to admit. I've some powerful force protecting me from harm. I swear to you, sir, it is like I am blessed with good fortune."

Richard set back to smile at his face. "And you bring your good fortune to me."

"Aye, sir. I did!" He chuckled.

* * * *

After their loving, Justin sat up and found his breeches. Twisting around to Richard, Justin cupped that amazing, strong, clean-shaven jaw in his hand and stared at those sea blue eyes. Eyes he never thought he would see again in his lifetime.

"Please stay," Richard whispered, "Though I seem content here, I am not. I have the things I had hoped for, but, something was always lacking, Justin. Now that you are here with me, I see that something was you."

* * * *

Across a jungle path of vines and flowers to a rough cobbled lane, Justin made his way back to his docked ship. Crossing the gangplank, he greeted his men who were wondering on what he had decided to do. Before he could speak to anyone about his plans, his pilot approached him with a young boy he was escorting by the shirt, nudging him to see the captain of the ship.

"Aye, sir, we found this lad stowed away on board," the pilot said.

The boy panicked and dropped to his knees before Justin. "Aye, Captain! Please, sir, you must let me stay. I have always wanted to sail the seas. I beg it of you, don't drag me off!"

Captain Justin Taylor rubbed his smooth jaw as he listened to the lad. "How old are you, boy?"

"Eighteen, sir!"

Reaching out his hand, Captain Taylor said, "Come here, lad."

The boy rose to his feet awkwardly and moved closer to him.

"I'll not give you any lectures or warnings. I'm the last one who should. But you need to be asking permission of the true captain of this rig, lad. That position is no longer mine. I've sailed my last voyage, shed my last drop of blood, and gathered my last doubloon." Patting his back, Justin brushed by him to gather his things from the cabin.

George glared at him as he passed.

"Please, sir, I beg of you. Don't let them drag me off!" the boy cried, running after him.

Hearing such familiar pleas, Justin paused and turned back to him. He stroked his long, soft, blond hair back from his bright blue gaze. "You are a very pretty lad. You will have plenty of misery living at sea. You may even be passed around like a maiden, you know. But like I said, it is not my decision to make. It is a decision I suggest you ponder well. For many have tried, and so many have died," he warned, then raised his head to view the rest of his crew. All their eyes were on him. Justin had prepared them for this inevitability so it would not come as a shock to them. When he set his gaze on George and caught his anger about to explode in a dramatic scene, Justin sighed tiredly and walked away.

As he continued to his cabin to pack, Justin could hear the lad still begging the crew. Gathering his things, he opened his chest to collect his booty. Justin put his logbook into his pocket and heard a light knock. Raising his head, he found his pilot.

"We'll miss you, sir, but we wish ye the best of luck."

"Thanks, John. You've been a great crew. I was honored to sail with you." He shook his hand, then spied another crewmate behind him. When the pilot found George there, waiting impatiently, he lowered his head and backed away, allowing him to pass inside.

Knowing he was there, Justin continued to gather his few personal belongings quietly.

"So? Ye have made yer decision?"

Stopping what he was doing, Justin tried to stand tall under the low ceiling but ended up hunched over. "George, I told you this was my plan."

"No! Ye said ye were just trying to meet up with him! Not leave the ship for him," he argued.

"I am sorry—" Justin was in no mood for this display.

"Sorry?" George choked in amazement. "I loved ye like no other fer the last three years of our service, and ye says sorry?"

"I never led you to believe there could be anything between us," Justin countered. "I've never given you any false hope."

"No!" George crossed the wooden boards to meet him straight on. "Ye ne'er gave me naught! Night after night, not a hand did you lay on me. In tears, I begged of ye to let me love ye, my Captain—yet ne'er did ye allow it. Why?"

Justin could not answer that question. He hated the idea of hurting this man, but what was he supposed to do? He hoisted his kit over his shoulder and turned towards him, when to his surprise, he found his beloved standing there behind the angry crewman. It was odd to see him inside the small confines of that cabin—the place where they had first consummated their affair.

When George caught Justin's attention darting behind

him, he spun around quickly. There, crouched over in the small confines, was an enormous, muscular man.

George backed up a step and accused Justin, "Is this him, then?"

"Aye, George. This is me Captain Jones."

Justin could tell Richard immediately checked to see if George was armed. A cutlass sword hung from George's hip.

"You need a hand, Justin?" Attempting to ignore the man, Richard gestured to Justin.

George confronted Richard angrily, pointing a finger into his handsome face and shouting, "Ye be getting the prince of *His Revenge*! Ye better appreciate it!"

"George," Justin admonished. "I am still in command on this ship until I remove myself off of it. One more arrogant word, and it'll be the cat o'nines for you."

"Ye think I care! Whip me! It'd be the last thing ye do to me, but at least I'll remember it."

"Lads..." Richard tried to intervene.

Throwing down his kit, Justin approached his crewman menacingly.

"No. Justin, calm down." Richard stood between them.

"Don't ye get yerself involved in this!" George shoved Richard away. "This is between me and me captain!"

"That's enough," Justin roared, making toward him in the cramped cabin. "Horacio!" Justin thundered for his boatswain.

"No! Justin!" Richard tried to stop him.

"Aye, sir?" The boatswain appeared at the doorway.

"What will it be, George?" Justin gave him one last chance.

Seeing he had no alternative, George spat on the floor and shouted, "Good riddance to ya then!" He shoved by the boatswain out of the room.

257

"Sir?" Horacio asked, confused by the scene.

Sighing tiredly, Justin mumbled, "Nothing now, mate. Be on your way."

"Aye, Captain." He took a look at Richard, then disappeared.

In the calm silence that followed, the two men stood alone.

Justin opened his mouth to speak, to apologize, but nothing came out.

As if overwhelmed with nostalgia, Richard gazed around the cabin, eyeing everything inside that was familiar or new, every inch bringing back memories to him, both wonderful and nightmarish.

Having a feeling Richard was reliving some moments, Justin lifted his kit, watching Richard closely. "You all right, sir?"

Richard found his eyes in the dimness. "It feels like another lifetime ago, Justin."

"Aye, sir, it was."

With an air of melancholy, Richard smoothed his hand over the wood surface of the desk.

As he stared at him curiously, Justin caught that smile. He tilted his head in question. "Was it a good one, sir?"

Richard looked up. "A good what, lad?"

"Memory."

Smiling brightly, he admitted, "Aye. It was of my cabin boy seducing me with his naked body."

Justin moved to him and wrapped his arms around him to kiss his lips. "I love you, my Captain."

Richard squeezed him tight and inhaled him deeply into his lungs. "Oh, my pretty, as I love you."

"Come. Out of these cramped quarters, once and for all." Justin reached for his hand.

Richard helped him with all his things as Justin shook the hands of the men he had sailed and fought with, thanking them for their service. Behind his back, Justin could still hear the lad going from one to the other, begging to be allowed to stay. Justin smiled and shook his head. "Aye, lad, if they let you, it'll be an adventure you won't soon forget! That I promise you."

He waved to them all, caught George's bitter grimace, then walked down the gangway. When he turned around behind him, his gaze found a very tall handsome man there with a grin as wide as a galleon's broadside. His heart burst with affection at that sight.

Justin peeked back at the men as they judged this handsome man their captain was giving up a life at sea for. And like his admirer, George, Justin knew some would never understand. He doubted he would care in the least if they did or not. One thing he had learned long ago, he was the master of his own destiny, and no one would decide his fate for him ever again.

While his crew watched him go, the first mate tried to get them all back to the real world and shouted for them to get the ship ready for sail.

The young lad was now crying as he was escorted off the deck.

"No young boys on board," the pilot told him.

As if saying farewell for the last time, Justin peeked over his shoulder once, then felt his lover's arm wrap around his waist.

Richard noticed his contented smile. "What are you thinking, lover?" Assisting Justin, he had the chest of booty tucked under his arm as they made their way back to the house.

"Not much, sir, just that maybe it's true that some pirate tales do have a happy ending."

Richard's eyes crinkled into a loving smile as they made their way into the starlit night.

About the Author

Award-winning author G.A. Hauser was born in Fair Lawn, New Jersey, USA and attended university in New York City. She moved to Seattle, Washington where she worked as a patrol officer with the Seattle Police Department. In early 2000 G.A. moved to Hertfordshire, England where she began her writing in earnest and published her first book, In the Shadow of Alexander. Now a full-time writer, G.A. has written over eighty novels, including several best-sellers of gay fiction. For more information on other books by G.A., visit the author at her official website. www.authorgahauser.com

G.A. has won awards from All Romance eBooks for Best Author 2010, 2009, Best Novel 2008, *Mile High*, and Best Author 2008, Best Novel 2007, *Secrets and Misdemeanors*, Best Author 2007.

The G.A. Hauser Collection
Single Titles

Unnecessary Roughness
Hot Rod
Mr. Right
Happy Endings
Down and Dirty
Lancelot in Love
Happy Endings
Cowboy Blues
Midnight in London
Living Dangerously
The Last Hard Man
Taking Ryan
Born to be Wilde
The Adonis of WeHo
L.A. Masquerade
Dude! Did You Just Bite Me?
My Best Friend's Boyfriend
The Diamond Stud
The Hard Way
Games Men Play
Born to Please
Of Wolves and Men
The Order of Wolves
Got Men?
Heart of Steele
All Man
Julian
Black Leather Phoenix
London, Bloody, London
In The Dark and What Should Never Be, Erotic Short Stories
Mark and Sharon
A Man's Best Friend
It Takes a Man
Blind Ambition (formerly The Physician and the Actor)

For Love and Money
The Kiss
Naked Dragon
Secrets and Misdemeanors
Capital Games
Giving Up the Ghost
To Have and To Hostage
Love you, Loveday
The Boy Next Door
When Adam Met Jack
Exposure
The Vampire and the Man-eater
Murphy's Hero
Mark Antonious deMontford
Prince of Servitude
Calling Dr Love
The Rape of St. Peter
The Wedding Planner
Going Deep
Double Trouble
Pirates
Miller's Tale
Vampire Nights
Teacher's Pet
In the Shadow of Alexander
The Rise and Fall of the Sacred Band of Thebes

The Action Series

Acting Naughty
Playing Dirty
Getting it in the End
Behaving Badly
Dripping Hot
Packing Heat
Being Screwed
Something Sexy
Going Wild
Having it All!

Bending the Rules

Men in Motion Series

Mile High
Cruising
Driving Hard
Leather Boys

Heroes Series

Man to Man
Two In Two Out
Top Men

G.A. Hauser
Writing as Amanda Winters

Sister Moonshine
Nothing Like Romance
Silent Reign
Butterfly Suicide
Mutley's Crew

Printed in Great Britain
by Amazon